FINAL
SECOND

BOOKS BY JOHN RYDER

THE GRANT FLETCHER SERIES
First Shot

FINAL SECOND

A GRANT FLETCHER THRILLER

JOHN RYDER

bookouture

Published by Bookouture in 2020

An imprint of Storyfire Ltd.
Carmelite House
50 Victoria Embankment
London EC4Y 0DZ

www.bookouture.com

ISBN: 978-1-83888-798-8
eBook ISBN: 978-1-83888-797-1

For my son, a young man who is easily my greatest achievement.

PROLOGUE

Carl Friedrickson ignored the early reaches of the Wisconsin autumn cooling the morning air and sprinted towards the small duck pond that lay fifty yards from his front door. The rubber boots a half size too large made his wild dash ungainly. He didn't even hear the squelches they were making as they moved on his feet. His entire focus was on the shape in the pond.

It was a shape he was more than familiar with. A shape he loved with all his heart. A shape he'd vowed to love, honor and cherish.

The cold water of the duck pond splashed up his legs unnoticed as he waded towards his wife, the now water-filled rubber boots heavy on his feet.

Carl could see Jane's blonde hair fanned around her head. Could see there was no movement in her body. Could see no reaction to his panicked shouts.

If she'd been face up, he would have carried hope with him. She wasn't. Her face was in the water, her back humped camel-like as her limbs hung down towards the pond's bed. His brain was telling him he was too late to save her, though his heart didn't believe what his mind was saying.

A duck swam past Jane, unaware or unconcerned by the human tragedy that had invaded its space.

Carl reached out a hand and snagged Jane's coveralls. His fingers grasping the sodden material as he hauled her body towards him.

She didn't respond to his touch. As he moved her limp body, a reddish stain remained in the spot where she'd been in the water.

His back arched as he wound his arms around her and lifted her free of the pond. Her body was inert as he carried her to the nearest shore, unresponsive to his shaking movements or his pleas for her to speak to him.

He laid her on the grass he cut every Sunday and started to perform CPR. As his hands went to her chest he saw the blood on the front of her coveralls. It was centered round where her heart lay. The heart she'd told him was his for eternity. The heart whose beat he'd listened to so many times, his head on her chest.

It was when he saw the blood and the wide gash in her coveralls that Carl realized that which he could not change. Jane was gone. He couldn't bring her back. Nobody could.

His first tear fell as he reached down to close her eyes and smooth the hair away from her face. Carl didn't notice the tremble in his fingers nor the peaceful expression Jane wore. Grief had turned to anger. To unbridled fury as he looked down upon her. The stab wound to her chest was bad enough to contemplate, but he'd remember the message carved into her forehead if he lived to be a thousand years old.

CHAPTER ONE

Zoey Quadrado's eyes were rubbed raw from all the tears she'd shed and her bottom lip stung as she chewed on it. As an FBI Special Agent she was no stranger to violent deaths, but this one was personal. Deeply, deeply personal. Jane Friedrickson had been her best friend since forever. Brought up on neighboring Wisconsin dairy farms, they'd been inseparable from kindergarten until they left college. While Zoey had pursued a career in law enforcement, Jane had returned to Wisconsin and married her childhood sweetheart.

Quadrado had wanted to fly back to Wisconsin and investigate Jane's homicide herself. The cops serving the town of Medford, on whose outskirts she and Jane had grown up, were known to be useless with anything more serious than traffic violations or bar fights, and she couldn't begin to have confidence they'd find Jane's killer.

But she was wrapped up in a large investigation into a series of homicides plaguing upstate New York and Pennsylvania, which meant there was no way she'd be granted any compassionate leave. All things considered, she'd be lucky to get the time off to attend Jane's funeral. For all she was FBI, she'd also have no jurisdiction in Wisconsin, so any investigation she undertook would be private and unsupported. She'd have no forensic help, no right to arrest and interview suspects, nor would she have backup if she identified the murderer.

It was all these factors that made her want to pull out her phone and dial a number she hadn't expected that she'd have to call nearly so soon.

Grant Fletcher was a man she'd met while on a previous case. He was a man apart from any other she'd met. A former Royal Marine, he worked construction while taking various mercenary-style jobs. Fletcher's brain was sharp, he was as smart as any trained investigator she knew, yet he lived by his own rules. His moral compass was strong yet uncompromising. If someone went at him, he deemed them responsible for the injuries he inflicted on them.

Most of all, though, despite having saved her life, Fletcher still owed her a favor and the investigation into Jane's death was how she planned to cash it in.

There were also other elements at play, so before calling Fletcher, she accessed a secret email address on her phone and started typing.

With the email sent, Quadrado turned to her laptop and set about reviewing her day's tasks.

Her phone pinged after less than five minutes. Fumbling with it, she saw there was a reply to her email. The speediness of the response made Quadrado assume her suggestion had been dismissed out of hand.

She opened the email expecting the worst. The reply had ten words that made her give an involuntary fist pump, and an eleventh that made her brow crease.

PROCEED AS SUGGESTED. FLETCHER MUSTN'T KNOW HE IS BEING TESTED.

SOTER

Fletcher answered on the third ring and listened while she outlined what she needed from him. Five pertinent questions later he'd set his terms and agreed to her offer of half his usual fee and a wiping of his debt to her.

As they so often did, her thoughts turned back to the last few months. In the aftermath of the case where she'd first encountered Fletcher, she'd been invited to visit the FBI headquarters on Pennsylvania Avenue.

Upon arriving she'd been ushered to a private room and kept waiting for an hour. She'd expected the axe to fall on her career. Instead she'd been taken to an out-of-the-way office where she was shown a video.

The video had shown three people in silhouette. From their hairstyles she'd guessed they were two men and a woman. The three people had each taken a turn to speak to her, their voices distorted by electronic software. Step by careful step they had outlined what she was to do regarding the Georgia case and Grant Fletcher.

He was to become their personal black ops operative if he wanted to evade jail. Compensations to him would be made, the largest of which would be the admittance of his daughter into any Ivy League college of her choosing. She'd be given an anonymous sponsorship through college and doors would be opened for her when she left college.

Quadrado had listened as the voices had detailed how she was to be Fletcher's contact and handler. That she was the one who must convince Fletcher to play ball. She'd realized as she was briefed that Fletcher's life was of no concern to them. That he was disposable and would only ever be used when there were legal implications for FBI agents. It was a good package Fletcher was being offered, too good for a man known to have committed first-degree murder. The generosity was suspect: the US government wasn't in the habit of giving such deals to its citizens, let alone a British-born killer. They'd want something in return for the money.

Instructions had been given as to how she'd be contacted by a secure email when Fletcher's talents were required. It was this address she sent her message to. There had been intimations the voices wanted to find a trial case for Fletcher though. So as a way to ensure her friend Jane's murderer could be caught, she'd offered up Jane's homicide as Fletcher's test case. The word "Soter" meant nothing to her so she supposed it was a name the shadowy figures went by. She knew it wouldn't be a real name, but it might have some twisted meaning, so she googled it. Soter was a Greek daemon associated with protection and guarding people from harm.

For all Soter might see themselves that way, Quadrado could only see Soter as someone who was manipulating and maneuvering both her and Fletcher. She understood that she was little better, that she was using Fletcher for her own ends, but as she was unable to investigate Jane's homicide herself, Fletcher was the next best thing, and she'd do whatever it took to bring Jane's killer to justice.

CHAPTER TWO

Fletcher pulled into the parking lot of Medford's sole motel. A flickering neon sign illuminated the front of the building and there was enough light coming from the streetlamps for him to not have to squint.

He'd known the call would come from Quadrado at some point. What he hadn't expected was that he'd be put to work with such efficiency. A couple of hours after her call, he'd been in the air. There had been scant time to pack a bag and inform his daughter, Wendy, he'd be away for a few days and that he'd arranged for her to stay with her grandparents.

He'd been met at Central Wisconsin Airport by a monosyllabic FBI agent who'd given him the keys to an SUV, a standard FBI issue Glock and a carryall containing spare ammunition, binoculars and a few other items he'd requested Quadrado equip him with.

The way she'd managed the delivery of these items spoke volumes. It could be that she was calling in, or laying out, a lot of favors, yet the speed with which Quadrado had everything in place to move him from his home in Vernal, Utah to Medford in Wisconsin spoke of either prior planning, or a previously unexperienced level of governmental efficiency. One way or another, he'd find out which. If the victim hadn't been a friend of hers, he'd have sworn she had backing from someone high up in the FBI.

A yawn stretched Fletcher's mouth as he walked to the motel reception. The journey had been tiring, not because he'd had to do much traveling, more because his brain had been on a hyperactive setting since he'd gotten Quadrado's call.

The job he'd been given wasn't anything like he'd expected. When Quadrado had intimated the FBI may be interested in using him as an off-the-books black ops operative, Fletcher was under no illusion about why he'd been chosen; he'd anticipated being used as a blunt instrument, not a precise scalpel. While this case had a personal edge to it with the victim being Quadrado's childhood friend, it was one he felt would fall within the realms of the local police department. Quadrado's reasoning that the local cops were useless didn't ring true to him. Yes, they might not meet her FBI levels of investigative prowess, but that was no reason to send him into the fray. A licensed private eye would be of more use. Especially if they had local connections. Therefore Quadrado wasn't telling him everything, which meant she had an ulterior motive he also had to consider. Whatever it was, he was sure it would become apparent in time, and until that point, he'd make sure to keep his wits about him.

As for the case itself, it was a straightforward homicide. He was a construction worker and a former Royal Marine, not a detective. He had received no formal training in investigative techniques, had no official standing to add weight to his dealings with members of the public and no illusions that he was the right man to look into a homicide case. For all his adoptive parents had been a cop and an investigative journalist, he wasn't sure what he could bring to the case that would make him any better than the cops Quadrado had dismissed as inept.

None of that meant he didn't have some ideas about what he should look for, the lines of inquiry he'd need to follow and who he'd need to speak to.

With his bags stowed, he sat on the motel bed and opened the file handed to him by the monosyllabic agent. The more he read, the more he became unsure as to whether the case really was personal to Quadrado.

CHAPTER THREE

By the time he'd read through the files, Fletcher had a better grasp of the challenge in front of him. The files were the police reports, most likely gleaned from the system by Quadrado or some office-dwelling analyst with a beige cubicle and a fondness for comic book heroes. Jane Friedrickson was twenty-eight, happily married to a dairy farmer and a well-liked member of the community.

Police inquiries had unearthed no enemies. There was no hint of scandal in her background, and Jane's husband had been at a loss for an answer when asked why he thought someone might want to kill her.

She'd gotten up and had gone out to join the guys who'd landed the early shift milking the two-hundred-strong herd at Greenacres Farm. Carl had remained in bed as he'd been up half the night treating a sick cow. He'd risen around seven and finding the house empty had gone out to look for his wife and check on the cow he'd been treating.

Instead of finding Jane, he'd found a bloodstain at the corner of his house. He'd looked around and seen his wife floating face down in the small pond at the end of the garden.

When questioned by the cops, the two guys milking the cattle reported Jane had never made it to the milking parlor. Neither had been out of the other's sight between arriving at work together and hearing of Jane's homicide. With the two workers alibiing each other, the only suspects left were the husband or an unknown third party.

Normally he'd assume the husband, but Quadrado had vouched for him as she'd known him since forever. According to conversations she'd had with Jane, the marriage was rock solid and they were trying for children. The idea that he'd killed her was preposterous in Quadrado's eyes.

Not knowing any of the actors in the drama, Fletcher tried to be more analytical, cynical even. So far as Quadrado knew, Jane or Carl may have been having an affair with someone. Quadrado had left town and for all she'd hear what her friends told her, she wasn't around to learn things for herself. If the affair had been found out, there would be tensions. Maybe she'd threatened to leave him and take half of the farm in the divorce? Perhaps he'd learned of her cheating and had killed her in a fit of jealous rage?

The more Fletcher considered the husband as the killer, the less he was convinced by his reasonings though. Quadrado had intimated that Carl was little more than a junior partner in the farm with his parents holding the controlling stake. This negated any threats made about divorce claims. There was also the closeness between Quadrado and Jane to factor in. If they were as tight as stated, Quadrado would likely have had some idea if Jane was experiencing any marital problems, and would therefore be accusing Carl.

To give himself a break from thinking about who, Fletcher bent his mind onto the how. The victim had been knifed in the heart outside the corner of her home. According to Quadrado, Jane was walking a route she'd traveled thousands of times previously.

Fletcher put himself in the position of the killer and worked out what he'd do in their place if he wanted to kill Jane. The corner of the house made sense. The killer would be able to lie in wait unseen until Jane rounded the corner. Then it'd be a simple case of stepping out and thrusting the knife forward. One stab to the heart and Jane would be as good as dead. How she'd ended up in the pond was more interesting though, given it was fifty yards from the corner of the house.

This method fit well enough for an amateur, but if Fletcher had been doing the kill, he'd have kept his back to the wall and delivered a backhand thrust to the heart, followed by a slash to the throat to silence any forlorn appeals for help. It would be easy to get the timing right; Jane's footsteps and the rustle of her clothing would alert the killer as to her approach. At the right moment, whack, the knife would plunge into her chest. It was what happened after that troubled Fletcher. The crime scene reports had told of a trail of blood drops leading from the corner to the pond. It was obvious the killer had stabbed Jane, then propelled her to the pond, possibly with a hand over her mouth to ensure her silence.

Once at the pond, the report stated she'd been pushed or thrown into the water and left to her fate. This scenario worked apart from one major flaw. The carving on Jane's forehead.

To Fletcher's way of thinking, the carving must have been done in the seconds before Jane entered the pond. No killer would give themselves a soaking, as it was just one more thing that'd be impossible to explain if someone saw them leaving the scene.

There was also the message sent by the carving. It didn't speak of anything personal to either the victim or the husband. Had Jane's killer carved "bitch" or "slut" into her forehead, it would have been easy to point the finger at Carl. Her killer hadn't done that. His message was far more worrying. It spoke of Jane Friedrickson being the first of several victims. Why else would he carve #1 in her forehead?

It was the message and its implications that gave Fletcher the most pause for thought. Was this a serial killer, trying to make a name for himself? Did he want to join the ranks of John Wayne Gacy and Jeffrey Dahmer, or was he trying to eclipse them and was numbering his victims so there would be an accurate count of his victims when his name went down in history?

CHAPTER FOUR

Fletcher was awake early and after a quick breakfast at Medford's diner, he'd climbed into the FBI SUV and set off to get his bearings. As he drove he found the same things time and again. Large empty fields, shorn of the corn grown to feed the cattle which gave Wisconsin its official nickname of America's Dairyland.

Flanking the fields were patches of isolated woods and farms with large sheds and silos Fletcher guessed were used for the storage of manufactured cattle feed.

To Fletcher the farms all looked to be well maintained, but he'd be the first to admit, agriculture wasn't an area where he had any level of expertise.

As he passed a wooden sign for Meadowfields, Fletcher made a mental note of the location as it was the family farm of the Quadrados. Quadrado had said to Fletcher she'd alert her brother, Peter, he'd be in the area and told him Peter would be a good source of local news. Speaking to Peter was high on Fletcher's agenda, but first he wanted to check out Greenacres Farm and speak to Carl Friedrickson if at all possible.

The mailbox at the end of the road leading to Greenacres Farm was in good condition. Painted white and stenciled with black writing, it told Fletcher he was in the right place. It also suggested the Friedricksons took pride in their farm. A mailbox wasn't an important thing and could last for years, yet they kept theirs in good condition, which intimated they had high standards and made the necessary effort to keep them.

Rather than drive down the track, Fletcher opted to park the SUV and approach Greenacres Farm on foot. The track curled away, dipping out of sight, but there was a silo Fletcher could use as a landmark, so he set off on a direct route. His line of thinking was that he'd be able to scope out the place slowly, to have time to assess the surrounding lands for points where the killer may have concealed himself before and after Jane's homicide. There were also the routes used for accessing and leaving Greenacres Farm to discover.

Nothing he saw gave him confidence he'd be able to discover what he was looking for. Once he'd crested the slight rise shielding Greenacres Farm from the road, he found the surrounding land was billiard-table flat. There were no ditches a killer could travel along out of sight, no folds in the land and no hedges or woods to conceal movement.

The layout of the farm supported his theory the killer had lain in wait at the end of the farmhouse for Jane to walk into his trap, as she'd have to go round the corner where she was stabbed to head towards any of the farm buildings.

At the back of his mind was his own independent research into Wisconsin farming. America's Dairyland was leading the country in the number of farms going bankrupt. At a daily average of two, there were more pressures than ever on the farmers. Low milk prices along with state and federal tariffs and taxes were cited as being responsible, yet Fletcher was sure that would only be part of the story.

As he walked Fletcher's mind was doing various calculations. As a place to attack or escape from, Greenacres Farm was a hard target. Although the killer had struck under the cover of darkness, he would still have had to travel to and from the farm. The nearest other building might be two miles away, but there were roads around the farm. It didn't make sense for the killer to have traveled down the dirt track from the road to the farm as he could have encountered a worker arriving for the morning milking shift. Meaning the killer almost certainly came across the fields.

The police report had listed no tire tracks in the immediate vicinity of Greenacres Farm that weren't accounted for by Carl or his workers, and suggested the killer must have hiked from a vehicle parked on the road.

Fletcher didn't like that idea. If it was him he wouldn't have wanted to leave a vehicle with an identifying license plate by the side of the road. He'd at least want it hidden and he'd also want to minimize the time he was at the farm or anywhere close to it. Had he been the killer, he would have driven a vehicle off the road and traveled without lights until he was a half mile from the farm and then walked the rest. This would have then left him a vehicle close at hand to aid a rapid getaway.

The binoculars Fletcher put to his eyes were good ones. He expected nothing less from the FBI's storage locker. Through them, Fletcher was able to examine each of the buildings and the farmhouse in detail. He'd learned long ago that it was often better to scope a place out from afar than close up. Standing on the ground looking up at buildings rarely gave as comprehensive a picture as seeing them magnified from a distance, as it altered the angle of inspection.

It was as he was examining the farm buildings that Fletcher heard a pair of familiar sounds.

Instinct and years of Royal Marine training saw Fletcher throw himself to the ground. He'd heard one gunshot and the impact of a bullet striking the ground near him.

As he rolled across the ground to prevent being a stationary target, Fletcher tried to work out if the bullet had missed on purpose or because the gunman was a poor shot. *Who* it was shooting at him was a minor matter at the moment.

CHAPTER FIVE

Rather than keep rolling in one direction and enable the shooter to lead his movements, Fletcher kept swapping from left to right. To further throw off the shooter's aim, he varied the number of times he rolled in any direction. It wasn't a plan for long term survival, but it kept him alive for the time being.

A second shot rang out as he changed direction and switched to a leftward movement.

The bullet was aimed in the direction he was traveling, yet it struck the ground a good five yards from where he was.

Instinct made him roll away from where the shot landed. He had no thought process about the action; his body's ingrained desire for survival and learned responses acted long before his brain could register the shot.

The next shot landed five yards to his right which had his reflexes propelling him left again.

Five times he changed direction without there being another shot.

Fletcher's brain was now working as hard as his body. Not on the evasive movements, his body had them covered, but on the shots that had been fired. The first missing him was something he'd put down to the gunman's inaccuracy. Now he'd had a moment to think, he realized the two follow-up shots were equally wide. For all his rolling around was designed to throw off the shooter's aim, the final shots had landed in areas where he'd never been.

This meant the shooter was either a catastrophically bad shot, or he was missing on purpose. Fletcher slowed his rolls and snuck a quick look towards the farm before resuming with his next change of direction. He had to squint due to the distance and the sun backlighting the farm, but he saw who he thought was the shooter.

The figure was standing in front of the farmhouse, his outline dark against the white of the building. His gun held in two hands above his head in the way Fletcher had been taught to carry a weapon through deep water.

Fletcher eased to a halt, his eyes never leaving the man by the farmhouse. The rifle stayed where it was so he eased himself up from the ground and onto his knees. Still the figure never moved. He rose to his feet, the binoculars gripped in his right hand.

A hand left the rifle and pointed his way and then to the ground by the shooter's feet. The message unmistakable.

Step by step Fletcher began walking to the farm. He was at the shooter's mercy and he knew it. There wasn't the smallest scrap of cover within three hundred yards, and even a zigzagging run wouldn't guarantee a successful escape if the shooter was as accurate as Fletcher suspected he was.

Once he got within two hundred yards, the figure moved the rifle from its aerial position and cradled it in the crook of his right arm as Fletcher approached. Fletcher's mouth went dry and he had to force his feet to keep moving forward.

The shooter was late twenties with ash-blond hair, a deep tan and sinewy muscles.

"Want to tell me who you are and why you're scoping out my farm?" The voice was tight with emotion. The anger that was a stage of grief was near the surface, yet submerged for the time being.

Even without the shooter laying claim to the farm, Fletcher would have known from his voice he was speaking to someone fighting to understand a sudden bereavement.

"My name is Grant Fletcher. Zoey Quadrado asked me to look into your wife's death." How the man reacted to Quadrado's name would be telling. This was the moment when he'd find out if this case really was personal to Quadrado, or if she'd fed him a string of lies.

.

CHAPTER SIX

Fletcher kept his face placid and his limbs loose as he neared the farmer. He had two objectives that were paramount to his survival. The first being to not provoke the farmer into shooting him, and the second to close the gap between them to less than twenty-one feet.

Twenty-one feet was the average distance someone could cover in the time it took an assailant to draw, aim and fire a gun their way. The rifle was already drawn, but unlike a pistol, it'd be slow to aim and slow to react to a moving target. On the other hand, at close range, a rifle bullet would do a hell of a lot more damage than one fired from a pistol.

To aid with the disarming tactics, Fletcher laced his fingers together and held them before his stomach.

"I assume I'm talking to Carl Friedrickson?"

"That's me." The gun never wavered.

"I was told you found your wife Jane in that pond," a side nod from Fletcher gave an unnecessary indication of the pond he was referring to, "on Sunday morning. I'm a… colleague of your wife's school friend, Zoey Quadrado." Colleague was stretching the truth to breaking point, but telling the man he was a mercenary wasn't likely to endear any great level of trust.

Bulbous knuckles whitened as they gripped the rifle. "You're the guy Zeke sent?"

"Zeke? I was sent by Special Agent Zoey Quadrado of the FBI. Her family own Meadowfields."

This was the clincher. This was the point where he'd find out if Quadrado had sold him down the river with her claims to be best friends with the victim.

"That's Zeke." The rifle was moved so it rested over Carl's left shoulder. "It's a nickname from her initials. Haven't heard her being called by her proper name since high school. Even her folks call her Zeke."

Now the possibility of confrontation was over, Fletcher saw Carl relax from being on high alert and show the grief he'd experienced. It was as if the man was shrinking in front of his eyes.

"I know that you don't know me, but Zoey has asked me to look into your wife's homicide as she doesn't have any faith in the local cops." It felt odd to Fletcher to use Quadrado's Christian name as he always thought of her by surname alone. And there was no way he was ready to call her Zeke, even if he was only referring to her. "If it's okay with you, I'd like to ask you some questions and then leave you in peace."

As much as he felt for Carl, Fletcher's thoughts were on the fact Quadrado's story had checked out. He'd been wrong to suspect her of playing him and knew he owed her an apology, even though he'd never given voice to his suspicions.

Carl's lips pursed as he considered Fletcher's statement and question. "The cops here are dumb as a stick. Anything you can do to find the asshole who killed Jane will be very welcome. Thought Zeke might have come herself, but if she's sent you, you must be someone she trusts. Ask what you need to ask." As he spoke, Carl moved the rifle until it was hanging from the crook of his elbow again.

"First off, I want to apologize for any questions I ask that distress or annoy you. I'm not trying to pry into your personal life, just get a picture of your wife's life, her friends and enemies."

"For all Zeke warned me you'd be coming, it still might have been wise for you not to try sneaking here." He flapped a hand to indicate that part of the conversation was over. "Jane didn't have enemies, everyone liked her." His voice caught. "Loved her."

"That's what Zoey told me. You're her husband though, you're the one she'd tell her day to. Had she fallen out with anyone? A friend? Or just someone in a store, a salesman or something like that?"

"Not at all." A rueful look hit Carl's face. "I'm the hothead who complains about servers and gets into it with salesmen. She is always the one who'll calm things down." Carl gave three rapid blinks. "It's not 'is' anymore, is it? It's 'was' now. It'll never be 'is' again."

Fletcher gave Carl a moment to compose himself, to clench and unclench his fists until the hurt was brought under a semblance of control.

"Which one of you was having the affair?"

"Neither of us, you son of a bitch." Carl's fists closed and Fletcher prepared himself to dodge the blow he expected to come.

Carl stayed where he was. The animosity slumping off him.

"Sorry, that was a bad question, but I wanted to catch you off guard. Tough as it might be for you to hear, most homicides are committed by someone close to the victim."

"I wouldn't kill her. For God's sake, we were trying to start a family. How can you think that?"

Fletcher kept his voice steady. "I don't, but the law of probabilities says you have to be a suspect, so I threw the affair question at you when you were low to get an unconsidered response." Carl gave him a blank look. "Was there anyone you're aware of who might have any reason to dislike Jane? An ex of yours? A rival from her school days? Someone who had a thing for her and got shot down?"

"There's nobody. Jane got on with everyone. Medford is a small town and all the folks in town and the surrounding area know each other. We tend to get along and if we don't care for someone, we keep out of each other's way. Once in a while there'll be something that gets settled with fists, but that don't happen much outside of the Tavern."

"What about potential suitors who might have tried their luck with her? Were there any you knew about? From the photo of her Zoey sent me, I could see she was a good-looking woman, so there's bound to have been some guys trying their luck with her." Carl's admission of being hotheaded made Fletcher wonder if Jane had kept such encounters to herself in an effort to stop her husband getting fired up.

A faraway look caressed Carl's eyes. "There were plenty of them and they all got the same answer. My Jane put them straight soon as she realized they wanted to shine their light on her porch."

"Okay. So, to theorize, maybe Jane's killer had another motive for killing her other than anger directed at her. You've admitted you're a hothead. Have you fallen out with anyone badly enough for them to have killed Jane just to hurt you?"

Carl's face turned ashen despite the deep tan. "No. You're not serious, are you? Do you really think Jane was killed because of me?"

"I don't know. That's why I'm asking."

Furrows appeared on Carl's brow as he worked through possibilities. "There's nobody. I fell out with a feed merchant over a hike in his prices, but every farmer around here did the same. I fired a guy who kept failing to show up for work, but he'd been fired from other places before that. Even so, there was hardly a shouting match. I said my piece to both guys and we parted ways."

"Anyone else?" Fletcher couldn't see either of the people mentioned being mad enough to take the huge step of committing homicide over a job or a lost customer.

"No. There's nobody I can think of."

"What about old enemies? Do you have any long-running feuds with anyone?"

"No." Carl's head sawed back and forth. "I've told you, we're a community. We stick together and help one another out."

"What about the carving on her forehead? Does that have any significance to you?"

"None. What kind of sick jerk-off does that? How could he do that to my Jane?"

It didn't go unnoticed by Fletcher that Carl had twice used the term "my Jane." It was a proprietary term and one he wasn't comfortable hearing from someone who ought to be a prime suspect.

"I don't know. But you can rest assured I'll be asking that question when I find him."

Carl's grip on the rifle tightened. His face shed its grief and allowed rage to show. "Don't ask him questions. When you find him, bring him to me. Let me have him."

Rather than answer Carl's request, Fletcher moved to a different subject. He had a final point to make before leaving. "I'd respectfully request that you don't tell anyone who I am and that I'm looking into your wife's homicide. As a stranger in town, I can pick up on things you've given up paying attention to and I don't want folks being guarded around me."

CHAPTER SEVEN

Meadowfields was every bit as well kept as Greenacres Farm and its land twice as flat. As Fletcher exited the SUV, he could hear the roar of a heavy engine working hard and the lowing of dairy cattle.

He walked up to the house and knocked on the door unsure as to what reception he'd get. He had no idea what Quadrado had told her family about him. She might have said he'd saved her life, or she could have described him as a killer. Both were true, but to a loving family, the difference between the two was huge.

The door creaked open and a woman opened the door. She was early-thirties and dressed in simple clothes her natural style made appear elegant. "You must be Mr. Fletcher, I'm Libby. Zeke has told us plenty about you. Do come in. Mom and Pop are out just now, but Peter's in the barn."

"Thanks, call me Grant." Rather than start with his questions, he waited until the woman had seated him at a large kitchen table, fixed him a coffee and called Quadrado's brother, Peter, to request he joined them.

Fletcher knew from Quadrado's emailed briefing notes that Libby was her sister-in-law. Libby was at home in this kitchen, her movements dictated with familiarity. The room itself was spacious with a high ceiling in the colonial style. A dresser the size of a cinema screen hid one wall, but other than the aged stove, it was the only item that wasn't modern. As Fletcher suspected has happened for generations, there's a baby asleep in a crib beside the dresser.

"Zeke let us know why you're here and asked us to help you in any way you ask of us. That was a terrible business with poor, poor Jane." Libby's bottom lip wobbled as she took a seat opposite Fletcher. From her he could see Jane's death had sent ripples of grief radiating out through the community.

"It was indeed. Other than your obvious shock and distress at her death, can you tell me your thoughts on the matter, please?"

"Of course. Jane was a good girl who grew up to become a fine woman. She and Zeke were apparently inseparable from the day they started kindergarten until Zeke joined the FBI. Jane married Carl who was her high school sweetheart and has never looked back. Never heard tell of her nor Carl making eyes at another, which is how it should be, of course, but often isn't. Jane was always one to raise money for charity or to help someone in need. A lot more folks than her family will miss her. Zeke was distraught when Peter called her with the news. How she'll manage without Jane is beyond me." Libby dabbed her eyes with a tissue. "I've always gotten on well enough with Zeke, but it was always Jane she confided in, never me, her own sister-in-law."

The door squeaked open and a Hispanic man strode in. His face grave and his right hand extended to shake. "I'm Peter."

Fletcher rose and took the hand. "Grant Fletcher."

Peter poured a mug of coffee and trailed an affectionate hand across his wife's shoulders as he moved to an empty chair at the table.

"So, Zeke has drafted you in." A look of respectful assessment was sent Fletcher's way. "She must trust you and your abilities. Whatever you need, just ask. We're all cut up about Jane and we all want justice for her, God rest her soul."

"Thank you. Your wife has told me a little about Jane, but I'd like to hear more about her, her husband and the pressures the pair of them may be under. From what I've learned online, dairy farming in Wisconsin is tougher than it's ever been."

Fletcher sat back in his chair and sipped at his coffee as Peter and Libby tag-teamed the information he'd requested. They gave a clear picture of the Friedricksons, their marriage and the struggles facing dairy farmers. A lot of what they said was of little worth, but collectively it slotted together to create a picture of a determined young couple who were in line to take over a family business and build on its solid foundations.

Libby threw a stern look at her husband. "There's the attacks on the farms, you need to tell him about them, Peter."

"What attacks?" As soon as he'd spoken Fletcher was wondering why neither Peter nor Libby had led with this information.

"A few of the local farms have been plagued with bad luck. Fires starting without explanation, more breakdowns than usual and some corn fields blighted."

Libby's hand landed on Peter's arm and gave it a squeeze. "It's more than bad luck, Peter, and you know it. You said as much yourself just the other day."

"Can you tell me a bit more, Peter? Is it bad luck, or actual attacks as Libby says?" There was no way Fletcher could let this thread go unpicked. "Has anyone been hurt before Jane Friedrickson? Is there any proof that it isn't a run of bad luck?"

Peter rose from the table and got himself a glass of water and rested his back against the fridge before answering. "It's more than a run of bad luck, but so far there's no proof. Maybe once a year, there'll be a fire somewhere. There's been six in as many months this year. Plus the number of breakdowns is way higher than usual. Nobody's been hurt and nobody's seen anyone skulking around or anything like that."

"Say these occurrences are deliberate, who would you think is behind it?"

A shrug. "Animal rights activists? Some wack job getting his rocks off by causing damage to hard-working farmers? Kids doing stuff for dares? Who knows? The local cops have looked into it, but they've found nothing."

Libby gave a scornful snort. "What do you expect? They couldn't find a cow if they were holding its tail."

Rather than try to process all this news as he heard it, Fletcher stored it away to mull over when he could give it his full focus.

Fletcher was climbing into the SUV when his phone started to ring; a glance at the screen showed Quadrado's name. With a bit of luck she'd have some further information that would help him work out who killed her friend. All he had so far were vague ideas and a distinct lack of suspects or even motives for someone killing Jane Friedrickson.

CHAPTER EIGHT

Fletcher drove away from Meadowfields with his cell at his ear. Quadrado was concise with her briefing, giving stark facts and proven details. Whether it was because she was trained that way by the FBI, or was staying professional to better control her emotions wasn't something he needed to think about. For all Quadrado's attempt at delivering a businesslike report seemed well put together, there was no mistaking the catch in her voice every time she said Jane's name.

Rather than pull onto the main road with the cell in his hand, Fletcher eased the SUV to one side of the bell-mouthed entrance to Meadowfields and cut the engine. He had questions for Quadrado and he wanted to be able to focus all of his brain on her answers.

"You said her coveralls were open at the front and the buttons of her shirt were torn loose, yet they were the only signs of a sexual element to the assault. Sounds to me like her killer planned to rape her and was interrupted."

"I agree." The two words were little more than a whisper. He got why. Jane had been Quadrado's best friend. As an FBI agent, Quadrado would have worked rape cases. She'd know all the horrors involved. As a woman she'd understand the fear her friend experienced in her last moments. As a human being she was dealing with a buttload of grief. In a lot of ways she was too close to the victim to be an effective investigator. Fletcher knew no Captain or Senior Special Agent would let her work the case if it fell in her jurisdiction. To him that was all bull. Because of the personal angle, she'd be the most dogged, most determined investigator any victim could possibly want. It was just up to him to keep a rein on her and make sure that her grief didn't cloud her thinking.

"If that's the case, it adds a different dimension to things. We know from the blood spatters she was stabbed at the corner of the house, then dragged to the pond. The cops from Medford reported an area of flattened grass by the pond, so it'd be fair to surmise that's where the hashtag and number were carved into her forehead." Fletcher didn't bother explaining to Quadrado that he'd sequenced her friend's homicide in his mind. She'd expect him to have done so and there was nothing except pain to be gained by walking her through it. "If she was to have been sexually assaulted, then either she'd been quick to repel her attacker in one sense, or we can assume that receiving the fatal stab wound was a consequence of her fighting to free herself."

"What are you getting at, Fletcher?"

"You said the coroner's report found no fibers under her nails. Other than the wounds inflicted by the knife, she was unharmed. Does that sound like someone who'd been trying to fight off a rapist to you? Because it doesn't sound like that to me." Fletcher paused to give Quadrado a moment to think.

"Go on, then. What do you think it was?"

"I reckon her killer had no intention of raping her. I think he wants to become infamous. The hashtag number one suggests he's planning more kills."

"Then why were her clothes torn?"

"To mess with our heads? To give the press a juicier story? To create a greater fear factor? You're the FBI agent, you know how these things work. Take your pick, but before you do, answer me one question: was her bra in the right place when her husband found her?"

"You know the answer. You've got the crime scene photos in your file. And as for messing with our heads, I don't get why he'd do that." Anger laced Quadrado's tone, although it was still underpinned with pain.

"To my eyes her bra was where it should have been. I asked Carl if he'd done anything to maintain her dignity. He said he hadn't and I believe him."

"So? The killer was interrupted when he tried to rape her. He wouldn't have had time to undo her bra."

"I disagree." Fletcher kept his tone neutral. "He had time to carve her forehead. Therefore he'd have had time to remove her bra, or at least push it out of the way so he could see or grope her breasts. He did neither of those things, or in fact actually sexually assault her in any way. Ergo, the attack wasn't primarily intended as a sexual assault. The torn clothes are a smokescreen we shouldn't be blinded by. You know as well as I do, rapists rape and killers kill. Rapists who kill still rape as well. That didn't happen."

"Damn you, Fletcher. You can be a real ass at times, but I hope to God you're right. It'd be one tiny crumb of comfort me and Carl could take from this awful situation."

Fletcher didn't comment. Quadrado had lost a lifelong friend. It was clearly rough enough for her to discuss Jane's homicide, so having to imagine her friend fighting off a sexual attack before she was killed was bound to be emotive for her. It was clear how close she was to Jane from the way she'd mentioned herself before Carl. It was normal for people to do this, yet Quadrado was trained to put that emotion aside and think of the victim and their family.

Until Quadrado was ready to speak again, he let his mind digest the broader details she'd told him regarding the autopsy. Jane had suffered a fatal stab wound to the heart. The cuts to her forehead were delivered postmortem. There were only minute traces of pond water in her lungs, which led the coroner to suggest Jane had died from blood loss before she could drown. There were no defensive or offensive wounds on her body and she'd not suffered any sexual assault beyond her clothing being torn.

"The cops out of Medford's best theory is that it was a drifter who happened to see her in town, followed her home, waited his chance, and then tried to rape her and got carried away when she fought back."

"The fact I'm here instead of at home in Utah tells me what you think of the Medford cops. Don't insult me by arguing their theories against mine. Your friend's killer is far cleverer than those cops. He may well be a drifter, but if he is, he's got his own transport. I've an idea I want to check out regarding how he arrived at and left Greenacres Farm." Fletcher explained his theory and got Quadrado's agreement. Although he was going to do it whether she agreed or not.

"If you don't think Jane was killed because she fought off a rapist, what do you think?"

"I'm not sure. I have a few half-formed ideas that don't seem likely. The best I can come up with is that someone tried to seduce Jane, got nowhere and turned nasty enough for her to threaten to inform Carl. That person then killed her, possibly to protect his reputation and possibly because Carl is a hothead who's not afraid to pull a gun. He fired three shots my way earlier today."

"Carl's a crack shot. He might have fired three shots near you, but believe me, if he wanted to kill you, he'd have done it with the first shot."

"That's comforting to know." Fletcher felt immediate shame at his sarcasm, but he didn't apologize. "Can you send the full coroner's report over? I want to take a closer look at a few points."

With the call ended, Fletcher put the SUV into drive and set off towards Greenacres Farm.

CHAPTER NINE

Fletcher parked in a place he figured wouldn't be in anyone's way and went looking for the widowed farmer.

Five minutes later he was climbing back into the SUV and setting off across the fields with Carl's blessing.

When he was a hundred yards from the farm he turned a wide circle and looked back the way he'd come. The SUV's tires had left distinct tramlines in the soil below the corn stubble. He completed his circle and drove towards the outer boundary.

Fletcher's starting point for a slow circumference of Greenacres Farm was a hundred yards from the road and fifty from the track leading to the farmstead. With the speed kept low, he followed a path parallel to the road.

He'd done the math in his head. The farmstead was at least a half mile from any of the roads forming its boundaries. To be certain of not being picked out by the headlights of vehicles on the road, he figured the killer must have parked at least two hundred yards from the road. By the same token, he reckoned Jane's murderer wouldn't have dared to get within four hundred yards of the farmstead lest his engine be heard.

A mile is made up of 1,760 yards. A half mile 880. Take away the 600 yards clearance, and there was a window of at least two hundred and eighty yards where the killer might have stashed his vehicle while he murdered Jane.

By keeping a hundred yards from the road, Fletcher was giving himself the best chance of finding where tracks might lead to or from the road.

He kept his mind clear and focused on the task at hand; thinking about the case could come later. Twice there were tramlines leading off the field. Fletcher dismissed these as belonging to tractors used when harvesting the corn as they were of a greater width than a vehicle like an SUV or pickup would create, and the tire marks forming the tramlines were far wider than the tires of road-going vehicles.

Halfway along the second leg of Greenacres Farm's square perimeter, he found what he was looking for. With the SUV halted he followed the tramlines to the road hoping to see a defined tire print in the dirt.

With there being none, he retraced his steps and followed the flattened stubble until the tracks led to another boundary road. Once again, the hard-packed dirt yielded no tire marks that might help to identify a particular vehicle and tie a suspect to the location.

As he walked back to the SUV he followed the tramlines hoping against logic that he'd spy something he'd missed on his way out.

What he found he didn't so much see as smell. At a point that was furthest from the two boundary roads the vehicle had arrived and left via, Fletcher's nose twitched at the somewhat familiar smell of engine oil.

He gave the area a thorough inspection and found one of the stalks of corn stubble was coated with oil and there was a viscosity to the ground below it.

Whether this would prove to be a solid clue or not Fletcher wasn't sure. All the same, he removed his jacket, and making it as tall as he could, tented it between the tramlines a foot away from where the oil was so he'd be able to find the spot again.

His next move was to patrol the rest of the perimeter in case someone had just stopped to use the field as a make-out spot and the killer had in fact parked in another area.

With his circuit complete, Fletcher pointed the SUV towards the farmstead. He had some follow-up questions for Carl and he wanted to replace his jacket as a marker. There was also the small matter of getting Carl to alert the local cops to the presence of the tracks and the oil. With luck they'd do a professional sweep of the area and take samples of the oil to build a case against any potential suspects.

When he got to the farmstead, Carl was standing by a tractor hooked up to a trailer with conveyors at the sides. Fletcher suspected the trailer was used to supply cut corn to the cattle in the sheds. The tractor's engine was running but Carl was staring at it as if he was either seeing it for the first time, or looking right through it.

"Hey." Not so much a greeting as a polite way to break the spell grief had cast upon the farmer.

"Oh." Carl looked his way, or at least faced him. There was no telling how well he was seeing what was in front of him. "Find anything?"

Fletcher caught the hope in the question, the desire for information, for some clue as to the identity of the person who'd broken Carl's life.

"A pair of tracks and what may be an oil leak where a vehicle was parked. I've marked the leak with my jacket, but we'll need to swap that for something more noticeable."

"Will it help?"

Again there was hope in Carl's voice. It tore at Fletcher to preach caution, yet he was all too aware how destructive false hope could be.

"I don't know. As clues go, it's not much of one. I need you to call the cops and pass off my find as your own. They can analyze the oil and perhaps use it to help secure a prosecution."

"I don't want a prosecution. I want to kill whoever took my Jane away."

Fletcher got Carl's desire for revenge. When grief was at its rawest point, it was a human reaction to want to take an eye for an eye. He would have no part in that though. He'd not deliver anyone up for vigilante justice. As much as Carl might want to personally avenge his wife's homicide, he'd be throwing his life away should he get caught for it.

"I know you do. But if the cops get the guy responsible, the oil, or a tire print they find, might make the difference between a prosecution and him being let go due to a lack of evidence. If you're planning to kill someone, shouldn't you demand the same level of proof?"

Carl's eyes pulled into proper focus for the first time since Fletcher's return to the farm. "I can see why Zeke drafted you. You're proper smart the way you're stopping me going after someone the cops might arrest and then let go."

"And you're nobody's fool to pick up on that."

With Carl being generous, Fletcher took the opportunity to ask what may have been a painful question. "I know we spoke earlier about your wife being the subject of someone's desire, can you think of anyone who may have been sweet on her but never acted upon it to your knowledge?" Fletcher gave a self-deprecating gesture. "I'm not sure it's the case, but at some level, most homicides are about money or sex. You're off my suspect list regarding money and I've heard from Zeke that you and Jane were trying for a baby, so you're cleared on both these counts. That leaves others for sex and money. As her husband, you'd be the main beneficiary if she was killed for money, so it makes no sense someone else would kill her for financial gain, which brings us back to sex. Is there anyone, a worker, a supplier or whatever you can think of who might have been hitting on her without you knowing?"

"None I can think of. Folks in these parts aren't like city folks jumping from one bed to another. We respect each other and don't go sniffing after another man's wife or girlfriend."

Fletcher had his doubts the area was as pure as Carl made it sound. He didn't push it though. That was the kind of detail Quadrado or one of her family could confirm or deny.

"What about her family farm? Zoey said she was in line to inherit that. Who's likely to take her place there?"

"Nobody. She was the only child of two only children. Her parents had her young, though, and are likely to be around a long time yet."

This was another bust, but at least it crossed a line of inquiry off Fletcher's mental list. All the same, he'd verify what Carl had told him with Quadrado.

Movement snagged at the corner of Fletcher's eye. He turned and saw a sedan barreling along the track from the road. A look at Carl showed both recognition and dejection on his face.

"It's my parents. They were on vacation in Europe."

The sedan yanked itself to a halt and spat out a couple who'd soon be entering their sixties if they hadn't already. The woman dressed in velour, the man head-to-toe in worn denim and a cowboy hat that made him look like the Marlboro Man's father.

"Damn sorry to hear 'bout Jane, son. Hell of a shame that. Woulda been back sooner but damned airlines weren't any help."

The man climbed into the tractor and shut it off as the woman embraced Carl, her assortment of bangles jingling as she moved. Not a single tear dampened her cheeks, but her face was crumpled in grief at both losing a daughter-in-law and the effect Jane's homicide had on her son.

Carl's father dropped to the ground and strode back to them. "No point in wasting good diesel. Let's go inside where we can talk. Mom can put the kettle on and we can get a proper coffee insteada that muck they serve in Europe." A flicked glance at Fletcher. "Who are you, a cop?"

"A friend of a friend." Fletcher was already taking a dislike to Carl's father. It may be grief that was making him so brusque and uncaring, but if there was any shred of decency in the man, or respect for his son, he'd not shown it yet.

It was a family dynamic Fletcher had seen before. A domineering parent and a child so used to being railroaded they no longer saw the level of control being exerted over them. Carl's father was a typical alpha male: confident in his position at the top of the pyramid and unafraid of challenges to his authority. In a few years if he became frailer and dependent on his son for physical help, his lack of control would be shown through bitterness and insults.

"Then get yourself gone. There's work to be done and we don't have time for strangers."

Carl's arm pointed at one of the empty drums stacked against a barn, so Fletcher gave a nod that he understood he'd been shown a replacement marker, and left the Friedricksons to themselves. From what he'd judged of Carl's father, it would be more like a board meeting than a family hug or a healing session.

CHAPTER TEN

Fletcher sipped at his beer and recounted his experience with Old Man Friedrickson. The more he thought about it, the less he liked the dynamic at play. Carl needed support and love from his family to nurse him through the darkest of times, and while Fletcher's mental jury was out on Carl's mother, he was in no doubt that Old Man Friedrickson would treat Jane's homicide as an inconvenience rather than a tragedy.

What galled him most of all was the way Carl let his father bulldoze him. It could be the burden of his sorrow had dissipated any desire to stand up to his father, or it could be a history of failing to do so that had left him so subservient. Either way, the confident shooter and the man who wanted to murder his wife's killer disappeared as soon as the door to his father's sedan had opened.

Time would help Carl overcome his grief. As healers went, it was the greatest of all. The desire for revenge would take longer to go. It had been more than fourteen years since a careless driver had precipitated the automobile crash which saw Fletcher's wife Rachel lose her life in the most horrific way. Those hundred and seventy-two months had eased the loss to a level that was manageable. What they hadn't eased were the fantasies about hunting down the other driver, or the guilt Fletcher carried.

Carl would have his own guilt. He'd blame himself for not getting up instead of his wife. He'd blame himself for not being there to protect her. Hour after hour until it became year after year, he'd point the finger of recrimination at his own chest. He'd think of what may have been. Imagine the kids they should have had, the vacations they'd have taken together and the journey they'd have traveled on side by side through life. All Jane's most annoying traits would be forgotten as irritants and rebranded as loveable quirks. She would be placed upon a pedestal so high no other woman could hope to climb it.

Fletcher had gotten through his own trauma by focusing on the needs of his infant daughter. Wendy had been the light to guide him through grief's darkest moments. Had it not been for her, he *would* have tracked down and killed the other driver. Her presence alone kept him on the straight and narrow, prevented him from seeking solace at the bottom of a bottle. Since Rachel… died—Fletcher couldn't think of it any other way—there had been no other women in Fletcher's life. He'd not been on a single date and hadn't found the desire to do so. On a couple of occasions, Wendy had engineered clumsy meetings with the single mother of her best friend, yet despite his daughter's obvious blessing, Fletcher wasn't ready to date again. Wasn't sure if he'd ever be.

Carl would have all this to face without the unconditional love Wendy had for him, and for this reason as much as the unsupportive father, Fletcher was sure Carl's darkest times were yet to come. Firsts were the hardest things to get over. On birthdays, anniversaries and festive holidays, the empty chair would seem bigger than usual. The Valentine's card with Jane's handwriting would never again adorn the mantelpiece. Every year on his birthday and at Christmas, Fletcher put the last cards Rachel had given him on display. Wendy, with all the wisdom of a teenager, had recently chided him that it was time to move on, but then he caught her looking at the cards, reading and re-reading her mother's loving messages.

As he always did when thinking of his wife and daughter, Fletcher's fingers caressed the locket he always wore. It carried their pictures and, other than Wendy herself, it was the one thing he'd save in a fire.

Fletcher pulled himself away from the melancholy thoughts, ordered another bottle of beer and cast a look around the bar. It was no more unique than a blade of grass. As a former Royal Marine, Fletcher had traveled the world and spent more than a few hours in bars of every kind.

The Tavern had a pool table, dartboard, laminated menus and a collection of disparate drinkers. There were men in jeans, a guy in a rumpled suit and a couple of women who looked as tough as any of the men present. A young couple sat in a corner, their fingers interlinked as they chatted, and an older couple sat in stony-faced silence as they drank. The pictures on the wall were a collection of local landmarks and gangs of workers engaged in rural tasks. A TV was showing a sports channel although the sound was muted. Fletcher had enjoyed many good nights in worse places and been thrown out of better ones.

The bottle of beer was cool and refreshing so Fletcher made short work of it.

He caught the bartender's attention and ordered another beer. When the bottle touched down on a napkin, he began his real purpose for visiting the Tavern.

"I hear there was a woman killed in these parts recently. Bad business that. What happened?"

The bartender cast a look around and kept his voice low. "Not sure. I did hear that she was walking about her farm early in the morning and her husband found her face down in the pond with knife wounds in her chest and 'first' carved into her cheek. As you said. Bad business."

Fletcher didn't miss how the bartender had gotten the details wrong. It was standard fare for each teller of a gruesome story to get something wrong and embellish facts a little to further enhance their version of events. The truth would soon be learned, but for the time being, the locals were creating their own theories. "That's awful. Who'd do such a thing?"

"Lot of sick people in the world today." The way the bartender rubbed the back of a finger against the underside of his nose, made Fletcher glad he wasn't drinking from a glass. "You ask me, whoever did such a thing to a good woman ought to face the chair."

"So you knew her then?"

"I knew her. Like I said, she was a good woman. Loved her husband and never let no one turn her head, although she was never short of offers."

"Interesting. I'm sure her poor husband is cut up."

"Course he is. Who wouldn't be?" The bartender's voice had risen to accompany the scorn of his words.

The additional volume had attracted the attention of two guys drinking at the far end of the bar.

They sauntered over. All macho image and beer fumes. One six and a half feet of gangle, the other a five foot sphere of burst capillaries topped by a bald head.

Gangle paused a yard from Fletcher, propped an elbow on the bar counter and spoke to the bartender while glaring at Fletcher. "This bozo giving you a problem, Don?"

"No. We're just jawing. Go back to your seat. Ain't no need for you to step in."

The bartender's tone intrigued Fletcher. Instead of being commanding it was subservient to the point of wheedling. Most bartenders could read their customers and were authoritarian enough to control troublemakers. Some were tough enough to deal with them head-on if the need arose. These were the bars where trouble was infrequent.

It would appear the imaginatively named Tavern was the kind of bar where the customers ruled the roost. Gangle and his pal Bald were types Fletcher had seen in bars on many occasions all over the world. They were the fighters, men who didn't consider a drinking session to be complete unless a few punches had been thrown. Fletcher had been chosen as tonight's target, and while he would never back down, he could well do without getting into it with a pair of local knuckleheads.

"It's cool, buddy. Like Don was saying, we were just chatting. No harm, no foul."

Bald stepped forward, his bulging gut framed by the suspenders holding his jeans up. "Didn't sound like chatting. Sounded like you was upsetting Don. We don't like Don being upset and think you oughta leave."

Fletcher eased off his stool ready for the fight that was now inevitable and stood belly to belly with Bald. If he left they'd follow him outside. In here there were plenty of witnesses to attest who'd thrown the first punch. Leaving would also mean he couldn't return to question the locals at another time without either local bully squaring up to him again.

There was nothing for it. He'd have to fight them.

"I think otherwise. But then again, I can count to twenty without taking my shoes off and I use a big boy pen instead of crayons."

CHAPTER ELEVEN

As expected, Bald and Gangle reacted to the insult Fletcher had tossed their way. Bald was closest so he was the first of the two Fletcher had to deal with.

There was no doubt in Fletcher's mind as to who would win the fight. All the same, he had to let Bald or Gangle be the ones to throw the first punch.

Bald had his own tactic. Instead of a punch, he threw himself forward, his entire body advancing, bulldozer style. Even though he was poised ready for a fight, Fletcher wasn't braced to withstand the impact of three hundred pounds thumping into him. He was driven backwards until his spine slammed into the bar. A left cross was thrown towards his head.

Fletcher blocked the punch with a forearm. He'd learned long ago that when fighting someone as spherical as Bald, throwing punches at the head wasn't a good idea as it brought him right into the man's orbit. With his back against the bar and Bald's huge belly pressing against him he couldn't dig a solid punch into the guy's ribs or gut.

A set of bony knuckles snaked past Bald's ear and slammed into Fletcher's cheek. Gangle had joined in.

Fletcher made as if he was trying to squirm right away from Bald and felt him shift his bulk to keep him pinned. The movement was enough to achieve Fletcher's aim of widening Bald's stance.

Fletcher's right leg powered upwards with all the force he could muster. He felt the flesh of Bald's flabby legs inhibiting his rising knee, but still managed to acquire his target with enough force to make Bald gasp.

A hard push on Bald's chest and Fletcher was able to free himself and get ready to deal with Gangle.

Gangle had taken a step back and was waving Fletcher forward. To follow his instructions would be foolish. Bald was hurting, but he wasn't out of the fight yet; if Fletcher did as Gangle wanted, the taller guy would be able to keep him at bay with a series of long-range jabs until Bald recovered enough to attack Fletcher's exposed back.

To counter that, Fletcher drove an elbow into the side of Bald's head. The way he was bent forward cupping his groin made the move simple to execute and very effective as Bald didn't see it coming.

With Bald now out of commission, Fletcher could deal with Gangle. Two steps brought him to a point where he was confident he was close enough to tempt Gangle into launching a punch, yet far enough away to have time to react to it.

There was a shift in Gangle. Nothing huge or telegraphed, just a minute change in his stance and a fleeting flicker in his eyes. To someone with Fletcher's training and experience it was as obvious as a distress flare.

Gangle feinted a rangy left jab, stepped forward and threw a right uppercut that had enough force to lift Fletcher off his feet and dump him in an unconscious heap. Or at least, that's what would have happened if the uppercut had connected.

The problem with exhibition punches like Gangle's uppercut was that if they didn't land on target, they left the person who'd thrown them exposed to a counterattack. Fletcher dug a left hook into Gangle's ribs then showed him how to land an uppercut.

Gangle didn't go down. He stood and wobbled on jello legs until Fletcher plucked a chair from the nearest table and eased him into it.

Bald was back on his feet, yet he was little steadier than Gangle. Fletcher sat an empty chair beside Gangle and pointed to it.

"Don." Fletcher waved a hand at the two men he'd beaten. "Get these guys a whiskey with a beer back, will you?"

Once Don had poured them, Fletcher handed the drinks to the still groggy men.

Bald took his drinks and eyed Fletcher with suspicion. "What you doing this for?"

"To show there's no hard feelings. You picked the wrong guy to fight. Between you, you landed one blow on me. I hit you both twice and you were out of the game. I could have hit you more. Could have hit you harder. I chose not to. Next time you step in front of me, I'll not be so lenient. Take the drinks, learn the lesson you've been taught and forget about bothering me again."

Fletcher sat back onto his stool and picked up his bottle of beer. Don was making himself look busy at the other end of the bar. After what had happened, he wouldn't want to be seen to be showing favor to a stranger over the locals. It made sense as Fletcher was aware that while he hoped to be back in Utah before long, Gangle and Bald would be here next week, next month, next year.

CHAPTER TWELVE

Fletcher pulled the covers over his body and lay his head on the pillow to continue thinking about why Gangle and Bald had been so quick to want to fight him. His early thought that they were a pair of bullies who liked to throw their weight around still stood, but only to a degree.

What he also had to factor in was a rural town mentality. Places like Medford could be insular; the locals would be used to strangers passing through, but they'd always keep them at arm's length, doubly so for the ones who asked questions about an event that would have shocked the community. Around these parts, farming was the main industry and there were many other businesses supported on the back of the farms. Sure, there would be realtors, lawyers and other professions same as any other place, but the majority of the work they'd do would be for the farms, the farm workers or those who worked on supporting businesses.

There were few tourist attractions in the area to draw strangers, so the community wouldn't see a large amount of visitors; the motel only having twelve bedrooms was testament to the scarcity of visitors and it wouldn't surprise Fletcher to learn the motel's main customer base consisted of specialist workers who'd come to the area to install some piece of equipment at a farm or the creamery in Medford.

For a popular local, as Jane had been portrayed, to have been killed would have sent a shockwave throughout the area. In places the size of Medford, everyone was no more than two degrees of separation from everyone else, and while they might not get along too well, they'd stick together. In a lot of ways, such towns were like families. They'd fight and bicker with each other all day, then at night stand shoulder to shoulder with each other if one of their number was under threat.

All the same, the response was heavier than needed. Don, the bartender, had failed in his attempt to calm the two guys down. The more Fletcher thought about it, the more he was reverting back to his original thinking. Gangle and Bald had been bullies spoiling for a fight. They'd gotten one they hadn't expected by challenging him. Even though he'd gone easy on them, he felt no remorse for the pain he'd inflicted. They'd come at him, therefore their injuries were self-inflicted.

In an odd way, Fletcher was pleased about the way he'd dealt with them; neither man had shed any blood, and there had been no damage to the bar, not even a spilled drink.

With his fingers drumming against his chest, Fletcher focused his thoughts on the homicide he was supposed to be investigating.

He was no closer to establishing a decent theory, let alone a suspect other than Carl. What galled him most was his growing suspicion Jane was chosen at random by an itinerant killer determined to make a name for himself. Not only would this support the thinking of the cops from Medford, it would greatly lessen the chances of him being able to identify and apprehend the killer.

To counter the dark direction his thoughts were taking, he tapped out a message to Quadrado asking her to search databases to see if any other homicide victims across the country had ever had similar messages to Jane's carved into their foreheads.

CHAPTER THIRTEEN

The ringing of his phone wasn't a sound that would make Fletcher move in a hurry. While he liked the connectivity cell phones gave, he loathed how they'd become so dominant in so many people's lives. He was more used to seeing the top of his daughter's head than her face, and it was the one thing they would fight about.

Regardless of this, he still dashed from the bathroom with a face covered with shaving cream and grabbed his phone from the bed when it rang. This early in the morning, it could only be Quadrado.

It was.

He put the phone to his ear and grabbed a pen and a notebook in case he needed to jot anything down.

"Your query about more victims with the hashtag message," a pause came down the line as Quadrado took a deep breath, "there were no previous cases, but... damnit, Fletcher." Fletcher didn't need to hear more. He could guess what was coming next. All the same, he didn't interrupt Quadrado. "A farmer has been found murdered. He'd been laid up with a bad back and his wife was overseeing the early milking. When she went back to the house she found him with his throat cut."

"Did he have the hashtag on his forehead?"

"Yeah. Hashtag two." Quadrado's voice lost composure and gained anger. "What kind of sicko does that to a man in his bed? To a woman on her way to work?"

"Where was the farm, Wisconsin or somewhere else?" Fletcher gabbled the question, as it was critical information.

"It was White Birch."

The way Quadrado didn't explain where the farm was told Fletcher it was local. There had also been a catch in her voice that said a lot. He thought of the signs he'd passed when looking for Greenacres Farm and Meadowfields. He didn't recall seeing one for White Birch, but that didn't mean he hadn't passed it and remembered it, since it wasn't what he was looking for.

"I gather that's near here. Do you know the farmer?"

"I know him, I've known him all my life. White Birch is next to Meadowfields. It's also opposite Greenacres at the crossroads."

Fletcher could place White Birch now. The tramlines he'd found at Greenacres Farm had cut the corner off the crossroads. This development meant the killer was operating in this area and targeting local farms. It was bad news all round; although, on a selfish level, Fletcher was heartened the killer's second victim hadn't been in another state as catching a moving target would be many times harder than apprehending someone in a localized area.

"What was the farmer's name?"

"Walt Renard." A sniff. "He was a good guy, Fletcher. He and my father have been friends as long as I can remember. Walt always had candy for me and Peter when we were kids. This feels like someone is going after my family's friends. I know it's wrong to think that, but that's how it feels."

"I doubt that's what's happening, but if it is, you have to believe me when I say we'll get him. Now, I need information from you. Need you to be at your best so I can find this guy before he strikes again. How was he regarded locally?"

"He was well-liked. He was one of those guys who didn't speak much, but when he said something, it was worth listening to. Everybody liked him. Everybody."

"Okay. What about his farm? Was it doing well or was it in trouble?"

Another sniff. "It was doing well as far as I'm aware. My father would know."

"In that case I need you to speak to your father at once. You need to trawl everything he knows about Walt Renard. About his farm, his finances, grievances with people and anything else you can think to ask or your father might mention, then feed that back to me."

"What are you going to do?"

"Go there and see what I can find out."

"You can't just go and ask questions. You have no jurisdiction. Nobody will give you the time of day."

"What else can I do? You're paying me to investigate Jane's homicide; we've got another the same, so I'm going to take a ride over there to see what I can learn. What else do you expect me to do?" Fletcher tried not to let anger creep into his voice, although he was pissed at the way his hands were tied. "I'm still going to go there. If what you're saying is true, then you'd better work out a way to get me a badge of some sort or I might as well go home for all the use I'll be." Fletcher had his own methods of getting information from people, and while he didn't want the confines a badge would bring him, it might prove useful to have one for a change.

"Please. Please don't go home, Fletcher. I need you to be there. To get to the bottom of these killings. My family live there. Peter or my mom or pop could be next. Or Libby. I've already lost Jane to this killer, I can't bear the thought of losing a family member to them."

"I get that." He'd have had to have been made of rock not to hear the desperation in Quadrado's voice. "But you either fix me up with some kind of ID or a badge so I can speak to folks like the Renards, or prepare yourself to deal with the shitstorm my methods usually leave behind."

Fletcher cut the call and thought about the conversation with Quadrado. He hadn't wanted to be hard on her, but his point stood. Without some kind of official approval, it'd be so much harder for him to run the kind of investigation she seemed to want him to run.

CHAPTER FOURTEEN

Quadrado eased back into her chair and powered up her laptop. As well as everything that was going on back in Wisconsin, her current case was grinding to a halt while her boss's demands for results were growing with every passing day.

Her father had been at White Birch with her mother to support Walt Renard's widow when Quadrado called him on her drive to work. She'd ended up imploring her dad to take precautions for the safety of the whole family. His grim reply had told her his mind was already thinking along the same lines she was.

None of the answers she'd gotten from him filled her with any kind of hope. Maybe Fletcher with his unique and cynical way of looking at things would be able to find a lead among them. She couldn't see any sign of one.

On a lot of levels, Quadrado knew she was too close to the victims to think with the necessary objectivity needed to conduct a professional investigation. Yet there was no way she was stepping back from the investigation. Walt Renard had been like an uncle to her. And Jane, Jane had been the sister she'd never had. Jane had been the one she'd giggled with about boys. Jane had known of her every childhood crush. It had been Jane she'd run to when her heart was broken or she'd reached one of life's milestones. Jane had been the one to cover for her when she'd snuck away to spend the night with Harry Sommers. Jane was the person who knew everything about her and was closest to her in every meaningful way. As she thought about Jane, she was oscillating between remembering the good times she'd spent in Jane's company, a burning fury that was compelling her to seek a vengeance she mustn't take, and giving in to the crushing grief threatening to overwhelm her.

Fletcher had that separation and, while he wasn't without compassion, he had a cold analytical way about him that smashed through any roadblocks emotion might construct.

While her laptop booted up, she used her phone to send a message to the shadowy figure who'd recruited her and Fletcher. She put forward every argument she could think of to get a badge or some kind of official recognition for Fletcher as well as giving a brief update on his progress and the fact a second victim had been found.

The first thing she did once her laptop was ready was email the key points of her conversation with her father to Fletcher. The sooner he had these details the sooner he'd be able to get his brain working.

A pinging sound had her reaching for her phone. In her haste, she knocked the cardboard cup of takeout coffee she always started her day with off her desk and onto the thin carpet tiles covering the floor.

Quadrado couldn't help but curse when the cup landed in a way that allowed its lid to split from the cup and disgorge its contents. She wasn't so much worried about the ratty carpet tiles as the loss of a good coffee. Today had been more than tough enough, without her caffeine crutch being taken away. Worst of all was the fact she knew she wasn't clumsy. She wasn't one who bumped into things, tripped over her own feet or knocked stuff over. She was precise in her movements and therefore recognized the clumsiness as being founded in her distraction.

The case she was on was one she no longer cared about. She just wanted it finished so she could head to Wisconsin, hug her family and offer condolences to Carl in person. She wanted to catch Jane's killer. To discover what had compelled him to take the life of such a special person.

It took her five minutes using paper towels from the bathroom to mop up the worst of the spill, although she was sure there would be another stain on the tiles when they dried out. It was a simple act, cleaning up the spill, but such was her fragile mental state, the fact she'd spilled the coffee had her on the verge of tears.

With the cleaning done and her emotions under a tight control, she returned her attention to the phone and let out a second curse.

Her request to get Fletcher a badge of some form had been denied along with the note that to ask again would be seen as offering up an excuse for future failings.

CHAPTER FIFTEEN

Fletcher stomped out of the motel room and made his way to his car. The first email from Quadrado had been bad enough due to its sparsity of usable information. As for the second, it had been the digital equivalent of a kick in the teeth with a steel-toe-capped boot worn by an NFL placekicker.

To hell with Quadrado. He'd just have to go to White Birch and do the best he could. Quadrado had promised to keep an eye on the local cops by scouring police databases as she'd done with Jane's homicide.

It was something, but not a lot as the information was old news by the time the cops had returned back to their station, written up their reports and the reports made it into the databases. They also missed out nuances and the cops' hunches, as no sensible cop would commit a hunch to a database until they'd done the groundwork to support their thinking.

The request for a badge had been his way of dealing with a thought that had been plaguing him since Quadrado had first called.

She was an FBI agent so it stood to reason she had friends in the bureau. At the least she'd have acquaintances she could call on for a favor or two. She might even have a marker or two she could draw in. Either way, she'd have proper law-enforcement-based folks she could call on before him. Yet she hadn't called on them. She'd drafted him in.

The email with the information had come separate from the answer to his question about a badge. He'd been speaking to her when he made those requests. There was no way she would be able to get him a badge. She didn't have the pull to do such things. He was a civilian, had undergone no investigative training and had a homicide rap hanging over him. She ought to have told him as much when he made the request. She hadn't though, she'd delayed the answer and had sent it separate from the information he'd requested at the same time. Which meant the decision for him not to get a badge wasn't hers. She'd asked someone else the question. Her direct boss and the FBI field office in Wisconsin would have both laughed at the request, which meant that she'd asked the question of someone else. Someone who had the pull to make such a thing happen.

The identity of the person or persons she'd gone to wasn't hard to figure out. It would be the shadowy people who'd gotten her to offer him a deal after what happened down in Georgia.

This also explained how she'd been able to arrange for FBI agents to meet him at the airport, give him a gun and the keys to an SUV.

Quadrado had never mentioned the shadowy figures, and he could only see one reason for the omission. He was being tested before they put him on a mission that mattered to them. Succeed and Wendy would be sponsored through college while he undertook missions. Fail and he might end up being sent back to Georgia to face homicide charges for the man he'd killed.

As happy as Fletcher might be for the cops to catch this killer, his own future depending upon him solving the case before they did meant he was in direct competition with the cops.

The way the shadowy figure or figures was hamstringing him by not giving him a shred of jurisdiction made Fletcher wonder if this was a forlorn assignment he was destined to fail.

As he neared the SUV, a cop car screeched its way into the parking lot and slid to a halt in a way that blocked Fletcher's vehicle in its space.

Rather than risk increasing his troubles by arguing with the cops that he needed his vehicle, he stopped his march and rested a butt cheek against the hood of a battered hatchback.

From the way the cops had arrived it was clear they were intent on making an arrest and were trying to get the element of surprise by coming in fast. In a couple of minutes they'd either have their target or would be moving off to try another location.

Two cops exited the car. One was young enough to have never used a razor and the other wasn't. The older of the two was heavier set than any reputable doctor would advise and had a mess of gray hair trying to escape the captivity of his hat.

It stood to reason the older cop would be the one in charge, and this was proven within seconds of him getting to his feet. The pistol in his hand pointed straight at Fletcher as he barked an instruction at Young Cop.

Fletcher reacted to the cop's aim by slowly moving his arms away from his sides and resting them on top of his head. Old Cop would have years of experience, but that didn't mean he wasn't the trigger-happy type who'd shoot first and ask questions later.

"Good morning."

"On your knees, Fletcher. Keep those hands where I can see them."

The fact Old Cop had used his name gave Fletcher all the information he needed at this moment in time. They were here for him. Their reasons were as yet unknown, but he was sure he'd learn why he was being arrested before long.

"Of course." Fletcher eased himself down onto his knees. Scrubbed his left knee side to side so it wasn't resting on a stone. "Just so you're aware, I have a pistol holstered on my right hip and a knife in my right boot."

If you're innocent, it's never a bad idea to forewarn cops pointing a gun at you where your weapons are; they only get pissed when they find them and the last thing you need with cops is to get off on the wrong foot.

"Don't get smart with me, sonny. One false move from you and I won't hesitate to pull the trigger."

Fletcher didn't make any moves, false or otherwise. Old Cop was just as Fletcher had expected him to be: an alpha dog keen to impress a pup while also burnishing his reputation.

Old Cop gave a series of terse instructions to Young Cop.

To keep Old Cop from pulling his trigger, Fletcher allowed Young Cop to remove his weapons, pat him down for others and handcuff him. Rather than antagonize Old Cop, Fletcher kept silent and amused himself by counting the times he could have broken free, disarmed and shot both cops.

The fact he got to four showed the extreme lack of competence displayed by the two cops.

Once the cops were walking him to their car Fletcher felt Old Cop had calmed down enough for him to speak without being shot. "Can I ask why you're arresting me?"

"Been two homicides in our area. You been spotted with a knife sticking out of your boot and you got yourself into a fight at the Tavern last night. Sounds to me like you're trouble. Odd that people start dying when trouble comes to town. We heard all about you asking Don at the Tavern questions about Jane Friedrickson. We know you've been out to the Friedrickson place. Heard about how you found some tracks and an oil stain."

This was more information about his movements than Fletcher had expected the local cops to have gotten this soon. As much as it might be a bad idea to try and grill Old Cop, Fletcher couldn't not ask more questions.

"Have you asked yourself why I went back to the crime scene if you think I'm the killer? Why I'd potentially help you by looking for the wheel marks and letting you know about them?"

"Don't try and be clever with me, Fletcher. I'm thinking you're one of those sickos who get off on seeing the grief they've caused. That you're finding so-called evidence so you can throw us off the track. You might think us rural folks are dumb as a stick, but you'd be wrong."

Fletcher ignored Old Cop's glare and let Young Cop put him in the back of the cop car. There was no point arguing; Old Cop had his theory and he'd bend his understanding of the evidence to make it fit.

It took more than an hour for the cops to get Fletcher booked into a Medford PD cell. Fletcher was compliant at all times as there was nothing to be gained from antagonizing the two cops. He answered the basic questions he was asked and his only comments regarding the allegations against him were that he was entitled to a phone call and he'd like to make that call at the earliest possible moment.

Old Cop sat Fletcher down at a cluttered desk, handed him the system phone and leaned back in his chair, arms folded with a smug look on his face. Fletcher reckoned Old Cop would expect him to call a lawyer or a loved one. He called neither of those.

From memory he dialed Quadrado's cell number and waited for a connection. He didn't get one.

When the service kicked in, he left a brief message about his arrest, where he was and the time.

He had nothing to gain by stating the time, but he wanted her to know how much of his time the arrest was going to waste.

CHAPTER SIXTEEN

The holding cell where Fletcher had been detained was functional, small and stank worse than ten-day roadkill.

Fletcher couldn't pace more than two steps in any direction so he sat on the bench that doubled as a bed and tried not to let his temper rise. The delay to his case was infuriating and all the time he was incarcerated in the cell, the cops investigating the homicides would be leapfrogging him. Or at least they would be in the time between realizing he was innocent and when they saw fit to release him. He knew that in the greater scheme of things, it didn't much matter who caught the killer so long as they were caught, but to him it was a matter of personal pride as he didn't accept second place in any situation. There was also the fact that if he was right in his suspicions about being tested, the cops solving the case before him would mean he'd failed.

The one consolation he had was Old Cop seemed to be in charge of things, and as much as he might try and make the evidence fit Fletcher as a suspect, Fletcher knew his innocence would be backed up by Quadrado, which meant the cops were wasting their time pursuing the wrong suspect. A counterpoint to this was the odds against catching a murderer increased at an exponential rate with every passing hour.

As well as the good it would do him to solve the homicides, it would also mean a killer was taken off the streets and the sooner that happened, the fewer victims there'd be.

The fact he'd not bothered to take many notes worked in Fletcher's favor as it meant he'd committed most of the details he'd learned to memory. In his mind he plotted out a map of the sites he knew.

Greenacres and White Birch farms faced one another on opposite quadrants of a crossroads. Both had had one of the farm owners' family members killed on site. On the other sides of the crossroads lay Broken Spur and Calvertsholm.

All four of the farms had been afflicted by the run of bad luck Peter Quadrado had mentioned, with Calvertsholm the worst affected until the homicides. Yet the farms at the crossroads weren't the only farms to have a higher-than-usual number of incidents in the past year. Meadowfields had been blighted with troubles as had a couple dozen other farms in the area.

The bad luck could be just that, or it could be something else. The question was, if it was something else, what was it?

Fletcher's next move was to compare and contrast the two victims. One was an elderly farmer, the other a young farmer's wife. From what he'd gathered from Quadrado about Walt Renard, Fletcher had surmised he'd be on the point of retirement, or at least, as close as a farmer can get to such a state. White Birch was largely being run by his son, although Quadrado had made it clear Renard Senior would still have a major say in things.

Jane Friedrickson's role at Greenacres Farm was a different thing altogether. From the way Old Man Friedrickson had treated his grieving son, Fletcher doubted Carl would at best have anything better than a supervisor's position. Jane might been seen as Carl's equal, but in Old Man Friedrickson's eyes that wouldn't amount to a glowing reference.

The more Fletcher chewed at his thoughts, the more he found they had a bitter taste. The fingers of his right hand stopped drumming on his knee to slam down on the bench.

The positions of the victims in the hierarchy of their farmsteads didn't make any kind of pattern possible as Walt was the real power in one, whereas Jane was at the other end of the scale. Therefore the run of bad luck and proximity of the kills to each other couldn't be discounted as the closeness of the two kill sites was the only connection that made any sense.

There might be no obvious link between the two homicide victims, but Fletcher was certain that somehow, somewhere, there was a thread tying Jane Friedrickson and Walt Renard together. All Fletcher had to do was get out of jail, find the thread and follow it until it led him to their killer.

CHAPTER SEVENTEEN

The looks Fletcher got from the two cops would have amused him in different circumstances. Young Cop had an expression of reverent awe while Old Cop's face was twisted in disgust as he released Fletcher.

Quadrado had come through for him and pulled the necessary strings to have him released. Old Cop had a clear issue with his best suspect having greater pull than he did, but that was his worry, not Fletcher's.

"You're free to go. Be careful out there."

Old Cop's words may have been civil, but there was no mistaking the anger underpinning his tone or the implied threat of the last sentence.

So far as Fletcher was concerned, Old Cop wasn't a threat on any level. If he tried to interfere with Fletcher's investigation or arrest him again, all Fletcher would need to do to get Old Cop to back off was remind him of the friends he had.

Young Cop led Fletcher to the squad car. As his SUV was still at the motel on the other side of town, a ride back would be appreciated and he was glad it was the younger cop who'd been appointed as his taxi driver. For all he was dominated by Old Cop, Young Cop seemed decent and there was a spark of intelligence in his eyes. With luck Old Cop would soon retire allowing Young Cop to work with someone who'd train him in a way that didn't involve leaping to dumb conclusions.

Fletcher chose to sit in the back rather than accept the offer to ride up front. He wanted to check his phone for email updates from Quadrado. While he'd been arrested, other cops might well have searched the site where Renard was killed, spoken to potential witnesses and a dozen other things Fletcher wanted to do. While Fletcher didn't think Young Cop would spy on his messages, he didn't want to give him the opportunity. Like it or not, he was in competition with the cops and his arrest had given them a minimum of a three-hour head start.

There were several emails from Quadrado. Each one bearing a different report.

The first email he selected detailed the coroner's initial findings at the second murder scene. Walt Renard had been killed in his bed. A stab wound to the chest and a slash to his throat were the major wounds recorded. The #2 on his forehead minor by comparison to the two life-ending wounds.

The coroner had refused to say whether it was the stab or slash which had ended Renard's life until he'd performed the autopsy, but he'd felt confident enough to state the stab to the heart had been the first injury he'd received.

The homicide method fit with Jane Friedrickson's homicide. A stab wound and then a mark on the forehead. The slash to Renard's throat was a new development. After a moment's thought about why he'd received an extra wound, Fletcher surmised Renard's throat had been cut to stop him shouting for help.

There's a period when after receiving a serious injury where the body's natural defense mechanisms take over. Before pain receptors transmit details of a wound to the brain, the body is already shrinking arteries at the wound site, dumping hormones to combat the pain and putting the victim into shock. The real pain follows a second or two later when the victim has realized the extent of the wound.

Jane had been on her feet when stabbed. It would have been easy for her killer to loop an arm around her neck and clamp a hand over her mouth. A tough old farmer lying in a bed wouldn't be so easy to silence. Despite the trauma to his chest, he'd probably had enough fight about him to try calling for help. Maybe it was a warning to his wife rather than a request for assistance. Either way, a slash to the throat would silence any cries he made.

That the killer had hung around to leave his message spoke of confidence, of a need to have his kills attributed to him.

The next email was a summary of statements taken from the White Birch farm workers and Renard's wife and son.

None of them had seen or heard anything as they'd all been at work in the milking parlor. The wife and son had known of no enemies and there had been no disputes of note with anyone in the last year. The two workers had been employed by the Renards for years, and like the guys at Greenacres Farm, they, along with Renard's wife and son, all provided alibis for each other.

Another email detailed when the autopsy was scheduled and gave a time for a briefing. It also stated that samples of the oil leak Fletcher had found had been collected and sent to the lab in Milwaukee. Test results were expected back by Friday afternoon at the soonest.

The final email was a list of officers and the tasks assigned to them. Fletcher was pleased to see there were only four cops working the two homicide cases and that one of them had been tasked with repeating Fletcher's search for tracks.

With all this new information to add to what he already knew, Fletcher sat back in his seat, closed his eyes, and let his brain wander along the various tracks the evidence had created. All seemed to be dead ends, yet he was sure there would be something to give him a solid lead to follow, he just had to find out what it was.

Young Cop was a steady driver and he got Fletcher back to the motel without any drama.

As Fletcher was crossing the parking lot to his SUV, he checked his phone again to see if Quadrado had managed to get him any more updates.

Her name was against an unopened email with a blank subject line.

He opened the email more with hope than expectation.

The email had a picture of a courtroom and a link. When he tapped the link he was directed to a Wikipedia page that detailed the state of Georgia's ruling on capital punishment.

It was all Fletcher could do not to launch his cell at the SUV. Quadrado hadn't needed to be so graphic when pushing him to solve the case. He might owe her a favor, but for her to pressure and threaten him in this way was both cruel and unnecessary. She might be paying him to be here, but Fletcher vowed that when he next spoke to her, she'd get every one of his thoughts on her crass behavior and damn the consequences.

CHAPTER EIGHTEEN

As much as Fletcher wanted to get cracking with his investigation, he knew he needed to calm himself before he spoke to anyone.

The shower was set to lukewarm as he stepped in and washed the jail smells off his body. The motel-supplied shower gel had an odd scent that was neither masculine nor feminine. It lathered though, and that's what mattered.

Now that the local cops knew he was investigating the homicides, he figured it'd only be a matter of time before the majority of Medford's residents learned he was freelancing the case.

This meant he could be more direct in his questioning as the need for discretion was eradicated the moment Old Cop had pointed a gun at him.

With a set of clean clothes on, and his sense of outrage largely dissipated, Fletcher climbed into the SUV and set off towards the town's hospital.

Medford Medical Center looked as if had been designed with a set of stencils. Everything about it spoke of repetition. The rows of windows all had the same blinds lowered to the same point. There were no splashes of individuality such as plants in the windows, and the cars parked out front were lined up as if soldiers on parade.

Fletcher didn't need any medical help, but he walked up and joined the line to the reception desk all the same. In front of him was a young mother trying to settle her crying infant while another child tugged at her pant leg for attention. The mother looked frazzled with the demands of parenthood, but she was patient with her kids. Ahead of her were an elderly couple; him with a cane, her with a walker and a defined stoop.

As he waited Fletcher took sly peeks at the receptionist. She was mid-forties, well turned out and wore her blonde hair in a neat ponytail. Her blouse was a corporate kaleidoscope of colors that spoke of someone trying to brighten up an otherwise drab workplace uniform. Efficient and friendly, she dealt with her customers with a smile and seemed to know who they were without being told. Rather than just dealing with each customer's request, she was having a brief chat with each person.

So far, so good.

Fletcher had learned from his reporter mother that receptionists in local doctors' and dentists' surgeries were often good sources when it came to local gossip. They met more people than most and had a constant supply of tidbits about people and events in a local community. He'd sought Quadrado's advice as to possible candidates for this source of info and she'd suggested he speak with the receptionist at the medical center.

If there were any undercurrents flowing through Medford, something told him this chatty receptionist would know all about them.

The old couple shuffled off towards the seats, him making sure he supported her.

Now he was a little closer, Fletcher could see the tag on the receptionist's blouse. Felicity was her name.

The mother stepped aside so Fletcher moved to the counter.

"Hello, sir. How may I help you?" Felicity's smile touched her eyes.

"I'm sorry to bother you. I was wondering if you could spare five minutes to answer a few questions." Fletcher pulled a helpless face. "I've been asked to look into Jane Friedrickson's homicide and I could really do with someone who can tell me about Medford and how the people get along. Who doesn't like who and so forth.

Your name was recommended to me as someone whom everyone confides in. Are you able to help?"

Felicity's eyes sparkled as she absorbed the compliments, although Fletcher felt guilty for delivering bullshit in a sterile medical center.

"That poor woman. So far as being able to help, I am, and I'm not." A hand gestured at the line behind Fletcher. "I can't talk just now. Can you come back around six? I finish then and will be happy to exchange what I know in return for dinner with a mysterious stranger who I've just seen checking me out."

Fletcher had no great desire to have dinner with her, but he needed to pick her brains, so he swallowed his distaste at her brazen date-fixing. "Six it is." As for her assumption he'd been checking her out because he was attracted to her, that was sure to lead to future complications so he resolved to set Felicity straight as soon as he could.

"That's a date then, Mister…"

"Fletcher. Grant to you."

CHAPTER NINETEEN

Abbotsford was another version of Medford. The buildings were as near identical as they could be without being classed as replicas. Both cities were located on major crossroads that acted as their main drags.

Fletcher had chosen not to dine with Felicity in a place where she'd be a known face. After the scuffle in the Tavern and his arrest, he was sure he wasn't too popular with the citizens of Medford and he didn't want to cause any trouble for Felicity by being seen with her.

A side bonus was that when she found out he had no romantic interest in her, being in a different city would make it harder for her to walk out on him. He knew he was manipulating her, and while it wasn't a nice trait to recognize, Quadrado's threat of incarceration was enough to make him overcome his misgivings.

As they'd driven to Abbotsford, Felicity had chattered to him about the residents of Medford as if he knew them. Not once had he tried to stop her, instead preferring to adopt the role of a listener to her talker. When he was asking her questions later, it'd be in his favor to already have an established set of roles.

The eatery recommended by Felicity was a bar and grill with a wide porch and a collection of large pickups in the parking lot. Its interior had a wood theme, but the tables were clean and there were delicious smells filling the room.

The laminated menu was filled with hearty, meat-heavy dishes. Fletcher opted for grilled bratwurst with peppers, onions and fries while Felicity chose the booyah stew.

As they were waiting for their meals to come, Fletcher turned the conversation to business.

"I'm sure you'll have heard all about the homicides. I was asked to look into Jane Friedrickson's, but as it looks like Walt Renard was killed by the same guy, I guess I'll have to look into them both to see if I can work out who killed them."

"I heard they were connected." Felicity lifted her glass until the straw touched her glossy red lips. "Such a terrible shame two good people were killed in such a horrible way."

"It is. What connections have you heard?"

"Just that they both had numbers carved onto them. I mean, how gross is that? Isn't that the sickest thing you've ever heard?"

"It's certainly up there." Fletcher took a pull of his soda. "What are the local folks making of the homicides? I'm sure you've heard all kinds of theories."

It was a stretch that someone would have the right idea, but the more ideas Fletcher could come up with or hear, the better there was a chance he'd find the right one, even if it was triggered by another theory.

"I've heard a few." Felicity glanced around as if worried she'd be overheard. "Most folks are blaming a serial killer who's traveling round the country. Some are saying the homicides are the work of whoever is behind the run of bad luck farmers have been having." She adopted a coy look. "And one or two folks have pointed their finger at you."

"And you? The fact you're having dinner with me tells me you don't think I'm the killer, so who do *you* think is behind it?"

"I don't know. But something tells me it's not you. My best guess is that a serial killer has decided that farmers make for easy targets and is doing his thing. It's so scary. Just gotta hope he gets caught soon before he moves on to us folks in town." Felicity gave a wide but nervous smile that formed mismatched dimples on either side of her mouth. "You're the guy brought in to look into this. Maybe I should be asking you who you think it is."

"You can ask, but I wouldn't have an answer for you." Fletcher lifted his soda to his mouth and took a drink. He wasn't thirsty, but the action gave him a moment to think without having to speak. Felicity was a first-class gossip, that's why he'd sought her out. It would be naïve of him to think she wouldn't try and get some tidbits of her own. She would have to be handled with care, and anything he told her would have to be information he didn't mind sharing. There was also the fact that for all she thrived on gossip, she was smart enough to work out his thinking from the questions he asked her. "At this stage I'm still trying to get a picture of the local community, the friendships, the rivalries and the people who are enemies. The cops will work the evidence found at the crime scene and match it to what they know about folks from Medford. I'm more of a left-field thinker brought in to examine the improbable and unlikely. Dollar to a dime says the local cops find the killer first."

Felicity's snort was enough to share her opinion of the Medford PD. Maybe she knew Old Cop personally. "I'm afraid you're gonna be wasting your time though. There's no real rivalries or enemies round here. Sure, a few folks are jealous of the farmers who are making money, but there's been enough that have failed for the most of them to have everyone's sympathy. You'll have seen the creamery, saw the places that sell or repair tractors and so on. Wisconsin is America's Dairyland and Medford relies on the milk that comes from the farms. One way or another, milk supports every man, woman and child in town."

"Okay. I get what you're saying. Is there anyone who used to make money from the milk or cheese industry who doesn't anymore? Someone who might be bitter, someone who'd have a heavy grudge to carry against the Friedricksons, the Renards or the farming industry in general?"

Felicity's lips pursed and her brow furrowed as she gazed across the bar. "Hmm. That's an interesting question. Everyone in Medford knows how vital the farms and creamery are to the local economy. I can't see anyone doing such a thing."

"Really?" Fletcher heard the disappointment in his voice. "There's nobody who feels they've been screwed over by the farmers?"

Felicity scrunched her nose as she thought. "Actually, there is someone."

"Who?"

"Mick Barkel. He was a contractor, had a lot of men and machines, but he's now little more than a barfly. From what I recall, his business fell apart when the drink got a hold of him. He'd send his men to the wrong farms, make mistakes with the bills and when his men called him out for his errors he was nasty with them. Called them worse than dog crap. The farmers stopped using him, and his men found work with the contractors who replaced him. He lost his home, his wife and every cent he had to his name."

"Sorry, when you say he was a contractor, what exactly does that mean?" Fletcher's first thought was that Barkel must have been in construction.

"Sorry. Contractors are guys who own a bunch of tractors, foragers and other farm machinery. They're hired by farmers to do all the plowing, corn silage harvesting and lots of other jobs like that. It saves each farmer the expense of buying foragers and all the other equipment they'd need. Mick Barkel was the biggest contractor in the county by quite some way until he lost his way."

"What does Barkel do now?"

"He kept one tractor and he does odd days here and there for a few farmers who felt bad about their part in his downfall. The rest of the time, he can be found in the Tavern saying how he's going to start up the business again. Show the farmers he can do the job." A knowing sigh escaped her lips. "He's been saying that for a long time now. From what I've heard, there's more fire and less conviction than there used to be."

"That's so interesting. I knew you'd be able to help me." Mick Barkel was the kind of person Fletcher had been hoping existed. Someone who'd have a genuine reason to hold a grudge against the farmers. By the sounds of him, he had enough desire to talk about recreating his business, but not enough to straighten himself out and do it. That was a dangerous combination. He'd no doubt carry resentment and Fletcher was sure there had been harsh words sent Barkel's way when he'd let down the farmers or overcharged them. All of these were breeding grounds for bitterness. For enmity and a desire for revenge. "Can you describe him? Physically, I mean. I'd like to recognize him should I run into him."

"He's about six foot tall, maybe two hundred pounds. His hair is thinning and his face is the face of a drinker. If you see him in the Tavern, he'll be the drunkest man in the room. In fact, if you see him anywhere other than a kegger or frat party, he'd still probably be the drunkest person around."

"Sounds like the drink has chosen him."

Fletcher had seen some of his Royal Marine buddies get chosen by alcohol. At first it was a way to relax, then it became a habit. Habit became dependency, and by the time his buddies had realized their reliance, it was often too late for them to escape alcohol's clutches.

"It did. But he sure helped make it easy for the drink."

The server brought their food and they munched their way through the large portions in amiable conversation.

As well as discussing the case, Fletcher noticed how Felicity was trying to probe him about his personal life. She didn't ask outright if there was a Mrs. Fletcher, or a girlfriend in his life, although she gave him every opportunity to disclose if there was. He supposed she was trying to find out if he was relationship material. Fletcher was cool with her probing; along with a few bucks for dinner, it was the price of the information she had.

With their meals finished and neither of them having stomach space for dessert, Fletcher got the check.

Even as they were walking back to the SUV, his mind was firing off in a thousand directions. Chief among his thoughts was the idea Barkel had started exacting his revenge against the farmers by subtle means that were attributed to bad luck, and had then escalated to homicide. The numbers carved in the foreheads of his victims could well be the order in which the farmers had stopped using him as their preferred contractor.

CHAPTER TWENTY

When Fletcher pulled up outside Felicity's house she was slow to unbuckle her seatbelt. There was an invitation on her face. But as pleasant a person as she might be, she held no attraction for Fletcher.

All things considered, Felicity was a good-looking woman; she was intelligent, friendly company and well-mannered. There was no reason—beyond the fact he'd be leaving Medford as soon as the case was solved—why Fletcher shouldn't date her.

He got all that. He'd told her he'd be on the first plane home as soon as an arrest had been made. She knew he was a single father, a widow and that he still loved his wife. None of these details had phased her.

There was nothing wrong with hooking up for a one-time night of passion.

But it was something he couldn't do. Even if it would be understandable. Normal. Long overdue.

"I'm guessing that you're going to say no if I ask you in for coffee."

"I'm afraid I am." Fletcher hesitated, unsure which of the many words weighing down his tongue would cause the least offense. "It's not that I don't like you. More that I still love my wife. If anything were to happen between you and I, I'm afraid I'd feel I was cheating on her and, I don't want to be that guy."

Afraid was a mild word. Terrified would be a better one. Petrified the most apt. He'd gone over the logic of snapping Rachel's neck a million times. It always stood up to his examinations. They'd been in a car crash and she'd been trapped after a collision with a tree. Rachel had asked that he end her life before the car slid into a river and drowned her. Drowning had been her worst fear and at her request, her insistence, he'd killed her to save her.

Felicity's lip wobbled. "You must have loved her very much."

"I did. I still do."

"She was a lucky woman to have known the love you gave her." Felicity leaned over and planted a gentle kiss on Fletcher's cheek. "Goodnight, Grant. I enjoyed having dinner with you. If you find yourself in need of some company or some more information, you know where I am."

"Thank you."

Fletcher wasn't just thanking her for the offer of more help and he was confident she understood that.

When he got round the first corner, Fletcher pulled over to the curb and plucked his phone from his pocket. He'd been desperate to check for updates from Quadrado, but he'd had enough manners to leave his phone alone when in Felicity's company.

An email from Quadrado shared the coroner's findings on Renard's autopsy. The farmer had been stabbed first and had then had his throat slashed. The stab wound had been deemed severe enough to be fatal in its own right, so Fletcher believed his theory about Renard's throat being cut to silence him was sound.

As with Jane's homicide at Greenacres Farm, no trace evidence was found by the CSI technicians. No fingerprints that didn't belong had been uncovered and the search around the farm's perimeter had again found tracks curling in from around the crossroads.

The contractor, Mick Barkel, might seem like a prime suspect on paper, yet the more he thought about how the crime scenes were devoid of evidence, the less probable it seemed the killer was a man known for his addiction to alcohol.

Fletcher started the SUV again and set off for the motel. After a quick shower, he planned to head back to the Tavern and see if he could engage Barkel in conversation.

First though, he put in a call to Wendy. After the unspoken offer from Felicity, he needed to hear his daughter's voice, if for no other reason than to remind himself why he was doing this.

CHAPTER TWENTY-ONE

The Tavern was busier than Fletcher expected it would be on a Wednesday night. The same bartender was on duty as the previous night and Fletcher spied Gangle and Bald sitting at a table with another guy.

With a bottle of beer in front of him, Fletcher sent a nod towards Gangle's table. He got one back from Bald, although he wasn't convinced they'd learned their lesson. To test their intentions, he left his beer on the bar and went to the men's room. Sure enough, twenty seconds after he walked into the men's room, Gangle, Bald and their buddy came piling in.

The buddy had the wedge-shaped body of a swimmer and while Gangle's and Bald's faces showed years of battle scars, Swimmer's face was handsome and unmarked. That was never a good sign. People who lost fights had crooked noses or scars where flesh had been opened and never healed quite right. Good fighters won their battles without taking any significant blows. Swimmer was toned, muscular and carried no obvious battle scars; therefore, as far as Fletcher was concerned, he was by far the most dangerous of the three. As such, he was the one Fletcher would have to deal with first.

Fletcher kept his back against a wall, the hand dryer pressing against his spine. He was on the balls of his feet and his hands were loose at his sides ready to react.

It was Swimmer who spoke. His voice deep and stentorian. "Hey, buddy. You're not welcome here. Not after what you did last night."

"Really, you're telling me I'm not welcome because I defended myself when I was attacked for no reason?"

"You seem to think you're a tough guy. Well, let's see how tough you really are." Swimmer gestured to himself and the other two. "Come on then, smartass, let's see what you've got."

"There's three of you. Last night when your two buddies tried to kick my butt, I stopped them with four blows and only caught one myself. I warn you now, I held back last night. I won't be holding back tonight. Any injuries you receive, the blame for them will be on you, not me."

For all his tough talk, Fletcher knew the odds were against him. To fight multiple opponents, you need space to move, to dance back and forth in a way that separates one of the combatants from the group so he can be taken down. Then it's a case of repeating that move until the numbers of the guys you're fighting diminishes to a point where those left realize what's happening and back off.

To fight superior numbers in a confined space is to ask for a beating. The one advantage Fletcher had over his opponents was that he had no need to worry about friendly fire and could attack in any direction if he found himself surrounded.

Swimmer flexed his muscles as Gangle cracked his knuckles. They were gearing themselves up to attack, although Fletcher hadn't missed the way Gangle and Bald had kept themselves behind their buddy.

Rather than wait for one of them to attack him, Fletcher took the fight to them. He took a rapid step forward, his back arching as he grabbed the lapels of Swimmer's sports coat.

The human forehead is designed to protect the brain. It's a solid slab of bone. When a solid slab of bone collides with a soft item like a nose, there's only one winner. Fletcher's forehead had momentum and muscle powering it forward.

Swimmer's nose erupted like a dropped watermelon. Fletcher knew he'd not just be stunned, but that his body's reflexes would have caused his eyes to water, temporarily blinding him. As he pirouetted to keep an eye on the other two, Fletcher threw a backhand elbow Swimmer's way with his right arm. It caught a glancing blow, but Fletcher had never expected to land a knockout; the elbow was more about keeping Swimmer occupied with defense rather than attack. A straight left from Fletcher landed on the side of Swimmer's exposed jaw.

The elbow had already spun Swimmer's head, adding to the trauma to Swimmer's brain due to the headbutt. The second and third blows from the elbow and the punch increased the trauma to the point where Swimmer's body shut down to protect itself. As he slumped to the floor, Fletcher screwed his body back towards the other two, his hands coming up ready as his eyes sought out their positions and looked for any attacks they might be about to make.

Bald and Gangle repeated their moves from the previous night. Fletcher was driven back by a charge from Bald that bent him backwards over the hand sinks. Heavy punches slammed into his body as Bald worked low. Gangle's long arms arced over Bald's back towards Fletcher's head.

To combat the twin assaults, Fletcher tucked his head into Bald's neck for protection and squirmed to his right. Once free of Bald he jabbed the point of his elbow into the man's kidney.

He didn't manage to deliver the debilitating blow he wanted to, but at least Bald was hurt enough to buy Fletcher a couple of seconds.

He used the time to go after Gangle. The longer reach of Gangle's arms meant Fletcher caught a jab that split his lip and had to duck a cross that would have knocked him clean out had it landed.

As soon as he was close enough, Fletcher threw a series of punches at Gangle's face. His intention was to drive Gangle back until he had nowhere to go and then get in close.

Gangle retreated until he was in a stall. There was less room for Fletcher to throw punches, but the long arms of Gangle were impeded more than his were.

Fletcher ignored Gangle's attempts at defense, grabbed his shirt and hauled Gangle onto his advancing forehead.

Gangle's nose went the same way as Swimmer's had, so Fletcher nailed him with an uppercut and went back to deal with Bald.

There was no need for further violence as Bald was slumped onto one knee and was emitting low moans. For all his size, he was nowhere near as tough as he made himself out to be.

Fletcher checked Swimmer wasn't playing possum, washed up and returned to the bar.

He lifted his beer, drained the bottle in a single pull and dropped fifty bucks in front of the bemused bartender. "For two beers and the extra cleaning your men's room will need."

With the beers in his hand, Fletcher crossed the room and sat opposite the bedraggled heap that was Mick Barkel.

CHAPTER TWENTY-TWO

The office lights didn't bother Quadrado as a rule. Tonight they were irritating her with their brightness. Lights twinkled outside the window, although she wasn't looking that way. No matter how she rotated her head, no movement she made could alleviate the stiffness in her neck from being bent over her laptop for the last four hours. The Caesar salad she'd had for dinner had filled her at the time, but the longer she'd remained, the more she found herself tempted by the candy and potato chips in the vending machine standing in the hallway. It was comfort food and would undo all the hard work she'd put in at the gym. Comfort was what she craved right now. With her family only able to offer well-meaning platitudes via messages and telephone calls, there were no arms wrapped around her. No hands held. Just endless hours of work and a constant fight not to give in to her emotions and permit the many tears she was fighting back to flow. In one sense having to work gave her a focus and a distraction from her grief, but the focus was growing ever harder to maintain and the distraction less compelling.

Her day had been a mixture of good and bad. It had started with a rocket from her boss demanding results on the case she was currently investigating, then she'd had to bail Fletcher out of jail and send him the exact response from Soter when she'd again requested some form of badge to help him navigate the Medford cops. While the possession of a badge would simplify things for him, she was also hoping it might add a level of constraint as

Fletcher was wont to take matters into his own hands. To round everything off, she'd searched all the databases she knew of and had found no instances of hashtags and numbers being left on homicide victims.

She knew she'd upheld her side of things by feeding Fletcher all the information she could find, she just wished she'd been able to send something his way that would help him. His responses had been terse at best and she expected that he blamed her for the threatening picture and link. Quadrado possessed enough self-awareness to know that if their positions were reversed and she'd received that response from him, she'd have felt abandoned, manipulated and, most of all, furious.

As it was she was already disgusted at the way things were panning out. She hadn't worked so hard to get into the FBI to become a handler for a loose cannon. Not once had she envisioned such callousness being a part of law enforcement. Yes, from the perps she was paid to catch, but never from the higher-ups. She had no idea who Soter was, but the fact she'd been appointed as Fletcher's handler after a trip to the Hoover building told her that, whoever he was, he either had sanction from, or pull over, the FBI director. Either way, she found the interactions with Soter depressing as it was clear that, so far as he was concerned, both she and Fletcher were tools to be used, and Jane's homicide was nothing but an opportunity to test Fletcher's resourcefulness.

The one positive she could point to was that her current case had broken a new lead and ought to be wrapped up in a day or two at most. She'd then be able to cash in some of her vacation time so she could fly out and join Fletcher. Her badge would enable her to protect and vouch for him and she'd be on hand to work the case with him. The small matter of jurisdiction negated by the fact she would be on vacation.

Quadrado powered down her laptop and left the office, her mind whirling between the intricacies of her own case and the one she'd parachuted Fletcher into. There were few similarities of note between the two cases, but she still looked at them as a pair in the hope something in the FBI case could trigger an idea for the Wisconsin one.

She found nothing worth the mentioning, but from the way he was looking into Jane's homicide, she knew it wouldn't be long before Fletcher had a suspect in mind. All she hoped was that he'd do the right thing when he had someone in his sights.

CHAPTER TWENTY-THREE

Mick Barkel was pretty much as Felicity had described him. His cheeks were decorated with burst capillaries that reminded Fletcher of tree roots and the thinning hair on his head was unkempt and lank.

"I'll not say no to your beer, buddy, but I'd 'preciate knowing who you are."

The slur in Barkel's voice was replicated in his limp posture. It was as if he was made from rubber the way he slouched in his seat. When he reached for the beer Fletcher had got him, his hand wandered side to side before he clasped the bottle.

"My name's Grant Fletcher. Your name was mentioned to me so I thought I'd introduce myself to you." A gesture at the bottle in Barkel's hand. "Don't know about you, but I've always found buying a beer always helps when meeting someone."

"Works for me." The bottle was raised to wet lips and drained of a third of its contents. "So, why did someone give you my name and what makes me a guy you want to meet?"

Fletcher gave himself a mental cursing for underestimating Barkel's intelligence. It stood to reason anyone who'd managed to run a company with forty employees driving expensive machinery would be nobody's fool. He knew that he'd need to proceed with caution as he didn't want Barkel to realize he was investigating him on suspicion of homicide.

"I heard how your business went bust and thought you got a raw deal. I had a team of ten guys working construction. My pops had built the business and left it to me when he passed. I worked night and day, but the folks who'd been Pop's customers for years started hiring other firms. No matter what I said, what I guaranteed, they apologized and told me they weren't going to use Arrow Construction anymore. Jerks." The fabrication of a similar story to Barkel's was a gambit, yet Fletcher was sure Barkel would bite; after all, misery loves company.

"I bet they was folks you knew most of your life. Same God damn thing happened with me. Sure, I made a couple mistakes. I'm human. Humans make mistakes. Lost my family business in just one summer. Folks I'd looked after for more than twenty-five years turned their backs on me overnight. Bunch of assholes, the whole lot of them. I'll show them, one day soon I'll start again. Build my business back up until they're begging me to work their farms again."

The bitterness layering Barkel's tone spoke of his deep-seated resentment. The fact he was responsible for his own downfall played no part in his assignation of blame. The talk of resurrecting his business like an agricultural phoenix was talk; nothing more, nothing less. He might have the intention when full of beer and bourbon, but the simple fact was, when push came to shove, Barkel would choose a barstool over a driving seat whenever he could.

"You do that. You show the jerks." Fletcher clinked his bottle against Barkel's in a show of solidarity.

"I will. Just you watch me do it." Barkel's glassy eyes tried to focus on Fletcher. "You gotta do the same. Gotta show those jerkweeds that you're a better man than the one they know."

This sounded promising to Fletcher. Barkel might be full of beer, yet there was a spark in him that wanted to prove himself to those who'd once employed him as a contractor. On a personal level, Barkel's fall from a position of respect within the community would be tough to accept. He'd been a boss, someone who gave orders. Fletcher didn't know the price of tractors or other agricultural machinery, but he didn't suppose they'd be cheap. With forty-plus drivers and countless machinery to manage, Barkel's contracting firm would be sure to have a seven-figure turnover. To lose all that and end up as a barfly would gall any man.

It was that line of thinking Fletcher was following. Even though he was responsible for his own fate, Barkel had a right to rue his mistakes and want to atone for them. Either that, or had he chosen to punish those he deemed responsible for his downfall?

The question was, had Barkel turned to mischief and then homicide to exact vengeance he didn't deserve?

The more time he spent in Barkel's company, the less he believed Barkel was behind the killings. The man was a lush. His shirt was buttoned out of alignment; his movements clunky and inexact. The idea that he was capable of sneaking around two separate farms and killing two people without leaving any kind of trace evidence was laughable.

The three guys who'd come at Fletcher in the men's room slouched their way into the room and headed towards the exit. Fletcher fell silent as he watched them pass, his body loose and ready to respond should they try another attack.

Once the last of them had left the bar he turned back to Barkel. "I heard there's been a couple of them farmers killed. That's a little bit of karma working for you, right?"

"Hell no." Barkel's head sawed left and right, then turned his attention back to Fletcher. "Jerks mighta screwed me over, but there's no way they deserved to be killed. 'Specially not a young woman. That Jane, I tell you, she could turn the head of any man in not just Medford, but the whole of Taylor County. Pretty as she was, she never acted like she was no different than anyone else. She was kind to those she met and I ain't never heard tell of her looking at no one but her husband. As for Walt, he was one of the last to leave me. In the end he had to get someone else 'cause my men were off like rats leaving a sinking ship."

The denial was too instinctive for Fletcher to not believe it. Barkel's testimony to the character of the victims backed up everything he'd heard from others. One telling point was his description of Jane's looks. It made it sound like he was attracted to her, yet there was the caveat that she'd remained true to Carl.

Fletcher raised two fingers to the bartender and when the bottles were placed on the counter he rose to collect and pay for them. He wanted a moment to think about his next question as he felt the wrong emphasis would close up Barkel regardless of how much beer he bought the man.

"I heard she was pretty. Bet she had a lot of guys hitting on her back in the day."

"She had her share. Used to knock their advances outta the park like Babe Ruth at the Yankee Stadium."

"So she never got her head turned?"

"Nope. One of my guys was mad crazy on her, but he never hit on her once. Guess he knew he'd get turned down. Then again, if he did win her heart, Carl Friedrickson isn't the kinda man you cross lightly. A good shot with a bad temper is an ugly combination, and Steve Heaton had the good sense not to hit on her."

Fletcher could vouch for Carl's accuracy. He'd seen no sign of the man's temper, although Carl had admitted to having one. The way he was domineered and belittled by his father would be a breeding ground for resentment and self-loathing. These were elements that festered in the mind; for years a temper could be kept in check, but sooner or later, all those buried feelings, the slights and insults would come to a head and there would be an eruption of emotion.

The ensuing rant or attack would be out of proportion to the event that precipitated it, but it would be the cumulative effect of too many bitten tongues that would fuel Carl's anger.

By following this line of thinking, it could also be suspected Carl had killed his wife. But it felt wrong to Fletcher, and it made no sense for Carl to have also killed Renard.

At the moment Steve Heaton seemed like his best suspect. Barkel's description of him being "mad crazy" about Jane could foster strong emotions and overreactions to being rebuffed. Where Renard came into the picture was uncertain, but given the location of the tracks where the killer had parked his vehicle, was it possible Renard had seen something and was therefore killed to ensure his silence?

Fletcher drained his beer and stood to leave.

When he stepped outside the bar he found himself looking down the barrels of a shotgun.

CHAPTER TWENTY-FOUR

Fletcher had left the Tavern prepared for the three guys he'd beaten up in the men's room to try their luck again. What he hadn't expected was a posse a dozen strong. And that none of the faces looking back at him were ones he recognized.

At this point the identity of the people in front of him was irrelevant. The only things that were relevant were the twin abysses of the shotgun's barrels, the forefinger caressing its triggers and the state of mind of the guy holding the shotgun.

Fletcher raised his hands to show a lack of threat. The shotgun was steady; in fact, had it been held any steadier, the guy wielding it might have been mistaken for a statue.

He was three feet from the door and six from the shotgun. It was possible he could dodge to one side and avoid getting hit by any of the shotgun's pellets. The odds were against that though. There was also the question of where he'd go. The bar only had one entrance he knew of. There could well be a back door where supplies were brought in, but he doubted it would be unlocked and ready to aid a mad-dash attempt at escaping.

Fletcher could try running down the street, ducking and weaving to present a moving target. That wasn't an enticing option either. Shotguns are designed to cover a wide area with their shot. At six feet he had a chance of moving before the long barrel could traverse to his new position. At twenty his movements would have to be greater and the shotgun's lesser. That was a bad idea all ways up.

"Call the cops. We got him."

The cops were good news. Fletcher's first thought had been that he was about to be the victim of a lynching. The second was he would be taken to a quiet location and given the kind of beating that would ensure he'd never again trouble the farmers of Taylor County.

"Hang on a minute." The voice of the guy with the shotgun was calm. A positive sign as someone strung out or wound up wasn't ideal to have pointing a gun your way. "He looks happy we're gonna call the cops." The tip of the shotgun barrel bounced an inch and returned to a statuesque condition. "Wanna tell us why you're happy?"

Fletcher did everything he could to keep his voice even and his words inoffensive. "I just walked out of a bar and found myself staring down a shotgun. A cop is exactly who I want to see right now. I have no idea who you guys are and what you're pointing the shotgun at me for. It could be because I beat up the three guys who attacked me in the men's room. I doubt that though as I can't see any of their faces in your posse."

Fletcher had used the word posse on purpose. It was a word that was associated with lawlessness and as one of them had mentioned calling the cops, his current thinking was the guys in front of him were trying to aid the cops rather than exact their own vigilante justice. As such he wanted to give them subtle reminders that what they were doing could be interpreted as illegal.

"Pah. You're full of bull, mister." The speaker was two to the left of the shotgun holder. "You're bluffing us. We know you was arrested this morning and let go because the cops had nothing on you. They're bound to have something on you by now. You're the one who killed Jane and Walt, and we're gonna hand you right over to the cops for your crimes. Hell, you just admitted beating up on three guys. We seen the shape of them. You handed their asses to them good and proper, and you just admitted it in front of witnesses. If nothing else, the cops'll have that on you."

The speaker had him there. Fletcher had made a mistake admitting to the fight, and if the cops were called, he was sure Old Cop would take immense delight in booking him for the altercation. Quadrado would, of course, smooth his exit from the cells again, but it'd be another black mark against him, and he wanted to lessen their number rather than increase them.

"You make sense, sir." There were times subservience and politeness were better than fists, boots and elbows. "Of course, you don't know my side of the story and I'm guessing most of what you've heard has been rumor or speculation. Do you guys know Peter Quadrado up at Meadowfields?"

"'Course we know him." The scorn in Speaker's voice was thicker than an elephant's butt cheek. "What of it?"

"I'm friends with his sister, Zoey, although you probably know her as Zeke."

"So?"

"You know she's an FBI Special Agent, right? You probably also know that she and Jane Friedrickson have been friends since kindergarten." Fletcher was sure they were capable of making the connections themselves, but he still felt compelled to spell things out for them. "Special Agent Quadrado is tied up on a big case, and as such she can't come out here herself to investigate her best friend's death. That's why I'm here."

Fletcher was making a point of using Quadrado's FBI rank whenever possible to hammer home the associated credentials.

"Okay." It was the shooter who was speaking now. "Real slow, show us your badge."

Fletcher had anticipated this request. "I'm not a cop, nor a feebie. I'm an investigator, I look into things for people. Special Agent Quadrado asked me to look into something for her, and I am. I have no credentials or license on me that can prove I am what I say. However, feel free to call Peter Quadrado, he'll vouch for me. So will Carl Friedrickson. You can call the cops if you like.

They won't thank you for it and they might also want to know why you're pointing your shotgun for no good reason at a guy who's doing nothing more than leaving a bar."

A cell phone appeared in Speaker's hand. He fiddled until he'd got the number he wanted and flicked it onto loudspeaker mode so everyone could hear.

Peter Quadrado's voice came through. A little tinny sounding, but unmistakably him. "Hey, what's up, buddy?"

A minute later the posse were muttering apologies and wishing him luck with his investigation. At least, most of them were as there were still some of the group who eyed him with suspicion as they went their separate ways.

As he walked back to the motel, Fletcher ran all the counter surveillance techniques he knew. It wasn't that he could hide where he was staying when there was only one motel in Medford, more that he wanted to check for tails and others who may decide to confront him.

CHAPTER TWENTY-FIVE

Fletcher tapped out a message to Quadrado requesting any and all information she could gather on Steve Heaton and then dropped his cell on the bed while he poured himself a glass of water.

As much as he felt the investigation was moving forward, he knew it wasn't progressing fast enough. There were various threads that made sense and others that made every theory he came up with fall apart when he tried to include them.

There was a definite shift forward with things, although the way the locals had turned against him wasn't good. Somehow or other he'd have to win them over to get their cooperation.

The biggest thing bugging Fletcher was that his suspect list was so short. As well as speaking to Mick Barkel himself, Fletcher had made his own calls to Peter Quadrado and Carl Friedrickson before going to the Tavern. He'd asked both farmers about Barkel and the order in which he'd been dropped by the various farmers. Carl had suggested that his father had remained loyal to Barkel longer than he ought to have, and Peter confirmed what Barkel himself had said, that Renard had been one of the last to drop Barkel as a contractor, and in fact was one of the only farmers who still used him when he needed a one-man job.

These testimonies laid waste to his theory about the hashtags denoting the order in which his customers had deserted Barkel.

As suspects went, Barkel fit several criteria, yet whichever way he looked at it, Fletcher couldn't imagine someone as gripped by alcoholism as Barkel was having the ability to exact two forensically clean kills.

There were also the hashtag markings to consider. Fletcher had researched the symbol online. Before it was claimed by social media it was used as a pound sign from the Latin *libra ponda* meaning *pound in weight*, and abbreviated to "lb", with a line through it to denote it as a contraction. Over time the pound symbol became the slanted tic-tac-toe board everyone is familiar with and was used by most people to simply denote numbers. In turn it became used by computer programmers to group items together until it took on its most modern incantation as the hashtag phenomenon after being used on social media for the first time in 2007.

With so many meanings attributable to the hashtag symbol, there was a world of possibilities as to the exact symbolism behind why it was carved into the foreheads of the killer's victims.

The killer could be anyone from someone who felt they were getting their Shakespearean pound of flesh by ending the lives of those he carved the symbol into, to a social media addict using the hashtag as both a counting and grouping mechanism as well as a signature to their kills.

Worst of all was the idea the killer was doing nothing more than using the symbol as a way to screw with the people he knew would be investigating his crimes. This would mean a lot of time would be wasted on theories that went nowhere.

A light tapping at his door made Fletcher abandon his theorizing and focus his full attention on the door. The pistol on his hip made its way into his hand. After the situations he'd encountered at the Tavern, he wasn't taking any chances.

CHAPTER TWENTY-SIX

The tapping was repeated. A fraction louder the second time, although that could be a trick of the mind as Fletcher had diverted his sensory perception towards his ears. In his mind, there were two possibilities as to who could be on the other side of the door.

The first was Felicity. She'd made no secret of her attraction to him, but even as he thought it, Fletcher dismissed the idea as being egotistical.

Possibility two was another posse. The soft knocks at the door nothing more than a test to see if he was awake.

The tapping happened a third time as Fletcher padded his way barefoot to the door. He kept the arm holding the pistol close to his body with the wrist an inch from his ribs. Only a fool goes through a doorway with his gun extended at full reach where it's easy to grab or deflect and tough to readjust onto a new target at close range. If anyone was acting in an aggressive fashion on the other side of the door, Fletcher had no worries about hitting a human-sized target at a range of five feet even if he wasn't looking down the sights of the pistol.

He took up a position at the side of the door, the barrel of the pistol lined up to aim at the gap that would form as soon as the door was opened.

His left hand grasped the handle, whipped the door open and clenched ready for action in the briefest of seconds. As soon as the door was opening, Fletcher's eyes were assessing the figure he saw standing before him.

It was neither a posse nor Felicity. A relief for Fletcher on both counts.

The man in the doorway was the last person he expected to see. "Can I help you, Don?"

A hesitant pause as the Tavern's bartender eyed the pistol in Fletcher's hand. "It's more like I can help you." A shaky finger indicated the gun as a thick bead of sweat ran down Don's flabby cheek. "I swear, I'm offering no threat to you. I'm here to help, but if you're going to point that thing at me, I'll turn round and go home."

The way Don was laying down the terms was odd as Fletcher was the one with the gun. Had he been of a mind to, he could have used the pistol and the obvious threat it carried to extract all the information Don might possess.

Once he'd checked Don was alone, Fletcher holstered the gun and backed out of the doorway so Don could enter the motel room.

Fletcher sat on the bed and offered Don the wicker chair. The bartender's reasons for visiting were a mystery to Fletcher, and his best guess at them was that instead of force he was here to advise Fletcher that he'd better leave Medford for his own safety.

"You say you're here to help. What makes you think I need help and that you're in a position to offer it?"

"You came to Medford to investigate Jane Friedrickson's homicide, then Walt Renard was killed in much the same way. Because of the similarities between their homicides, you're looking into them both." Don paused, licked his lips and blinked twice. "Well, until a week ago, Walt Renard was sleeping with my sister."

This revelation was gold dust as far as Fletcher was concerned. At last a secret had been uncovered, and in the process had given him a possible lead. Of all the things he'd expected when he heard the tapping at the motel room door, this was the last.

Fletcher took a moment to assess the information. It made sense for Don to not tell him this in a public place. First off, he'd want to do what he could to protect his sister's reputation. Second, it would do him no good to be seen as speaking out of turn regarding the personal life of a homicide victim as it would further distress his widow. Third, he wouldn't want his regular customer base to know he'd helped the out-of-towner none of the locals knew or trusted.

"Can we back up a little? You're right in what you said about me looking into Jane's death. I never told you that though, so how did you learn about it?"

"You hear lots of things when you tend bar. My hearing is none too clever so I learned to read lips. First time I met you, you talked about Jane Friedrickson's homicide. Then I heard you were arrested. I also saw you were asking a lot of questions about the two homicides. When you started talking to Mick, I figured it was worth paying attention to what you were saying. I reckon you fed him some bull to get him talking. I also reckon you were figuring he had a grudge against the farmers for putting their business elsewhere. It makes a lot of sense except I'm the one who sells Mick his beer. Every night when he leaves the Tavern he's like a puppet with the strings cut. The nights those folks were killed, he was as wasted as he was every other night. A man who can hardly stand isn't one who's fit to go killing and not get caught."

"I came to the same conclusion about him myself." Fletcher gave Don a direct look. "What's the story with Walt Renard and your sister?"

"Annie works for a cattle market on the edge of Merrill. They hit it off and whenever he was in town they'd hook up." A look of shame covered his face. "Sounds like a teen thing. It pains me to say it, but two people their age ought to be past all that kind of thing. They should be settled, not sneaking around like horny teenagers."

"How long were they seeing each other?"

"Best part of a year so far as I'm aware."

Fletcher didn't comment on their behavior because he didn't want to disagree with Don in case the bartender refused to tell him anything else. So far as he was concerned, Annie was free to do as she liked if she was single. Renard cheating on his wife was wrong no matter how you looked at it, but for all they knew, the Renards could have had an open marriage. He'd never been comfortable passing judgment on other people's personal lives, so Fletcher had made it a rule of his to keep out of all discussions unless invited to share his thoughts by one of the main protagonists.

"You said before they broke up a week ago. What happened there?"

Don hesitated. Licked his lips, blinked and looked at every part of the room except where Fletcher was sitting on the bed.

CHAPTER TWENTY-SEVEN

Fletcher could see the inner turmoil Don was experiencing by his expressions alone. It was one thing to try and help a stranger solve a pair of homicides, another to lay bare your sister's love life.

"Walt's wife found out about the affair and gave him an ultimatum. Annie or his wife. He chose his wife." Another lick of the lips was again followed by a double blink. "Annie was heartbroken. She's not been to work since and there's nothing anyone has said to her that's helped. One of our cousins is staying with her, but being frank with you, Annie's not in a good place. She's suffered with her mental health in the past and I'm worried about her. About what she might do. Sooner or later Walt's wife will let something slip to the cops, and then they'll start wondering if my Annie has anything to do with his death."

"I doubt it." The words were as bald a lie as Fletcher had ever told because he was thinking the very thing Don was afraid the cops would.

"Really?"

The hope in Don's voice speared Fletcher's conscience. It also made him realize Don was here as much for his sister's sake as to help him.

"Let's slow down a moment. You've just thrown me a huge curveball and I need time to process what you've told me." There was no lie in Fletcher's words this time.

Three main scenarios ran through his head. Renard's wife had taken the opportunity to deliver a brutal punishment to her cheating husband, after Jane's homicide had given her something to replicate and she'd stabbed her husband before leaving the house; Don's sister Annie could have followed the same reasoning, snuck into the farmhouse and exacted her own revenge for being dumped. Or, and this was the most probable theory, neither of the women in Renard's life had killed him and his homicide was the work of the same person who'd killed Jane: her killer had struck a second victim.

The question facing Fletcher was how he could explain these ideas to Don. He put what he hoped was a sympathetic expression on his face. "I've had a chance to think now and I can see why you're worried." He gestured at Don. "Forget for a moment that Annie is your sister. Who do you think the cops will look at for Walt's homicide when they learn of his affair?"

"Annie and his wife." A meaty paw washed over Don's face. "I knew it. Annie's fragile. If the cops give her a hard time they could push her over the edge." He looked at Fletcher, his eyes full of desperation. "She's tried twice in the last three years to… to take her own life. I think they were cries for help, but I'm afraid being accused of homicide will tip her over the edge. Please. You've got to help me prove she's innocent."

"I'll do what I can, but I can make no promises." Fletcher lifted his right hand in a loose fist. "Here's the options as I see it. One," he extended his forefinger, "we do nothing and hope the cops never hear of the affair. Two, Annie goes to the cops herself, explains about the affair. Three, we investigate Annie as a suspect ourselves to establish if she has an alibi for the night Renard was killed. Four, you speak to Annie, explain the cops may come knocking on her door and prepare her to face their questions." Only Fletcher's thumb was left curled against his palm, and as much as he wanted to find a reason to extend it, he'd run out of ideas.

"Our cousin could provide an alibi. She's been staying with Annie since Walt broke it off with her."

"Okay. Let's be practical about this. How long does it take you to drive to Annie's place in Merrill?"

"An hour or so depending on traffic."

"Right. So allowing extra time to get to White Birch from here, that's say two and a half hours' travel time on a round trip. Plus time at the farm."

Fletcher ran the numbers in his head as if he was the killer. Ten minutes to get to the farm's homestead. Five to get to the house unseen. Perhaps an hour to wait for either Walt or his wife to appear for the morning milking. Five minutes to make sure Mrs. Renard wasn't coming right back. Another five to enter the house and find Walt in bed without alerting him to the intrusion. Two to five to make the kill and leave the message on Walt's forehead. Two more to get back out of the house. Another two to get back to the darkness. Then fifteen to locate the parked automobile. A total of an hour fifty. Say two and a half hours as he was trained in such matters, whereas Annie wasn't. Although it could be as little as one if Annie had known when to expect one of the Renards to leave the house.

"Say one hour minimum and two and a half hours tops at the farm. That's a window of between three and a half and five hours for Annie to be out of the house."

"What does that mean exactly?"

Fletcher raised a hand. "Hold on, I'm not done. We know Walt Renard's wife found him around six in the morning. And that she'd gone to the milking parlor at four thirty. So, that's a gap of an hour and a half. Starting at four thirty, I reckon the killer would have waited five minutes before entering the house and then been inside for no more than ten. They'd also have to have been gone before Mrs. Renard came back. This shrinks the window of opportunity to eighty minutes. Say he was killed at four forty. We give the killer twenty minutes to return to where they'd hid their car. Five o'clock. We've already worked out it takes an hour twenty to travel from White Birch to Merrill. That gives us a time of twenty after six as the earliest Annie could have returned home. If she'd waited until the other end of the eighty minute window where Renard was alone in the house, it would be seven forty when she got home." Fletcher looked at Don. "Is your cousin an early riser? Because that's your sister's best chance of proving her innocence."

Don gave a helpless shrug. "I don't know. I'll need to speak to her. To Annie. What should I do? What should I suggest to them?"

"Sorry. That's your call. I can help with the logical side of things, but you know your sister."

Don got up and left without another word, although he did shake Fletcher's hand on his way out.

Fletcher's heart went out to the troubled bartender. He'd done what he could to help him and had kept certain parts of his thought processes private. He could have mentioned the fact Renard's wounds would have spurted blood onto his killer. That if Annie had killed him she'd have either returned home with her lover's blood on her hands and clothes, or she'd have had to have made a stop somewhere to clean up.

The cops on the homicide cases might not be the brightest, but they'd know to look at Annie's clothes for traces of Renard's blood. They'd examine her car, the knives in her kitchen and maybe even the filter on her washer. They'd give her a hard time to try and get a confession. If her state of mind was as fragile as Don suggested, she might even give them a false one to end her torment.

As much as Annie might be a suspect in the cop's eyes, she wasn't high on Fletcher's list. In his experience, fragile people didn't have the low cunning shown by the person who'd killed Renard and possibly Jane as well.

Fletcher was certain that if a different person had killed Renard, it was more probable that it would have been his wife than his former mistress.

He lay on the bed and ran through his plans for the next day. First off would be a trip to speak with Jane's erstwhile admirer, Steve Heaton, then he'd drive to Merrill and see what Annie and her cousin had to say for themselves. Working out who killed Walt Renard wasn't what he'd been hired for, but there was a strong possibility that a breakthrough regarding Renard's homicide could help lead him to Jane's murderer.

CHAPTER TWENTY-EIGHT

Fletcher ordered a plate of ham and eggs with two sides of toast from the server. Protein and carbs, his stock food groups. Medford's diner wasn't busy this early in the morning so he had peace to gather his thoughts and try to herd them into a recognizable shape.

While he waited for his breakfast to come he read through the email Quadrado had sent him. There was an address for Steve Heaton and a list of his misdemeanors. He'd been in trouble twice for stalking women he wanted to date. The alarm bells were ringing in Fletcher's mind. Heaton's record hinted at either someone who didn't know how to take no for an answer, or someone for whom attraction turned into obsession.

He picked out a short reply to Quadrado, bringing her up to speed with intel about Don's sister and suggesting that, while he'd leave the decision to her as to whether she inform the local cops, he was going to visit with Annie to see what her story was.

Annie's involvement and Don's worries about her fragile state of mind gnawed at Fletcher. In his mind, his success at finding Jane's killer would also bring a resolution to the Renard case as the two were sure to be linked.

This in turn added an extra pressure. The sooner he could find the killer, the sooner Annie could be exonerated from any scrutiny she came under.

His breakfast came and he dug into it. The eggs a perfect sunny side up and the bacon a shade less than crispy, just as he'd ordered.

As good as the food was, he stuffed it into his mouth as if he hadn't eaten for a week rather than taking his time and savoring it. It was part a holdover from his Royal Marine days when he'd learned to eat and sleep whenever he got the opportunity, and part a dislike of food that wasn't volcanic lava hot.

With the plate cleared, Fletcher drained his coffee, picked up the last piece of toast and left the diner. He was sure that while dairy farmers started their days early, contractors like Steve Heaton would probably be a little later to get to work as they'd have to wait for daylight or at least until the early morning dew was burned off.

CHAPTER TWENTY-NINE

The building that stood at Steve Heaton's listed address was little more than a converted shack. A power line connected to a raised gable and there were the remains of a fence surrounding what may once have been a colorful garden. Where the siding had faltered or rotted it had been replaced with random-sized boards that lacked any form of treatment.

A large pickup sat to one side of the shack, its front festooned with spotlights and its body jacked up on after-market shock absorbers. Unlike the shack it was well cared for. Not just clean, but polished enough to gleam and shimmer in the early morning sunlight.

The presence of the pickup was a good sign. It meant Heaton must be home.

As a precaution to the contractor leaving without having answered any of the questions he planned to put to him, Fletcher made sure he blocked the pickup's exit path with his SUV. Once he'd parked and got out, the first thing Fletcher did was drop to one knee and tie the bootlace he'd loosened before climbing out. As his hands went through the familiar routine, his eyes were searching under the pickup. They found what he was looking for. A series of dirty marks where leaking oil had stained the dirt.

Fletcher was on high alert as he walked forward. It wasn't that he was scared, more that he knew he might be facing down a killer at any moment and it would be foolish not to anticipate some level of violence or sudden attack from Heaton if his thinking was on the mark.

The other side of the shack was littered with a number of small outbuildings whose condition was dilapidated enough to make the shack look palatial by comparison.

The path to the front stoop wasn't maintained, but it showed enough signs of use for Fletcher to be confident it was Heaton's regular route in and out of the shack. The stoop itself had a wooden handrail that was adorned with snake skulls. It was only as Fletcher followed the path, stepped onto the weathered stoop and rapped his knuckles on the front door that he could see they were real snake skulls rather than manufactured copies. He tried to pick one up only to find it was fixed to the rail.

As he waited for Heaton to answer, Fletcher took a step back and kept his hands by his sides. The last thing he wanted was for Heaton to see him close to the door and get the wrong idea about his reasons for visiting. To further relax the man inside, he moved back until he was beside one of the posts supporting the stoop's roof. If Heaton was the killer, the last thing he wanted to do was get on his wrong side and have the man attack him. To this end, putting distance between himself and the door made extra sense.

Nobody answered the door. No shadows moved inside the house.

Fletcher stepped forward, repeated the knock with a little extra vehemence and then returned to his position by the post.

There was the same lack of response to his second knock as the first.

When he considered the snake heads on the stoop's railing, Fletcher realized they were serving a dual purpose. They were showing Heaton's skill and bravery as a hunter while also sending out a definite warning to all who might come and disturb the contractor.

With no answer forthcoming from the knocks on the door, Fletcher left the stoop and started to circle the shack. He was calling out Heaton's name as he went. When he rounded the side of the shack he had to navigate a narrow passage between two of the outbuildings.

The yard at the back was festooned with various pieces of ancient farm machinery that were undergoing restorative work. One of the outbuildings had a double wide door propped open by a block of lumber.

"Hello, Steve, are you there?"

The only answer Fletcher got was a knife sailing past his ear and embedding itself into the wall of the house.

CHAPTER THIRTY

Quadrado took her seat at her desk, her head a mess of the different cases. Her boss had granted her an audience to explain her thinking and, as was his way, he'd probed at every little piece of her logic until he was convinced of the theory she was putting forward. Once the interrogative briefing was complete he'd done his usual thing of leaning back in his chair with his eyes closed and his fingers laced across his stomach.

It was his way of zoning out to process his thoughts and, while it worked for him, Quadrado had spent the five minutes of his thinking time resting her eyes anywhere except on the nest of hairs sprouting from his nose.

When he'd returned to a more vertical position he'd nodded once, paid her a backhanded compliment for reaching the conclusion she had, and then fired off a list of instructions to her and her partner.

It was those instructions that were foremost in her mind as she keyed in her laptop's password and started putting the first wheels in motion.

A muffled ping came from her jacket pocket. It wasn't the regular doink her phone made for emails. It was *that* ping. The one which denoted a message from Soter.

She tossed a look over her shoulder to check she had privacy and opened the message. It was a reply to the update she'd sent after receiving Fletcher's emails.

Like all good FBI agents, she'd covered her ass and sent the decision regarding arresting Annie up the chain of command to Soter. Her orders were to anonymously inform Medford PD about the affair between Annie and Walt Renard. It was a sensible idea, although she'd felt crappy doing it. She was an FBI Special Agent, not some lowlife informing on others.

The second part of the email was the most concerning. Soter had also dug into Heaton. This told Quadrado Soter had access to information and databases that were closed to her unless she could obtain warrants. As the case was off-the-books so to speak, she'd not been able to go down this route. She guessed Soter either had a tech wizard at his disposal, or a level of clearance high enough to negate the need for warrants.

Her grip on the wireless mouse tightened as she read how Steve Heaton had served time in a juvie detention center for stabbing a salesman who'd knocked on the door of the family home. The guy had only survived the attack as the knife Heaton had thrown at him had struck a rib rather than a soft part of his flesh.

Heaton had pled out and served a three-year sentence topped off with parole. His parole officer had no problems with Heaton whose conduct he'd described as exemplary.

None of the words Quadrado was reading made her feel good about Fletcher going to knock on Heaton's door, so she dashed off a warning email and crossed her fingers it reached him before he got to Heaton's place.

CHAPTER THIRTY-ONE

The gun was in Fletcher's hand before he had the chance to think about reaching for it. Muscle memory was a wonderful thing, not that Fletcher was thinking about it as he searched for Heaton or whomever had thrown the knife.

Fletcher's world was confined to two sources of focus: the view beyond the sights of his pistol and the thumping of his heart. He'd gotten a fright. There was no question about that. He'd seen no sign of anyone. The knife could have easily hit him. It had embedded itself deep into the siding of the house. Had it been aimed four inches across and struck his head, it would have killed him. He didn't waste a millisecond wondering if the knife had missed his head on purpose or by accident. The only thing that counted was making sure another didn't come his way.

A figure he guessed was Heaton stood between two of the outbuildings. Maybe ten, twelve feet away. He had another knife in his hand. Heaton was dressed in store-bought combat fatigues, had a wispy beard and a mess of hair best described as a greasy tangle.

There was no reaction from Heaton as he stared down the barrel of Fletcher's pistol. For all the emotion on his face, Fletcher could have been handing him a beer instead of pointing a deadly weapon at him.

Heaton's left hand held another throwing knife. It was held sideways by the handle rather than the blade, which made Fletcher relax the barest fraction.

There are a lot of misconceptions about throwing knives. The biggest one being that in flight, a thrown knife will rotate many times before striking its target. A well-thrown knife ought to rotate to increase its stability in flight. Fletcher knew there was a formula for the number of spins required for various differing distances. At the range between him and Heaton, one spin would be all. The longest recorded knife throw was over a hundred feet and had involved around fourteen spins, but Fletcher wasn't a fan of throwing a knife. He'd much sooner keep his knife in his hand and use a gun as a distance weapon.

Another myth is that knives are only thrown when gripped by the blade. A proper throwing knife like the one in Heaton's hand was designed to be thrown from both handle and blade. The duality allowing for half turns in flight to alleviate the jump in the number of rotations between varying distances.

Held as it was, the knife in Heaton's hand couldn't be thrown at Fletcher without a significant movement. Fletcher needed a fraction of a second to react and a smaller fraction to shoot. Heaton didn't stand a chance.

"Drop that knife. Right now."

"Screw you." Heaton's face, tone and body language were full of defiance. "If you were gonna shoot me you'd have done it by now. Same as I chose not to kill you, you made a decision not to pull your trigger."

"You chose not to kill me?"

"Damn straight I did." Heaton's empty hand pointed at the knife by Fletcher's ear. "Take a look. I aimed for the knot."

Fletcher threw a rapid glance at the knife embedded into the wall. It bisected the center of a knot in the siding and stood out on what appeared to be a perfectly level plane. Heaton had skills with his knife.

"Why don't you drop the knife, I'll put my gun back in the holster and explain why I'm here."

"I know why you're here. Whole damn county knows why you're here. You're supposed to be this most superior investigator sent to find who killed Jane Friedrickson."

"Drop the knife and I'll explain why I'm here." Fletcher pointed at the dirt under his feet. "Why I've come to see you."

"Screw you." Heaton's defiance was being replaced with anger. "It's obvious why you're here. You're here to plant something on me. To set me up for Jane's homicide. To accuse me of killing the most awesome, most beautiful, most superior woman who ever walked on God's green earth."

"I'm not here to do anything of the sort." As he spoke, Fletcher was considering pulling his trigger and saving everyone the hassle of dealing with Heaton. As well as his previous counts of stalking, his obsession with Jane Friedrickson was clear. His speech patterns were off kilter and his skill with knives marked him out as a threat.

For someone who could throw a knife with Heaton's accuracy, sliding one between ribs and across a throat would be a cinch, as would the carving of a message onto foreheads.

"Yeah right. And I've got the most superior role in the next Hollywood blockbuster." Heaton pointed in the direction of the trail Fletcher had followed to get to the shack. "Go on, get back in your SUV, give it *Full Metal Jacket* on the gas pedal and don't come back. You had some real evidence linking me to the deaths, there'd be a dozen cops with you. You're here by yourself because you're pissing in the wind and wondering where the rain's coming from."

It gouged at Fletcher to admit it, but Heaton was right in a lot of ways. All the same, he kept his aim on the contractor as he backed away. He made a change to his plans; he now wanted to speak to Mrs. Renard before he went to Merrill to see Annie as he wanted to try and get Mrs. Renard's take on the contractor.

CHAPTER THIRTY-TWO

The road to Merrill reminded Fletcher of a lot of the roads he'd traveled before he left the UK. It was a basic strip of asphalt with a lane going in each direction. The sides of the road were grassy verges separating the asphalt from the bordering fields. After a while the fields gave way to large woods full of slow-growing trees like birch.

If he wasn't so preoccupied with his thoughts, he'd be feeling nostalgic. It was more than a decade since he'd been back to the UK to visit his adoptive parents, and while they Skyped or FaceTimed one another, it wasn't the same thing. His mother's fear of flying prevented them coming east, although she'd used Valium to enable her to visit after Rachel's death.

The conversation with Mrs. Renard hadn't gone well in any fashion. It was possible grief had made her haughty, but Fletcher doubted that was the case. Every attempt to speak with her in private had been thwarted by either her standoffishness, or the presence of her daughter-in-law who protected the older woman with a ferocity akin to a lioness guarding her cubs.

He'd got the same details from Mrs. Renard as he had from the file Quadrado had sent him, and there was no way he was going to broach the subject of Walt's infidelity with another family member in the room.

Fletcher knew it was uncharitable to understand why Walt had found comfort in the arms of another woman, but the pernicious Mrs. Renard had stripped him of his desire to see her in a positive light. From the pinched mouth, to the straight back and haughty manner, everything about her made him think of the word harridan.

By the same token, he couldn't see her as the killer. He figured that would be too quick, too painless for a woman like her. That she'd be the type who'd gladly cut her own nose off to spite someone else's face. She'd want to make her husband suffer, to have him regret his dalliance every time she gave him a look or chastising word. She would prefer to execute him with a thousand verbal cuts than a knife to the heart or a slash to the throat.

He'd looked around White Birch as he'd visited, but other than the general layout of the buildings, it was little different to Greenacres Farm and Meadowfields.

Quadrado's email informing him of Heaton's fondness for throwing knives at people was a day late and a dollar short, although he was pleased to read she'd held off from making the anonymous call until nine o'clock. By his calculations, it'd take the Medford PD at least an hour from getting the information to speaking to their counterparts in Merrill and getting Annie picked up.

The areas of Merrill Fletcher passed gave the impression it was a decent place that spoke of affluence and a respectable community. Yards were tidy. Bushes and lawns were trimmed and he saw little graffiti or areas where there were obvious issues with crime.

He rounded a corner and drove along Lake Street until he found the house he was looking for. It wasn't hard to find. The cops leading a distraught woman towards a squad car were sign enough. For once in his life, Old Cop must have acted with something approaching competence. What that would mean for Annie was yet to be defined, but Fletcher was confident she wouldn't enjoy the next few hours.

CHAPTER THIRTY-THREE

The air was filled with the smell of charcoal and woodsmoke as Fletcher approached Calvertsholm Farm. Calvertsholm was one of the other two farms abutting the crossroads where the Hashtag Killer – as the press had named him – had left the road to hike towards the farms of his victims. As he drew towards the buildings he could see a pair of fire trucks and four of the huge tankers farmers used for spreading manure. Off to one side were a dozen of the pickups favored by the local farmers. The fire trucks were spraying water over the embers of a farm building, while the tankers were being used as water tanks to feed the fire trucks with a constant supply of water.

He'd never thought about it before, but Fletcher realized that for farms and other rural buildings, fire hydrants weren't common things, therefore alternative supplies of water would have to be sourced by other means.

A knot of men were standing by the rear of one of the tankers. Most stood still, with grim faces. One of their number, who Fletcher guessed owned the farm, was gesticulating at the remains of a shed with fury and despair written all over his face.

Fletcher could pick out the shapes of some vehicles among the debris. One had the defined shape of a tractor and another looked to be a large cattle trailer. This indicated to him the timber shed had housed farm machinery before it caught fire.

He couldn't help but wonder if the fire was another piece of the bad luck plaguing Taylor County farmers or if there was someone behind it. And if there was someone behind it, was that person the same guy who'd killed Walt and Jane?

His suspicion was that the locals believed everything was connected. He'd learned of the fire from Peter Quadrado who'd urged him to swing by.

As he pulled to a halt, he saw Peter separate himself from the knot and walk his way. There was a grimness about Peter he'd not seen before, although the last time he'd seen him, only one of his family friends had been murdered.

"This is getting out of hand, Grant. As well as this fire, there was another over at Mile End during the night. Burned right through the milking parlor. It'll be weeks, maybe months before they can milk there again."

"First things first. Was anyone hurt, either here or at Mile End?"

"No, nobody."

"What about animals on the farm, were any of them caught in the fires?"

"Nope." Peter's voice was tense with fury. "Whatever jerk was behind this released the cattle, both here and at Mile End. It's the only positive any of us can take from this."

Peter's words sparked an idea in Fletcher's mind. "Are you sure they were released and didn't just escape? Or that they weren't let out by one of the firefighters?"

"Absolutely. There's no way they got out of the sheds without someone opening the doors." He gave an exasperated sigh. "The firefighters here and at Mile End all said the cattle were already evacuated when they arrived. Say they did manage to escape without any human help, what do you reckon the odds are they just so happened to effect a once in a lifetime escape at the very same time there was a fire in the next building?"

"Too high to contemplate."

The fact the cattle had been released was significant. It spoke of direct human involvement. It was always possible, if not probable, that a passing drifter or vagrant had done a good deed upon seeing the fire. But Fletcher's thinking was this pair of fires were arson rather than accident.

With a human responsible for the cattle being loose, and no one claiming responsibility for freeing the animals, it stood to reason whomever freed them was also responsible for the fire.

This led Fletcher to backtrack to the so-called run of bad luck that farms in Taylor County had experienced. It could well be these fires were someone starting out as an arsonist. That's not what Fletcher was thinking though. He suspected the unknown arsonist had also been behind some of the troubles other farms had previously experienced. The difference between then and now was he'd proven himself to exist by saving the cattle.

A car pulled up and disgorged a young woman and a guy with a professional-looking video camera. "Oh no. What's she doing here?"

"Reporters?"

"Yeah. She's the roving reporter for WITV. You can tell she thinks herself far too good for the stories she covers and that she's always looking for a break that'll get her a national contract. I heard tell she was as good as run off by Carl Friedrickson's old man and that she's been plaguing Elsie Renard as well."

Fletcher wasn't surprised she'd come to cover the story. Fires made for good visuals even if they were nothing more than smoking embers being doused by dirty-faced firefighters. When you threw in the proximity of the fire to the sites of two recent violent homicides, there was lots of room for conjecture that might just get her noticed.

A closer look at the reporter showed her to be mid-twenties, with a tousle of auburn hair that fell onto the shoulders of the mauve two-piece suit she wore. Her looks and styling were caught halfway between girl-next-door and professional businesswoman.

For all Peter's evident dislike of her, Fletcher saw no reason why the reporter shouldn't have ambitions and dreams. His own mother had fought to earn her place as a national newspaper's number one investigative journalist, and she'd had to do so in a time when most women in the workplace were seen as nothing more than secretaries or eye candy. People like this young reporter might have virtually no idea of the sexism or glass ceilings encountered by the people who'd blazed the trail of equality for them. Peter's life ambition might be to stay in Taylor County and work the farm, but that didn't mean others couldn't have aspirations of their own.

With an eye for the dramatic the reporter positioned herself so her back was to the smoldering fire, allowing the cameraman to frame it in the background of her piece to camera.

One of the guys who'd been talking to a firefighter came over to join Fletcher and Peter, his face grim beneath a John Deere baseball cap.

Peter lifted an eyebrow at him. "Well?"

"They're saying the fire was set. They reckon it's burned too evenly for a natural fire."

This was all the confirmation Fletcher needed. The only question he was focusing on now was whether or not the person targeting the farms was the same person who'd killed Jane Friedrickson and Walt Renard.

CHAPTER THIRTY-FOUR

Although he'd spent half of the day traveling and the majority of the rest speaking to people, Fletcher was restless in the motel room. No matter how he tried, he couldn't get himself into a position that felt comfortable for more than a few minutes and there was an irritability to him he wasn't used to.

He possessed enough self-awareness to know it was the lack of progress that was affecting him. As well as the threat to his liberty and indeed possibly his life, he viewed defeat as unacceptable regardless of the odds stacked against him.

Steve Heaton was a prime suspect for Jane Friedrickson's death, yet Fletcher wasn't aware of a motive for him also killing Walt Renard. The same logic applied to his involvement in the sabotage-style attacks on the farms. Heaton was weird on a galactic scale, yet beyond a probable genuine psychosis, Fletcher couldn't think of a reason why he'd damage the places where he earned his livelihood.

A lot of the same logic also went against the unknown arsonist. It was one thing to damage a few tractors, another to set fire to sheds, but it was a huge step forward to two counts of homicide. Also, people on a mission tended to escalate their actions as their campaign progressed. If the arsonist was the killer, then he'd started off with small pieces of sabotage that could be viewed as accidents, taken a giant leap up to a double homicide and then regressed back to arson. To Fletcher this was counterintuitive and the best of his thinking was aimed towards there being two separate entities at play. One a killer, the other the arsonist.

But why someone would be spending their time causing trouble for the county's farmers was a question he couldn't answer.

The lack of communication from Quadrado was another thing needling him. He'd hoped she'd have been in touch regarding Annie by now, but he'd heard diddly from her. No news might well be good news, but he was desperate for new information.

One step at a time, he went back over everything he'd learned since arriving in Medford. Beyond Heaton he couldn't think of a credible suspect and that galled him as he wasn't convinced of Heaton's guilt. The idea there was a serial killer operating in Taylor County was one he kept returning to and then dismissing. America had more than its fair share of serial killers, yet a sleepy area like Medford and its satellite towns wasn't a killer's normal hunting ground. Urban areas where a new face could be lost in the crowd worked best for those who wanted to remain unnoticed. Medford was altogether too small for a stranger to hang around for any length of time without the locals being aware of them. His own encounters with the locals proved that.

Likewise there were no real places where a killer could camp out without being discovered. The area was flat farming land, shorn of its crops and devoid of significant areas to remain out of sight. The woods fringing some of the fields were narrow strips of trees maybe fifty yards wide at most; too sparse to provide cover for any length of time. Fletcher knew he'd be able to hide out in them unseen for days, but to do so would require a lack of all creature comforts such as a fire or even a tent to keep him dry should it rain. The killer had a car or truck, he'd established that fact right off the bat. While a person could hunker down and disguise themselves, hiding an automobile was a different thing.

It could be the serial killer was a local, or they were hiding out in the next town or city. There were so many possibilities in Fletcher's mind, he was in danger of bamboozling himself.

He needed more information and there weren't a lot of sources. The Quadrado family and the Friedricksons were the most open with him, the barman, Don, was reticent to be seen talking with him in public and he'd feel he was taking advantage of Felicity by calling her.

Fletcher laced up his boots, intent on going to see Peter Quadrado. His various thoughts and conclusions had opened up a bunch of questions and Peter was the closest reliable source.

Before he lifted the keys to the SUV, he fired off an email to Quadrado reminding her that he was doing her a favor and would like to see her show that she gave even the smallest portion of a damn by keeping him updated. The wording of his email was harsh, but not so harsh as the email she'd sent reminding him he was over a barrel.

CHAPTER THIRTY-FIVE

Fletcher found Peter Quadrado in Meadowfield's milking parlor. The air was filled with a mixture of mechanical noises, farmyard scents and an oppressive heat Fletcher judged was caused by the number of cattle in a low-roofed area. A radio played a local station and there was a muted news report being read as Fletcher went to join Peter.

The center of the parlor was divided in two sections three feet lower than the stalls which flanked the low areas. A quick count of one set of stalls told Fletcher there were thirty-two cows being milked at any one time.

The area was a lot more sterile than he'd expected, although he had to leap out of the way to avoid being splattered when a cow lifted its tail as a precursor to emptying its bladder.

Peter was busy dealing with a rebellious cow who kept kicking at the collection of suction nozzles as soon as they were placed on her udders. After the third attempt, Peter reached up to an overhead rail and retrieved an odd-looking piece of equipment, shaped like a "C" written in a futuristic font that was all straight lines and angled corners. Peter climbed up to the level of the stalls, hooked one end under the front of the cattle's back leg and then raised it until the other end looped over its hip.

With the gadget attached, Peter dropped back to the lower level, lifted the collection of nozzles and fit them to the cow in a way that spoke of long practice. The cow's foot lifted, moved forward and then stopped. The gadget seemed to be digging in enough to deter the cow without going so far as to cause it pain so long as it didn't kick out.

"Can you spare ten minutes?"

"Give me five first, yeah?"

"Sure." Fletcher glanced round the lower reaches of the parlor, found a place he'd be able to watch without getting in the way or being soiled by any of the cows and observed Peter at his work.

Peter worked with the kind of efficiency that's bred by familiarity. Every part of each task he completed was done with simple practiced movements. A yawning sound made Fletcher's head turn and he saw a collection of the nozzles being drawn upwards from the last cow on the right to have them removed.

A gate clanged open and the cows to his right filed out only to be replaced by another eight. Peter reached up, pressed buttons on a small console suspended from the ceiling and Fletcher heard the rattle of pellets in a tube. Surmising it was cattle feed of some description, Fletcher watched as Peter walked along the line of cattle fitting sets of nozzles to their udders.

"Right. You got five minutes and then I'll have to start over again."

"Do you know Steve Heaton?" A nod from Peter. "What do you think of him?"

"Never had too much to do with him directly. I know he's a bit off-the-wall, but he's damn good at his job. He drives a forager when he's here and I've never had an issue with him, although I do know he's been in a spot of trouble. I remember hearing he was off the chart when it comes to book smarts. Heard quite a bit about that now I think back."

In a spot of trouble was a mild way of describing it. A knife thrown into someone's chest and two counts of stalking weren't what Fletcher would call spots.

"You ever hear of him being fixated with Jane Friedrickson?"

"Not in any specific context." A grimace. "Heaton's got that odd streak about him. He's well known for having an eye for the ladies, but not the gumption to talk to one. Much as he might leer over them, I never heard tell of him being seen out with anyone bar the guys he works with. So far as I know, he's never so much as been on a date round here."

Fletcher filed the news away for later pondering. "I met him earlier. He seems to have a thing about knives. And snakes."

"You've been to his place then. Never been myself but I've heard plenty about it. Legend is when he's not working, he spends his time out hunting snakes with his knives."

"And you don't think this is odd?"

"Of course I do. Everyone thinks he's one step away from being a certified wack job; thing is, a lot of us understand how the mind needs stimulus. You do the same thing day in day out for twelve or fourteen hours a day, you go a little stir crazy. He drives a forager back and forth for months on end. The guys trailing the corn from field to farm, they get to see different sights. Heaton, he sees the corn in front of him and the same two views above the corn all day." Peter huffed a breath upwards to flick hair from his face. "I told you he was super-smart, now try to imagine doing his job with all its monotony and a brain that's big enough to earn an MIT scholarship at the age of twelve. The man is sharp enough to be working for NASA and he's driving up and down the same fields day after day. Yeah, he does crazy stuff when he's not working, but he's good at getting corn in fast, and round here, that's pretty much all anyone cares about regarding him."

Fletcher did his best not to pull a face at Peter's frank assessment of Heaton and how the man was viewed in the community. It made a certain amount of sense, and as long as he didn't bother individuals, he'd be tolerated, even if he wasn't liked.

The man's intellect was a subject he hadn't expect to come up, much less for it to be revealed Heaton was so clever. As much as any other point, it made the contractor a prime suspect as there was no doubting the fact the killer was smart. The lack of evidence found at the crime scenes said as much. As did the way he'd gotten in and out again without being seen by anyone.

"Anything else you can tell me about him?"

"Nothing of worth."

"Okay." It wasn't, but there was no point trying to get information from Peter that he didn't know. "What about the spate of bad luck: do you or any of the other farmers have any idea who might want to cause you all trouble? Is there a common link between all the farms that have suffered attacks, like a feed merchant or contractor you've all stopped using?"

"There's Mick Barkel. Most everyone used him at one time or another." A shake of his head. "I can't see him causing trouble, though. He's too drunk most of the time and I can't see why he'd kill anyone."

"Is there anyone else you might suspect?"

"For the homicides? Or the attacks on the farms?"

Fletcher scratched his nose. "Let's stick with the attacks for the time being."

"Well. A few of the guys have pointed a finger, so to speak."

"Who at?"

"Nobody in particular, more a group of people than one person." As Peter hesitated Fletcher rolled a hand for him to continue. "Well." A look of consternation hit Peter's face. "There's a lot of people who don't like the way we farm. Eco warriors and animal rights activists who disapprove of the way our cattle are kept in sheds all the time. Some of the guys have wondered if the attacks on the farms were their way of hitting back at us."

The idea sounded plausible to Fletcher as he knew activists could be known to act outside the law, such was their conviction in their beliefs. What he couldn't see was how they would be tied in with the homicides. No matter how he looked at things, he couldn't picture animal rights activists sneaking about murdering people. They were about preserving life for animals and humans. For the elimination of factory farms over free range ones.

"That makes sense."

"So does what's being planned. A lot of us are of the opinion that things are going to get worse before they get better. And the cops can't guard our farms so we're going to. So far there's twenty-eight of us all planning to stand guard at night. We've got a group text and we're going to band together to catch the jerkweed who's been attacking our farms."

"Just make sure you don't get hurt, and that anyone you catch is in one piece when you hand him over to the cops."

Peter didn't answer so Fletcher let the matter drop. He'd made his point and, considering his own vigilante actions in the past, he could hardly step onto a pulpit and preach to people trying to protect their livelihoods.

Fletcher tried a couple more questions, but Peter was back in work mode, so he left the parlor and went outside to his SUV.

Once inside he checked his cell, hoping rather than expecting an email from Quadrado. There wasn't one, although there was a message from Felicity inviting him to dinner again.

Felicity was good company, but she wanted more than he was prepared to give, so to see her would be wrong. On the other hand, he'd like to pick her brains about Heaton, and also test the farmer's theory about the animal rights activists with her. He sent a positive reply and steeled himself for another evening of potentially batting away unwelcome advances.

CHAPTER THIRTY-SIX

Fletcher put the SUV into drive and pulled away from Felicity's house with a wry grin on his lips. She'd warned him about her lack of culinary skills and then proceeded to serve up a mouth-watering meal. Fair enough, it was just steak with a salad and homemade fries, but every bite was delicious, as was the apple pie she'd cooked for dessert.

Felicity had set the tone from the moment he arrived by telling him that she was happy to enjoy his company as a friend, but so long as he was in Medford, she'd be there if he wanted more.

Her candor was appreciated. They both knew where they stood, and once Fletcher had gotten his answers from her, they'd relaxed into each other's company.

The break from the investigation was more welcome than Fletcher realized. It was the first hour he'd spent not thinking about the homicides and what clues he must follow since arriving in Medford. The change of focus wasn't just beneficial to his stress levels, it also helped him gain a fresher perspective when he again bent his mind to the problem at hand.

Felicity's answers had also given him a different set of questions to ask himself. It turned out Steve Heaton did have history with Walt Renard.

Three years ago he and Renard had come to blows when the farmer caught Heaton looking at his college-aged daughter in a way he didn't approve of.

Fletcher got Walt's position. As the single father of a teenage daughter himself, he didn't like the way some grown men looked at Wendy. It was a tough situation: Wendy had to be allowed to cope with life herself and to grow up unhindered by paternal overprotectiveness, yet his every instinct was to protect her.

The daughter had been a final addition to the Renard brood and had come along a full decade after her nearest sibling. She was the baby of the family and treated as such by her father.

Words such as "leering" and "pervert" had apparently spilled from Renard's mouth upon following Heaton's eyeline as his daughter walked past.

Heaton had denied he'd been looking, but Renard's blood was up. When his fists came up and connected with Heaton's face, things had gotten ugly, and fast. According to Felicity, it had taken five other contractors to separate them, and by the time the two men were pulled apart, there was a knife in Heaton's right hand, though Felicity's source said that Renard had fared better than the younger man.

Angry words had been exchanged and Heaton had never been welcome back at White Birch.

While any humiliation for Heaton at being bested by a man twice his age was now three years old, there was nothing to say it hadn't festered. If Heaton was the one to have killed Jane, perhaps he'd gotten a twisted rush from it and had decided to settle an outstanding score.

Fletcher knew his theorizing was at best circumstantial, but there was little doubt in his mind Heaton was now the prime suspect.

With the SUV parked on the road's shoulder, Fletcher retrieved his phone, cursed at the lack of text or email response from Quadrado and tried calling her. Heaton ought to be picked up as soon as possible. It was a job for the local cops, although he'd be happy to personally bring the contractor in if needs be.

Quadrado didn't pick up. Didn't have chance to, as her cell went straight to her voicemail. He left a sharp message sharing his discoveries and stating the date and time as he believed their communications would be monitored by whomever had got Quadrado to cut him the deal, or one of his minions.

With the message left, Fletcher repeated it via email and set off traveling again. His path was aimless at first, but the more he drove, the more he was tempted to go towards Heaton's shack of a home and set up a surveillance detail.

A further insight into Heaton's mentality was a plan he'd let slip to someone when being teased about his lack of success with the opposite sex. The way Felicity had told it, Heaton's goal in life was to marry a farmer's daughter. Not any farmer's daughter, but the eldest daughter of a farmer who had no sons. In time he'd take over the farm and run it as his own.

Jane Friedrickson fit this criteria, which would only increase her attraction in his eyes. She'd be the perfect candidate as she'd not only be the sole inheritor of her parent's farm, but if Heaton could persuade her to divorce Carl, she'd be sure to walk away with either a significant lump of cash, or a share of Greenacres Farm.

It was all anecdotal, but the more he heard about Heaton, the more Fletcher was sure he was behind the homicides.

The other thing chewing at Fletcher's mind was Felicity's thoughts on the animal rights activists being involved in the attacks on the farms. She'd scoffed at first and had then changed her mind when she gave it some thought.

She'd spent a vehement five minutes explaining to Fletcher that while the cattle might not get out into the fields on a regular basis, they were still well cared for. Each of the stalls in their shed had special cattle mattresses, fogging devices to keep them cool during the fierce heat of summer and a diet that was calculated for each cow. Yes, they might be animals who were only being kept for the milk they produced, but at two thousand bucks apiece, they were valuable assets to the farmers and were looked after as such.

Like so many people whose community is supported by a sole industry, Felicity couldn't see an alternative point of view regarding any possible failings of that industry.

Fletcher was driving along ten miles below the speed limit when a large vehicle of some description appeared in his rearview mirror. He couldn't see much of the vehicle because its headlamps were high enough to shine right through the back window of his SUV.

The road ahead was empty in the darkness, so Fletcher kept his speed the same and waited for the vehicle to overtake him.

It didn't. Instead there was a sudden glare of full beam lights backed up with what Fletcher could only imagine was every spot lamp in North America.

Darkness turned to daylight for Fletcher as the other vehicle's lights illuminated a large area around his SUV.

To avoid being further dazzled, Fletcher leaned forward in his seat to remove his eyes from the brightness reflected at him via the SUV's rearview and side mirrors.

Fletcher bumped the signal stalk with his fingertips and moved towards the shoulder so he could pull over. The jerk who was scared of the dark could damn well drive around him.

The first nudge from behind was gentle.

The second was enough to make the SUV squirm across the asphalt.

CHAPTER THIRTY-SEVEN

Fletcher wrestled the steering wheel until the SUV was more or less straight then stomped on the gas pedal as hard as he could. Heaton's use of the movie title *Full Metal Jacket* flashed back to him as he wrung every last drop of acceleration from the SUV.

The SUV responded as best it could. In a race it would have romped against the ageing sedan parked on Fletcher's drive back in Utah. But against the monstrous vehicle that had twice rammed it, the SUV was a knife in a gunfight.

Fletcher had recognized the SUV as being a base model; comfortable enough with an array of gadgetry that would keep most people happy, it was a workhorse of the type bought in bulk by whichever rental company the FBI had sourced it from.

His pulse thumped and he could feel his mouth turn dry as sweat prickled all over his body. The adrenaline dump from his natural fight-or-flight reflexes was something Fletcher had experienced many times before. He knew how to control it, how to harness its energies into direct action.

A slight bend in the road wasn't sharp enough for Fletcher to need to slow down, yet he saw the pursuing vehicle back away.

Seventy, eighty, ninety. The speedometer kept climbing without any thought for the speed limit. Fletcher's boot stayed hard down on the gas pedal as the needle rose towards the hundred-miles-an-hour marker.

The slight bend had taught Fletcher the big vehicle was not as good in the corners as his SUV. The problem with that was most of the roads in this area were arrow straight.

At the speed he was traveling, he was upon junctions and turnings before he had a chance to react. With the other vehicle twenty feet behind and closing, there was no way he'd have time to slow down enough to make a successful change of route.

Another option was to go off-road. Which sounded easier than it was.

To keep the maximum amount of land farmable, whoever had laid out this road had positioned it beside the ditches which drained the fields. Either side of the asphalt was lined with a fringe of uncut grass and a three-foot ditch.

Even if there were no ditch, there was a one-foot difference in height between the asphalt and the field. Not a problem at twenty-five mph, manageable, if uncomfortable at fifty, and a disaster waiting to happen at a hundred plus.

The vehicle behind was closing again. Its daylight-creating lights clawing forward and preventing Fletcher from keeping too close a watch on its movements.

He was sure the vehicle would try to ram him again, which left him with two choices. Stay where he was and hope to ride out the impact, or not be available to be hit.

Both options had their pros and cons. A straight hit from behind was unlikely to cause too much of an issue provided he could keep the SUV lined up on the road. By the same token, any kind of lateral hit at these kinds of speeds would spell disaster. The paved road wasn't that wide, certainly not wide enough to provide room for him to correct a change in direction before he encountered a ditch.

The vehicle behind him was larger so it stood to reason it'd carry a weight advantage. As much as he knew evasive driving techniques were necessary, there was still a huge risk with taking them.

As the pursuing vehicle closed in, Fletcher let the SUV drift across the road a little. The other driver stayed where he was, dead center of the road.

Fletcher judged there was four feet of clear air between the vehicles.

He eased the wheel over until his passenger side wheels were as close to the edge of the asphalt as he dared take them. The other driver moved across as if preparing to nudge the SUV off the road.

Three feet.

"Come on, you heap of junk, get a move on."

Fletcher didn't get a response from the SUV. Not that he'd expected he would. His exhortations channeled his fear into anger. It would soon be the moment of truth. He had a plan. A risky idea he calculated had no more than a fifty percent chance of success.

Two feet.

Fletcher counted to five and then made his move.

With the fenders of the two vehicles less than eighteen inches apart, Fletcher jerked the SUV left and as soon as he was across the road and had corrected the SUV's desire to go into a slide, stamped on the brake pedal hard enough to send a reaction juddering back to the top of his thigh.

The SUV squirmed under the major shift in momentum. Its tires fighting for purchase as the anti-lock brakes did their thing. Even as the brake pedal first chattered back at his foot, Fletcher was bracing himself for the impact he knew was coming. The pursuing vehicle was abreast of him and coming his way, its driver having reacted to his jink left by copying the move and slamming on his own brakes.

The rear of the vehicle brushed the front panel of Fletcher's SUV. Tall wheels bashing metal and removing paint.

Fletcher had the lighter vehicle. It was more modern than his pursuer's. The advantage was with him.

He stopped a good ten feet before the other vehicle could, rammed the lever into reverse and got the SUV facing the other way.

The whole maneuver had taken less than ten seconds from wrenching the wheel to setting off in the opposite direction.

Ten seconds was an age in a battle situation, yet Fletcher was pleased with his work. He'd achieved his two main goals.

Number one: identify his aggressor. That was easy, the highly sprung, souped-up pickup was driven by Steve Heaton. He'd expected as much, and while it was good to have suspicions confirmed, Fletcher would rather have learned Heaton was trying to harm him in a way that carried less potential for death.

Number two: buy some time. The ten seconds it took him to turn would be quick in comparison to Heaton's pickup. Its longer wheelbase and wider turning circle would make it much harder for him to turn in one movement without putting a wheel into a ditch. Then it'd be back to a straight race. Up to around sixty, the SUV had superior acceleration until it kicked into its top gear which was designed for cruising.

Fletcher would have preferred a stick shift. Sure, the automatic would make sweeter gear changes under heavy acceleration, but it would have been programmed to be kind to the engine. With his life on the line, Fletcher had no mechanical sympathy for the SUV's internal workings and would have happily revved its engine to within a fraction of explosion if it meant he got away from Heaton.

For the first time since Heaton had rammed him, Fletcher took his eyes off the road and directed them to the passenger seat. It's where he'd left his cell and pistol.

Neither were there.

One or other of the jolts or swerves he'd made must have dislodged them from the base of the seat and sent them tumbling.

He couldn't summon help and nor could he fight back. It was now about straight-line speed or animal cunning. And Fletcher didn't have the speed advantage.

As hard as he was pushing the SUV, Heaton's pickup was reeling him in.

Desperate for a solution, Fletcher trawled his memory for markers that might indicate where he might turn off the road and onto a different route, be it cross-country or to a farm where there would be witnesses to Heaton's aggression.

Heaton was closing faster than before which suggested he had thrown caution to the wind and was thrashing his own vehicle harder than earlier.

Fletcher spied a signpost he remembered passing. It denoted a side road. Where it led didn't matter so long as it wasn't a dead end. The twistier the route, the better his chances of escaping Heaton.

The anti-lock brakes kicked back at his foot for a second time in as many minutes. It was going to be close. The false daylight Heaton's spot lamps created was bringing a violent dawn his way as the speed bled from the SUV so he could make the turn.

Fletcher spun the wheel, released the brake pedal and gave the gas pedal everything he had.

Heaton's front wing clipped the rear of Fletcher's SUV and then it all became about momentum.

Momentum is a quantifiable force measured by the multiplication of mass and velocity. Heaton's pickup was well over two tons and traveling at least fifty miles an hour.

Fletcher's SUV weighed less and was moving across the pickup's direction of travel.

Momentum will only dissipate if an external force works against it.

Heaton's pickup carried a lot of momentum that it transferred to the SUV, bowling it out of the way with a crashing thud that lifted its rear and sent the SUV whirling and skidding as its own momentum exacerbated the impact.

The pickup reacted much the same way as the impact locked one wheel while its remaining momentum sent it into a similar tumbling roll to the SUV's.

CHAPTER THIRTY-EIGHT

The SUV came to a halt on its roof with Fletcher suspended in an untidy tangle of limbs supported by the seatbelt.

With a hand braced against the steering wheel to guide his descent as much as possible, Fletcher reached the other hand round and fumbled to release the buckle.

Somehow every part of his body that made contact with the SUV when he dropped seemed to find a sharp edge. The passenger door was open, so he squirmed around until he could crawl towards it. There was a stickiness in his hair and the talcum powder used to prevent the airbags binding together was catching the back of his throat, but other than a slight grogginess, there was no serious injury for him to worry about.

Fletcher had to bat down the exploded airbags to exit the SUV. He didn't mind the inconvenience; they'd saved him from greater injury, he was sure of that.

What Quadrado would make of the wrecked SUV could wait for another day. Right now, his priorities were getting clear of the vehicle, as he could smell gasoline, and finding Heaton.

Foot by foot he crawled his way out of the SUV. His body a cacophonous riot of aches that kept his teeth gritted.

As he left the SUV, he pulled at the open passenger door to haul himself upright.

A shake of the head to clear his blurry vision proved to be a mistake as it made matters worse.

He blinked. Once, twice and then a third time.

They say the third time is a charm. It was and it wasn't for Fletcher. His vision improved, but the first thing he saw was Heaton's fist arrowing towards his face.

He tried rolling his head to the side, but it was too little, too late. Heaton's knuckles reopened the split on his lip and loosened at least one tooth.

Fletcher rounded the car door and went for Heaton. With the gun still somewhere in the SUV, he needed to stay close to Heaton. If he gave the man any room to throw a knife he was done for without a distance weapon of his own.

As much as he wanted to crash his forehead onto Heaton's nose, Fletcher didn't dare run the risk of his grogginess returning. The same applied to taking more punches to the head.

To this end he fought smart as well as hard. The punches he sent Heaton's way were all aimed at the nose or above. It meant his own torso was exposed, but until he was sure he was no more than lightly concussed, he had to protect his head at all costs.

A hammer blow landed on Fletcher's ribs as he landed a right cross on the bridge of Heaton's nose. This is how he wanted the fight to happen: trying to knock Heaton out while Heaton tried to wear him down with body blows.

For Fletcher, there was no standing back and picking accurate punches; this was an all-out brawl to prevent the contractor pulling one of his knives on him.

Three more times they exchanged punches with neither combatant landing a blow that would finish their opponent.

When Fletcher's next blow went unanswered his joy turned to panic in an instant. A knife had appeared in Heaton's hand and was arrowing upwards towards his chest.

The only way Fletcher could avoid the knife was to push on Heaton's shoulder to widen the gap between them. Both men staggered backwards, but Fletcher's foot caught on debris from the wreckage that sent him tumbling to the ground.

Before he'd even landed, Heaton was arcing towards him, the knife in his hand aimed directly at Fletcher's face.

CHAPTER THIRTY-NINE

Yet another late night at the office on the back of an early start had Quadrado yawning hard enough to make her jaw crack. She'd had little more than junk food for days and was longing to eat a proper meal with a knife and fork at a table, rather than a sandwich at her desk.

The idea she'd had for her case had paid off and today had been all about closing the net on the suspects and making arrests. Other Special Agents on the team had been handed the job of interviewing the suspects, but she was the one feeding them questions while also compiling the necessary evidence to secure both confessions and convictions.

With her laptop powering down, she turned her attention to the Wisconsin case and checked her phone. There were several emails from Fletcher, each with an increased urgency than the previous. His tone was also changing to become more sarcastic as he awaited her responses.

"Screw you, Fletcher." Her phone slid across her always-tidy desk. She didn't need his sarcasm. She needed a result. A person in handcuffs so she could stop thinking about Jane's homicide as a case and start to grieve for the friend she'd lost.

As soon as the phone reached a halt she was leaning forward to retrieve it. Fletcher wasn't by nature a caustic person; he was pragmatic, ruthless and smart, but he wasn't nasty.

He'd needed her and she hadn't been there for him. She had got him involved, and she'd deserted him as her own case broke open. He was out on a limb investigating Jane's homicide and she was his gateway to information. A gateway closed by the pressure of having to finish off her own case.

A memory of Jane flashed to her. The two of them had been sitting on a gate chatting about boys. Jane, as she always did, was talking about Carl. Quadrado couldn't remember which boys she'd been discussing but she could—in that instance—remember exactly how Jane had looked. They were fourteen at the time. Jane's hair had been its usual shock of curls and the freckles on her face had been deepened by the summer sun. As she thought of Jane's wide smile and infectious laugh, Quadrado had to bite her lip to stop herself from breaking down.

When she'd pulled herself together and checked what else was on her phone, she saw there was a missed call from Fletcher, and the message he'd left her was to the point on every level imaginable and made her blush with shame as she realized how well he'd done despite her lack of support.

The Heaton guy he was talking about was someone she wanted picked up right away. Jane had mentioned a contractor who'd been attracted to her, but had laughed it off without naming him. She now guessed Heaton was who she'd been referring to. With what Fletcher had learned about the man, there was a case to be made against him for both homicides.

She made a note on her pad and checked the email timeline. The bulk of Fletcher's messages had come before his call suggesting Heaton be picked up at once. She'd been in the room overlooking the interview suite when the call had come in which is why she'd missed it. All the same, she felt guilty not to be on hand to learn of such an important lead.

His earlier theories about the animal rights activists being responsible for the attacks on the farms made sense, and while he wasn't saying they had anything to do with the homicides, he'd suggested they could have killed Jane if she'd disturbed them as they were about to carry out one of their attacks. As a stand-in for Carl, it wouldn't be unreasonable to think she'd be the first person to be out and about on the farm the morning she was killed.

His request for more information on activists in the area was now a moot point, although—if they were responsible for the arson and earlier attacks—she knew a lot of farmers who'd be grateful if Fletcher could use his talents to stop them.

The woman from Merrill, Annie, who'd been having an affair with Walt Renard had been released after a brief interview. Both she and her cousin had told the same story. Unable to sleep, Annie had risen early and had distracted herself from her sorrow by baking. The noise she made had roused the cousin around five and the two of them had chatted, although the cousin had admitted she was less than happy at the lack of sleep.

Quadrado typed out responses to all of Fletcher's questions and promised to have Heaton arrested as soon as the Medford cops could get a warrant, and that she'd look into the activists the next morning.

She left the office and thought about the next day. There would be another early start, but with a fair wind, her case ought to be wrapped up around lunchtime. Then she'd be able to get a flight home to Wisconsin. By then Heaton would be in custody and the case should be all but closed. All the same, she wanted to see her family, and to visit Carl and offer him her condolences in person.

CHAPTER FORTY

Fletcher raised his arms to protect himself from the knife hurtling towards his face. Together they formed a bridge that blocked Heaton's wrist from plunging the thrusted knife into his cheek.

The knife in Heaton's hand was a hunting knife with the blade held outwards from the wrist, its top edge a line of jagged spikes designed to tear flesh. Blood ran past Heaton's eye from a cut in his hairline and there was a disheveled yet ferocious look about him. As they grappled, Fletcher could smell Heaton's sweat and the bourbon on his breath.

Rather than allow Heaton the chance to use the back of the knife's serrations against him, Fletcher slid both his arms outwards until he had both of his hands wrapped around Heaton's wrist.

He now had two hands to keep the knife away from his face compared to the one Heaton was using to hold the knife. However, he was on his back with Heaton's weight on top of him. His movement was limited whereas Heaton had freedom. Heaton also had a spare hand. All the advantage was with him. He could take the knife in his other hand, pull out another, or, simply add his hand to the struggling knot and force the knife down into Fletcher.

A punch from Heaton's free hand twisted Fletcher's head to the left.

The knife progressed an inch downwards as Fletcher reeled from the blow.

Heaton gave a wicked grin and threw another punch. Fletcher was ready for this one and while it still rocked him, the knife didn't move as far down. For all he had two hands pushing upwards on Heaton's knife arm, his elbows were bent and he could only apply the strength of his triceps.

Three more punches landed and another inch-and-a-half's progress was gained. Fletcher's muscles flexed against Heaton's weight, but the combination of the crash, the punches he was taking and the younger man's strength meant he wasn't able to halt, much less reverse the knife's path.

To make matters worse, Heaton had bent his wrist so the tip of the blade was aimed at Fletcher's eye.

Fletcher knew that if he was to survive this encounter, he'd have to change from defense to attack. The problem was, it was all he could do to defend himself and he was losing at that.

Behind Heaton's back, Fletcher planted his right foot flat on the ground and prepared to tense his already strained muscles even further.

When Heaton wound up his next punch, Fletcher made his move. As well as the upward force preventing the knife from getting any nearer his face, he pulled left with his left hand while pushing in the same direction with his right. To complement the lateral movement, Fletcher used his planted foot to thrust upwards, bucking Heaton's body the same way he was already pressing him.

Heaton went past the point of no return and rolled onto his back, his knife leaving no more than a slight cut on Fletcher's cheek. Rather than allow the man to roll away from him and spring to his feet, Fletcher moved with him. But he was on his back, so Fletcher couldn't stand without giving Heaton time to do the same. He rolled and squirmed his way on top of Heaton until they were both lying on their backs.

The knife twisted towards Fletcher's gut and he felt Heaton's muscles coil as he started to again apply a downward pressure.

Rather than get into another trial of strength, Fletcher held onto Heaton's wrist with his left hand and slid his right arm downwards until the elbow of Heaton's extended knife arm was in the crook of his own elbow.

Heaton realized Fletcher's intent and used his left hand to claw at his face. With his eyes screwed tight as protection against the scrabbling fingers, Fletcher pressed down with his hand while lifting with his right arm.

Elbows are a hinged joint. They're designed to bend one way and one way only.

Heaton screamed and cursed as Fletcher bent his right elbow the wrong way, snapping bone with a thunk that was audible over the man's wails.

He was still wailing as Fletcher rolled off him, patted him down in case there were any more weapons and lifted the knife away from his reach.

Fletcher was thinking all the time. He handled the knife by the top of its blade so as not to corrupt any fingerprints on the handle or the sample of his blood along the blade.

As soon as Fletcher was on his feet he delivered a solid kick to Heaton's groin that caused a fresh bout of screamed curses. The whole point of the kick was to keep Heaton in one place while he sourced his gun and cell phone. He could snap an ankle or a shin bone to do the same, yet that was more brutal than he wanted to be. He wasn't being caring towards Heaton; so far as Fletcher was concerned, Heaton's actions had more than earned him the punishment of further broken bones. But numerous injuries to Heaton would take more explaining to the cops, and Old Cop already had a grudge against him so he didn't want to give the lawman the slightest excuse to make his life more difficult.

With Heaton moaning and unsure whether to massage his groin or support his arm, Fletcher ducked back to the upturned SUV. He found his cell phone and the pistol resting on the ceiling below the back seats.

He checked them both. The cell had signal although there was a large crack on its screen where it had collided with something. The pistol was in good order and when he racked the slide after removing the magazine, there was no sign of any damage that would hinder its action.

Quadrado's cell was the number he dialed. She picked up on the second ring. Her tone was frosty to begin with, but when he explained what had happened she put any issue she had with him to one side.

He gave her the gist of what had happened and requested she give him five minutes to call the events in and then begin smoothing things over with the local cops for him once again.

Heaton maneuvered himself up to a sitting position and was cradling his injured arm with his good one as Fletcher cut the call to Quadrado and dialed 911. He wasn't sure of his location, but that wasn't an issue. The cell would be tracked as soon as the call was answered.

CHAPTER FORTY-ONE

Fletcher drained the last of the coffee in the paper cup and tried not to think of how much nicer a cool beer would have tasted.

The cops were treating him with a certain amount of respect. Quadrado had delivered for the first time today, and even by the time they'd arrived on the scene, they'd been aware of him and the fact he was one of the good guys.

To make things even better, Old Cop wasn't anywhere to be seen. Maybe he was off shift, or maybe, Fletcher thought optimistically, he'd retired and was on his way to Florida where he would spend his days complaining about the heat, and his nights boring people with exaggerated tales of his former importance as a cop.

For all he'd been extended a great deal of professional courtesy, Fletcher still had to go through his story several times. Heaton had been taken away by EMTs, although he'd had a police guard with him as he'd stepped into the ambulance.

The part of the story to take the most telling was how Fletcher had found evidence connecting Heaton to the homicides. The cops had gone over those parts way more times than Fletcher felt they needed to. He got that the information he'd gathered was nothing more than circumstantial, but Heaton's attempt to kill him tonight would give the cops something to push at him for, and with a real live suspect to go at, they'd be able to look at matching forensics and other evidence.

According to the cops Fletcher had spoken to, Heaton had attacked him because in his own twisted mind he thought Fletcher was the one to have killed Jane and he thought Fletcher was using him as a fall guy. Heaton was at the Medford Medical Center having his elbow set and then he'd face charges for the assault on Fletcher.

The one emotion Fletcher was feeling more than any other was delight. He'd solved the case, squared his debt with Quadrado and made a few bucks while doing so. There would be other missions to come in the future he was sure of that. For all his debt to Quadrado had been repaid, there was still a far larger account he needed to settle. At some point he'd be seconded for a black ops mission with full deniability. There was no way the shadowy figure behind the offer Quadrado had made him would deliver unless he did the same for them.

Fletcher knew better than to show his pleasure at having achieved his aim when setting out for Medford. Not to the cops whose case he'd solved. Not to men who'd all resent his presence, let alone the fact he'd outsmarted them and beat them to a solution on their home turf.

Best of all for Fletcher was the fact he'd be able to head home tomorrow, or the next morning at the latest.

Time after time he'd been over the same story. Related the same details and mapped out not just his investigative methods, but his thought processes at each stage. By the time he was finished he wasn't sure if he was being interrogated, or teaching his questioners how to run an investigation.

He was heading for the door within seconds of being allowed to leave.

As he passed the front desk, he saw from the corner of his eye three cops all reaching for their hats and rising to their feet.

The overheard phrase "not another one" was enough to suggest there'd been another attack on a farm. At least, that was Fletcher's primary thought. Then he realized he'd just handed Heaton over to the cops and that they were most likely talking about a drunk driver, or a fight between two guys in a bar.

CHAPTER FORTY-TWO

The shrill ring from his cell phone woke Fletcher a lot sooner than he'd planned. There was no number on the screen so he grunted a greeting and listened to what his caller had to say.

He was swinging his legs out of bed before the caller had finished speaking and was still buttoning his shirt as he walked outside.

The caller was waiting for him beside an SUV that was a double for the one he'd wrecked last night. Dressed as he was in a black suit with white shirt and black tie, the caller was either an FBI Special Agent, or an out-of-work actor who was about to attend an audition for a remake of *Reservoir Dogs*. He tossed Fletcher the keys and got into the passenger side of an idling black sedan and left.

Since he was now up and fully awake, Fletcher saw no point in trying to get more sleep. He returned to his motel room, showered, shaved and dressed in clean clothes. He also went through a set of stretching exercises to ease tired and bruised muscles.

Today should be about tying up the loose ends. It was over to the cops now. They'd interview Heaton, build their case against him and make sure he could never kill again. As for him, he planned to spend his day being on hand to answer questions, passing on what information he had to Carl Friedrickson and Peter Quadrado.

It was a day for recuperation and rest.

To that end, when he set off to get breakfast at the diner, he didn't just choose to walk, he chose to take a circuitous route. Part to invigorate a tired body and mind, and part to enjoy the morning sunshine.

As much as he was trying to wind down, Fletcher's brain was still running at a high level. The replacement SUV was among his chief thoughts. He'd spoken to Quadrado around ten or ten thirty. Eight hours later he'd been furnished with a new vehicle. No quibbles, complaints or admonishments had come his way about the cost or inconvenience in him having wrecked the previous SUV. Fair enough, it hadn't been his doing, but by the same token, he hadn't requested a replacement. There was also the logistics of getting another vehicle to him. Someone with serious clout had mobilized a pair of agents to procure a new set of wheels for him. The closest FBI field office to Medford would be Eau Claire. Eighty or so miles away, it would be at least an hour and a half to drive which meant the agents had been given their errand in the middle of the night. Why they'd done this when the case was solved and they could have put him on a Greyhound to get back to the airport was a mystery.

It all spoke of great efficiency and not for the first time, he wondered about why he'd been given this case. Yes, it was personal to Quadrado, but she was a lowly Special Agent at the start of her career. She'd progress through the ranks, he was sure of that, but at her current station, Quadrado wouldn't have the pull to arrange the new wheels in the middle of the night.

The mysterious figure behind Quadrado would, which also told Fletcher they were in direct and regular contact with her.

None of this answered why he'd been drafted to investigate the homicides. By rights, a team of homicide detectives ought to have been dispatched from one of the major cities in Wisconsin. That hadn't happened. He'd been sent. In fact, not just sent, but supported with resources, if not a badge to smooth his passage.

There was no question in his mind this whole case had been a test of his abilities. He was confident he'd passed as he'd found the killer before the cops had, yet there were still question marks in his mind as he took a seat in the diner. How involved was Quadrado?

Was she complicit with the mysterious figure's schemes, or a pawn the same as him? Would every mission or case he was given see him left to his own devices? Or would he get a more direct route to Quadrado and the resources the FBI had at their disposal? Who was the mysterious figure anyway? And finally, how soon could he get home to Wendy?

CHAPTER FORTY-THREE

The server brought him his usual: ham, eggs and toast with coffee. A pleasant woman in her forties, she kept her hair up in a messy bun and had a natural smile she wore often.

With time to savor the food, Fletcher ate with enjoyment as he watched the rest of the diner's patrons go about their business. A man in a sharp suit had a laptop in front of him and was typing with one hand as he used his other hand to shovel food towards his mouth. An elderly man looked out of the window with unseeing rheumy eyes and a group of men in coveralls dug into huge platefuls of food as they talked over one another with full mouths.

It was a typical scene and one he could appreciate.

His phone dinged so he picked it up. Although snatched would be more appropriate as he was keen to get back home and he hoped the email would be Quadrado letting him know Heaton had confessed.

When he read the email from Quadrado it was all he could do to lay the phone on the table rather than launch it through one of the picture windows at the front of the diner.

Quadrado's email didn't give him permission to go home. Quite the opposite, it informed him of a third homicide where the victim had been killed on a farm and left with a carving on their forehead.

The words he'd overheard upon leaving Medford PD last night came back to him. "Not another one." He'd thought it referred to an attack on a farm, but now he realized it had been the cops learning about the latest homicide. This explained the new SUV, but it didn't explain why he hadn't been informed of the third a lot sooner. The best he could figure was that Quadrado hadn't learned of it until this morning.

He reread the email and started building a timeline. Marcia Jamieson had said goodbye to her boyfriend and a group of friends around midnight and returned to the family farm. At four thirty, she'd been discovered beside her father's pickup truck. A stab wound to her heart and #3 on her forehead.

As the last person to see her, the boyfriend had been brought in and questioned, but he'd woken his parents clumping his way into the house at ten after midnight. An argument about the noise with his father had lasted until 1.00 a.m. As Marcia's farm was twenty minutes away and given the estimated time of death, there wouldn't have been enough time for him to travel there and back, so he couldn't be the killer.

The Jamieson farm wasn't local to Medford though. It was on the outskirts of Greenwood, some forty or so miles away. Fletcher's first impression was that he wasn't sure if it was a good or bad thing the latest homicide had taken place away from the localized area where the first two had been committed. In one sense it gave those already affected by homicides in their close vicinity a spot of respite, but at the same time, if it was a traveling killer, it would be far harder to predict where he'd next strike.

With another life forfeit due to someone's homicidal tendencies, the most frustrating part of this latest homicide was there was no way Steve Heaton could be the person who'd killed Marcia Jamieson, because he'd been under police guard in a hospital bed at the time she was murdered. This, of course, threw into doubt his guilt for the first two homicides. Fletcher knew that until either Heaton's guilt had been proven, or someone else was found to be behind the homicides, he wouldn't get to return home anytime soon.

With his meal finished, he sat back with a refilled coffee and bent his mind to not just the case, but what his next moves ought to be.

His first instinct was to fire up the SUV and drive to Greenwood to see what he could learn at the site of Marcia's homicide. This made practical sense, although his gut feeling was that instead of chasing the killer, he should be trying to leapfrog ahead of him so he'd be able to predict where he'd strike next, or at the very least, try to understand his motivations. To do that his energies would be better spent looking at all of the homicides as a whole, rather than investigating them in isolation.

To do this, he considered the victims. Jane Friedrickson, twenty-eight; farmer's wife. Walt Renard, sixty-two; farmer. Marcia Jamieson, eighteen; farmer's daughter. Listed in such a fashion, there was no real connection between the three other than the fact they all lived on farms and belonged to farming families.

Jane and Walt lived within a mile of each other whereas Marcia was over forty miles away. It crossed Fletcher's mind the killer might be operating on a two-by-two kill cycle. If that was the case, the next person to be killed on a farm would be close to the Jamieson's farm.

After that the killer would move on to yet another area. Whether this third site would be aligned in some way to the first two or would be random wasn't something he could guess at.

Were Quadrado actively involved in the case instead of being a support at the end of emails she took her sweet time to answer, he would have requested she use one of the FBI's psychological profilers. He could still ask, but there was an immediacy that was lost by doing everything via email and he wanted results at once.

Again, the disparity between the victims came to his mind. A wife, father and teenager had little in common other than their family professions. The initial report on Marcia Jamieson's homicide suggested there were no signs of sexual assault, but that didn't mean anything. Until there had been an autopsy, nothing could be ruled out.

As for Fletcher's own next moves, he had a few ideas, but he wasn't ready to commit to anything just yet. He sent Quadrado a short email saying he needed to think about the latest homicide before coming back to her, but until he gave a full response, he wanted her to do whatever it took to get a psych profiler on board.

Fletcher paid his check, leaving a decent tip for the friendly server, and set off to buy a number of supplies. It was his intention to work the first two cases alone, until he had either more information on Marcia Jamieson's homicide, or the help and support of an FBI profiler.

CHAPTER FORTY-FOUR

Fletcher taped the large-scale maps to the walls of his motel room and used the packs of sticky notes he'd also bought to mark out certain places. The first thing he marked were the farms where the attacks had taken place. Next he drew on approximations of the tracks that had been found at the Greenacres and White Birch farms.

Seeing the farms delineated on a map gave him a far better overview. The crossroads bisecting the farms was on perfect compass point alignment. Greenacres was between north and east while White Birch was in the south and west quadrant.

As he worked, Fletcher would pick up a notebook and add a question or two to add to the email destined for Quadrado's inbox. He had not yet had a response from her regarding the profiler and he wasn't holding out a lot of hope, but if you didn't ask, you didn't get.

With the homicide sites marked, Fletcher reviewed everything he knew about the first two homicides. He went over all the notes he'd taken, reread every email he'd been sent and recounted all the conversations he'd had since arriving in Medford.

None of the information he recapped gave a new clue or a different perspective on any of the ideas he'd already pursued.

To approach from a different tack, he put in a call to Peter Quadrado and got a list of as many of the farms afflicted by an attack as Peter could remember. Some of the details he heard could be regular bad luck or mishaps, but in the greater context, there was a similarity to a lot of the issues. Fires, machinery breakdowns due to a failing that shouldn't have happened and petty incidents like the tanks which held the milk having their coolers switched off causing the milk to spoil. The Quadrado farm, Meadowfields, had also suffered a couple of incidents.

The one constant with the alleged attacks was the lack of harm to any of the affected farms' livestock. One or two humans had received minor injuries when repairing damage or extinguishing fires, but not one human or animal had received any direct harm from the attacks.

Due to the number of incidents, Fletcher dropped the sticky notes on the bed and lifted a red pen from the collection of stationery he'd picked up. A circle was placed around every farm to have suffered an attack in the last few months.

The more he worked, the more crowded the map became. Some farms had two circles and one had three.

When he'd finished the extensive list, Fletcher took a step back to get an overview. What he saw didn't fill him with confidence.

There was a definite grouping on the farms within five miles of the crossroads, but there were also incidents several miles further away. Some of the examples away from the general area occurred in clumps whereas others were adrift of the nearest victim by at least four miles. By far the worst affected farm in terms of attacks was Calvertsholm, owned by Robert Kearney, which was sited in one of the quadrants of the crossroads bisecting Greenacres and White Birch farms. The farm where there had been the fire recently.

There being so many occurrences within a specific radius, it made Fletcher wonder if he ought to rethink his position on the farm attacks and the homicides being linked.

As much as it made sense, there would have to be a huge jump in the commitment shown by animal rights activist to escalate their campaigns to homicide. It wasn't a connection he was convinced of, but no matter how he approached the question, he couldn't find another reason for the attacks on the farm if they weren't committed by the killer.

The timescale also told a story. The first real incidents had started several months ago with maybe one a week, escalating to up to five incidents a week over the space of two months.

That the farmers now felt compelled to protect their farms by staying up on guard spoke of the damage the attacks were inflicting. It also made Fletcher worry for the farmers. Either they'd become a victim, or they'd find themselves on the wrong end of assault or homicide charges.

No matter how he looked at it, there was definitely a hotspot centered on the crossroads. Not just for the farm attacks, but also the homicides.

The questions Fletcher was left with gnawed at him. Were there also attacks on the farms around Greenwood, and specifically Greenwood? If so, how far back did they go? Was it all the work of one person, or were there a group of people involved? Would the attacks in Taylor County end now the killer had moved on, or was the crossroads the epicenter of something far bigger than he was currently thinking?

CHAPTER FORTY-FIVE

Fletcher typed out the email to Quadrado with his thumbs. He'd have much preferred to send such a lengthy email from a device with a keyboard, but there was little point in wasting brain space wishing for something he didn't have.

Along with all the points he had to make about the homicide cases potentially being linked to the farm attacks, he also reiterated his request for an FBI profiler, specifying a geo-profiler might be the best person to ask as there was a definite locality to the areas most affected by both the attacks and the homicides.

His suspicion that the crossroads was key to things guided his requests. He wanted information on the finances of each of the four farms that filled the quadrants formed by the crossroads. He was looking for a link between them, or something that stood out from the norm.

He also wanted Quadrado to do the same examination for the Greenwood farm and others adjacent to it. Fletcher didn't know exactly what he was looking for, but he was confident he'd recognize it when he saw it.

Another thing pulling his mind was the victims' status in their respective families. Jane Friedrickson's husband Carl was the put-upon only son of a guy who'd come across as a loud-mouthed jerk in the short time Fletcher had spent around him. It was Carl's parents who owned the farm, so there could be no direct financial motive to killing his wife for anyone other than Carl, or the person or persons her parents might choose as their heirs after losing their daughter. To kill on the off chance you'd be named in a will is extreme and highly improbable, so Fletcher canned that idea for the time being. Walt Renard had been the top dog at White Birch, supported by a middle son after the others had flown the coop. His wife would inherit and then his children. Adding infidelity into the mix, it could be that his wife had decided to cash in and get revenge at the same time. That didn't fit with the pattern though. If Mrs. Renard had seized an opportunity and mimicked the person who'd murdered Jane, it didn't explain why Marcia had #3 on her forehead. If Marcia had been killed by the same person as Jane, they would have been more likely to carve #2 onto her rather than take credit for a kill that wasn't theirs.

Should Mrs. Renard have murdered her husband, there were also the killer's thoughts on the matter to consider. He might not approve of having his signature appropriated to cast blame onto him for a crime he didn't commit. The counterpoint to this was the first killer might enjoy others building his legend for him. That he might get a kick from the idea of getting a free kill. He might enjoy the irony of a kill being attributed to him that wasn't his. In terms of the cops coming after him, a false claim would muddy the waters. Maybe he fancied himself as a modern-day Charles Manson and wanted others to commit crimes on his behalf?

Marcia Jamieson was the youngest daughter of a farmer with four sons. As yet there was no proof of sexual assault, and there was no way there could be any financial gain from her homicide.

All of these thoughts were making Fletcher think the killer was someone who was out to make a name for himself rather than someone looking to gain from the homicides.

With nothing but thinking to occupy his time until Quadrado got back to him, Fletcher took a walk to the library. He planned to scour back editions of the local paper to see if there was anything brewing in the community the locals had overlooked telling him.

It was a long shot, but there was nothing else he could think of that might yield the information he craved.

CHAPTER FORTY-SIX

Medford's library was a single-story building set back from Main Street. Fletcher made his way in and spoke to the woman behind the counter. Like so many other librarians he'd met, she had a pair of reading glasses hanging against her chest on what Wendy referred to as a "granny chain."

The librarian was pleasant and helpful. There was no hesitation from her when he asked to see the last six months' copies of the *Taylor County Gazette*, although she did ask him to help her carry them through from the back room where they were kept.

Seating himself at a table and with two boxes of newspapers to go through, Fletcher set to work. For the task at hand, a library was the perfect place. Serene and peaceful, the books on the shelves around him suggested he had the wisdom of the ages at his disposal as well as escape routes to fantastical lands. His adoptive parents had been huge advocates of reading and as a child he'd spent many hours poring over the shelves of his local library in search of a new adventure. As an adult he still read, although he now tended to read more nonfiction than he used to as his thirst for knowledge had never waned.

The weekly issues of the *Gazette* carried the same kind of information all small town newspapers did. There was a headline or two about local events, a roundup of births, deaths and marriages, and a collection of minor articles about petty crimes.

All in all there was little to hold the interest of anyone who wasn't a local. There were multiple articles on agricultural events and a host of ads for everything from local restaurants to a place that sold tractors.

The back pages had the traditional sports news and the pages before them had information on cattle sales. It was these pages that Fletcher suspected were the main reason the locals would buy the *Gazette*.

Hour after hour he pored over the newspapers. His eyes scanning the pages for anything that might be of use to his investigation. The crime pieces were all small beer and showed no indication of any feuds that might have developed. Medford wasn't big enough for gangs to have moved in and there was little mention of there being a problem with drugs.

Fletcher searched but he found no verified examples of animal rights activists causing real problems in the county. A guy called Bill Clay had been pictured leading demonstrations against what he classed as factory farms, but from what Fletcher read in the paper there was no real evidence Clay was anything more than a peaceful protestor.

All the same, he logged on to one of the library's computers and ran several searches to get a better picture of who Bill Clay was.

Bill Clay was a fervent supporter of animal rights and easily the most visible within five hundred miles. Which equated to over three quarters of a million square miles. Clay preached to disciples where and whenever he could. He held rallies, had an extensive blog where he posted opinions, statistics and called out anyone he felt wasn't putting animal welfare front and center of their plans. He was scathing on Twitter and other social media platforms, and seemed to be a regular speaker at rallies held by other activists. While he always stayed within the bounds of the law, the examples of his incendiary rhetoric Fletcher read suggested that Clay wouldn't be averse to direct action. Clay's latest slogan of choice, "Milked to Death," fronted what seemed a direct campaign against dairy farms and all of his most recent posts had been a condemnation of the way dairy cattle were treated. He might be in Minneapolis, but that wasn't too far away and there was no telling what he encouraged his followers to do by way of demonstrations, break-ins, disruption to the businesses involved or actual sabotage in a less public setting. If it was animal rights activists attacking the farms, he was confident Clay would know who the activists were and how to get to them. Due to the activist's mindset and fervency of purpose, Fletcher had a strong feeling he might have to be rougher with Clay than he had with others to get the answers he needed, but he was okay with that.

CHAPTER FORTY-SEVEN

Fletcher carried the boxes of newspapers back for the librarian and left. His searches had taken him only baby steps forward and he was again wondering if he was right to assume the attacks and homicides were connected.

His investigation was in danger of stalling, so before pursuing the animal rights question, he decided to go back to the start and go see Carl Friedrickson again. He also planned to try speaking to Mrs. Renard for a second time and to visit both the other farms bordering the crossroads. It was a vain hope that he'd learn anything, but it would give him something to do until Quadrado came back to him.

He'd already messaged her requesting more information on Bill Clay. On a certain level he knew she was busy with her own case regardless of how much she might want to be helping him, but he found it infuriating to be kept dangling when he could be progressing with finding Jane's killer. Every minute he spent waiting on Quadrado's responses was a minute he was delayed from returning home.

As he walked back to the motel for the SUV, his stomach rumbled. He reasoned it would be bad form to have it happen again when speaking to the bereaved families so he ducked into the diner.

The burger and fries brought to him by the server were first class and he ate them with economy. Though, as delicious as they were, they were little more than fuel to him. After he'd finished eating, he stayed for an extra cup of coffee. He'd had less than his usual amount of sleep since arriving in Medford and knew the meal he'd just consumed was likely to make him feel sleepy before long.

As he was about to rise, the reporter—who he'd last seen at the fire at Calvertsholm Farm several days before—walked into the diner and made a beeline for his table, the heels of her shoes clacking on the tiled floor.

"Mr. Fletcher, may I have a moment of your time?"

Fletcher held up his cup for a refill as the server passed by with the pot in her hand. "I'll give you as long as it takes to drink this coffee, Miss…"

"Drake, but please, Mr. Fletcher, call me Idaho."

"Grant." He gave her a level look as he picked up his cup. He guessed the name was a professional pseudonym she'd adopted to make her more memorable. "So, what do you need a moment of my time for, Miss Idaho Drake?"

She planted herself opposite Fletcher and gave him a wide smile as she pushed some auburn hair away from her face. "I've been hearing about a mysterious stranger who's been busy investigating the homicides. A mysterious stranger who also got himself into an automobile crash with a deranged knifeman he suspected was the killer. A mysterious stranger who disarmed the knifeman with his bare hands." Somehow she managed to widen her smile while still talking. "You've quite the rep, Mr. Fletcher. Two bar fights. One arrest and one fight with a knifeman in the four days you've been in Medford. Tell me, are you trouble yourself or do you attract it?"

"Are we on or off the record here?" Her answer didn't matter to Fletcher, he'd treat every word he spoke to her with the caution any sane person uses when talking to a journalist.

"I'd very much prefer on." She wafted the front of her blouse and used the action to undo the top button. "What do you prefer?"

Fletcher ignored the suggestive tone of her voice and kept his eyes on hers. "Off." He leaned back in his seat and folded his arms across his chest. A deliberate attempt to open distance between them, offer closed body language and thwart any attempts she might make to use further seductive techniques on him. "However, you already seem to know a lot about what I've done since arriving in Medford, so I'm happy to go on the record with you, if that's what you want."

"What can you tell me about the case? Are you getting any closer to catching the Hashtag Killer?"

Fletcher had no intentions of giving the reporter anything she could use. "I'm afraid I can't tell you anything more than the cops could."

"A recap from your perspective would be greatly appreciated."

She was fishing. The cops wouldn't have given her anything she couldn't have gotten from a crime scene report or press release. It may have been that a cop fed her information about him, but they wouldn't likely extend to sharing anything they could get into trouble for.

"Why don't you tell me what you know first so I don't waste our time?" Fletcher tilted his cup so she could see it was now only half full.

Idaho spoke for a couple of minutes. She did her best to make the scant information she had sound more than it was, yet it was obvious to Fletcher she knew very few of the real details.

"Sounds to me like you have things covered."

"Please, Grant." Another wide smile and a flap of the blouse. "I need more than I have already. The major networks will be here soon and I want to have the jump on them." She gave a coy smile that fooled nobody. "I'd be very grateful to you for helping me get the inside track and would be more than happy to compensate you for anything you can help me with." She moved her hand towards the purse she'd placed on the table between them.

Fletcher took a long pull on his coffee and put the cup down with enough force to create a noticeable clatter. "I don't take bribes,

Miss Drake. I'm here to investigate one homicide in particular and—only then, when I've caught her killer—any others that may be connected to it."

"I think you misunderstand me." She pulled a tube of lipstick from her purse and pouted before applying a smear to each of her lips. "I wasn't offering… money."

Fletcher rose from his seat. "It's still a bribe, and while my opinion may not matter to you, for what it's worth, I don't believe any career is worth offering what I think you're offering. Damnit, I'm old enough to be your father."

Drake's suggestion was one that gave him the cold sweats. On the one hand it was flattering to think a pretty young woman felt she could picture herself bedding him, but his overarching emotions were disgust at the idea of being so easily bought and pity for the way she thought so little of herself that she'd use her body the same way she'd use an everyday object like a pen. It could all be an act and she was planning nothing more intimate than a few kisses to get him to spill his guts before reneging on the promise of more. He had no interest in her, and even if he had, he was far too wise to be played by her.

She looked up at him without a hint of shame. "And that's one of the reasons why you should accept my offer." She held out a card he didn't take. "Anyway, you've told me plenty for now. I now know you were drafted in for the Jane Friedrickson homicide and that you're working on the theory the Renard and Jamieson cases are connected to her murder. You might want to rethink your position on my offer, because I've got someone looking into exactly who you are and how I make you look will very much depend on how much you help me."

Fletcher answered her by walking out of the diner.

Once he'd checked she hadn't followed him out, Fletcher pulled his cell from his pocket and checked it. There was still no reply from Quadrado, so he sent off a terse message requesting she give him the information he wanted or cut him loose so he could go home.

CHAPTER FORTY-EIGHT

Quadrado's fingers drummed on the desk as she read all the messages from Fletcher. She got that she'd been slow to respond, that she'd not acted with his levels of efficiency or alacrity. Did he not think she felt guilty about not being able to give him what he needed as soon as he asked for it? Did he not realize that she was trapped in an impossible position? That her brain and body had to be in New York, but her thoughts and heart were in Wisconsin? Did he not realize that her heart was breaking and until she closed the current case, she couldn't begin to grieve for Jane? She understood he needed her to furnish him with information and that he'd be kicking his heels without it. What she didn't get was why he had to be so rude; after all she wanted him to catch Jane's killer far more than he did.

Since Jane had been murdered, she'd been working sixteen-hour days, juggling her own case and Fletcher's demands for information as well as circumstances allowed. She'd had to keep the Wisconsin case a secret from her colleagues and immediate boss. This had involved lying, sneaked searches to learn what Fletcher wanted to know and a level of subterfuge she was unfamiliar with.

Now her own case was resolved, she'd be able to fly back home to Medford, to join Fletcher. First though, she had to do this research for him.

Top of her agenda was to look into Bill Clay. Like Fletcher had admitted in his emails, she was unsure of a link between the attacks and the homicides, but she knew it was something that had to be checked out.

The details of the finances of the farms requested was also easy to acquire. A dip into the IRS files got her what she needed. She downloaded the files and then emailed them onwards to Fletcher along with notice that she'd soon be out there to join him. Maybe a few hours studying spreadsheets would dampen his ire.

One by one, she worked her way through the things on Fletcher's list. For the most part the information was easy for her to source with the resources at the FBI's disposal.

It was the last item on her list that troubled her the most. She'd had specific instructions from Soter that the only help she could offer Fletcher was logistical support such as hardware like vehicles and weapons. Her own expertise was a given, as was information she could retrieve using official databases.

What she couldn't do was use any of the FBI's specialist services. Profilers, analysts and other such experts were all out of bounds.

She had a plan, though. A way to get round the restrictions placed on her. It would cost her an expensive favor, but it was the least she could do for Jane, and she knew that underneath all the animosity she was feeling towards Fletcher at his barbed emails, she owed him.

With the office empty, she lifted her cell and picked out the number she needed.

Quadrado's friend, Heidi Yorke, was the best profiler she had worked with. Astute, insightful to a level that was borderline clairvoyant, and smarter than any one person had a right to be, she was the right person to go to.

Quadrado had dealt with a neighbor who'd been bothering Heidi. Nothing overt like stalking, just hanging out, making suggestive comments and generally making enough of a nuisance of himself to make Heidi feel threatened.

It had taken a half hour of Quadrado's time to knock on his door, badge and threaten the neighbor in a way that made sure he stopped bothering Heidi.

To get someone as hesitant as Heidi was to break the rules, to use her talents for an off-the-books investigation, was a far greater favor than scaring off a creepy neighbor though. The balance of power would swing back to Heidi and Quadrado would be in her debt.

Quadrado didn't beat around the bush with Heidi. "Hi, it's Zoey. I need a favor."

"What can I do for you?" Heidi was all business and that was perfect for Quadrado as she couldn't cope with a sympathetic ear right now.

"I need a profile on a killer. But… it needs to be off-the-books. A friend of mine is working a case in Wisconsin and he needs help. I can't go through the channels as he's not law enforcement."

"I see." Heidi's matter-of-fact tone gave Quadrado hope she would deliver. "That's a big favor, Zoey, you'd owe me."

"I kinda guessed that would be the case." This kind of favor trading went on all the time. It wasn't a system Quadrado agreed with, but that was a fight for another day. Right now it was all about Jane. About doing everything she could to support Fletcher. "I'm happy to owe you one."

"Yeah, well, you won't owe me for long. My brother is coming to town in a couple of weeks. You know he's sweet on you. How about you say yes to that date he keeps asking you about?"

"You mean Eric? I guess, that's something we can do. We'll talk when he's here, yeah?"

Yes, she'd let Heidi's brother take her out for dinner. Eric was handsome, had a rakish smile and was personable enough until he started talking about his job as an accountant. Some people might find tax returns, profit and loss adjustment and expenses a fascinating subject, but she wasn't one of those people.

Eric might not be the ideal dinner companion, but that didn't mean Quadrado couldn't go on the date, play nice and then give him a gentle letdown at the end of the night. So long as he didn't take her to a steakhouse, it shouldn't be too hard.

"Deal. Okay, honey, give me what you've got."

With their deal struck, Quadrado related the list of information Heidi needed and promised to send it over at once.

By the time she'd finished sending everything to Heidi, Quadrado felt more like a secretary than a Special Agent. She'd been glued to her keyboard for what seemed like hours and had missed the first evening flights to Wisconsin.

But she'd be on the next flight, and at last could give Fletcher the support he craved as well as doing her best to help solve Jane's homicide.

CHAPTER FORTY-NINE

Fletcher drew the SUV to a halt two blocks away from Bill Clay's house in the Ventura Village neighborhood of Minneapolis. Before he got too close he wanted to have a proper recon of the area. It was never a good idea to enter a potentially confrontational situation without knowing your escape routes, where the cover was and what potential hazards lay in wait for you.

He got out and took a circuitous walk around the blocks until he was on 23rd. Clay's wasn't the most salubrious neighborhood he'd ever visited, but nor was it the worst. The houses were all showing signs of neglect, the gardens unkempt, a number with windows boarded up. However, there were few of the other signs that marked a bad neighborhood, and when he cast his eyes into the nooks and crannies he saw neither drug dealers nor even any discarded needles.

The drive from Medford to Minneapolis had been uneventful. Two and a half hours of straight roads and thinking time.

Quadrado had come through for him by the time he'd spoken to the four farmers, or at least tried to in the case of Mrs. Renard. She'd had him turned away at the door by her daughter-in-law. Of the other three, Carl and his parents had nothing new to add, Bettsina and Ken Pickworth at Broken Spur had been accommodating but had little information to add to what he already knew. Robert Kearney at Calvertsholm had been friendly enough, but without being rude, hadn't given Fletcher much of his time. His barn still lying in ruins from the fire, he'd had the baggy eyes of sleep deprivation. He'd suffered at the hands of the attacker more than the other three farms and he was frank about the fact he was spending his nights guarding his property with his rifle.

Fletcher had the good sense not to tell any of the people he spoke to that he was looking into their finances. Nor did he tell them their properties were at the epicenter of the attacks, although he was sure they'd worked that out for themselves.

Before setting out for Minneapolis, he'd tried to take a look at the files displaying the farms' accounts. The screen on his cell was fine for a lot of things, displaying spreadsheets and accounts in a way that was readable wasn't one of them.

He'd struggled on with them for a half hour before admitting defeat. In the end, he'd stopped at a motel on the outskirts of Minneapolis and bribed a young receptionist with a pair of twenties to print them off for him.

Her printer had clacked and rattled for so long he'd felt compelled to add a third note for the hefty sheaf of papers she handed to him in a ledger. She'd not just printed them for him, she'd segregated them into individual farms and separated them in the ledger with dividers.

Fletcher had heard many people grumble about millennials, but if they were all as hardworking and efficient as this girl, there was every chance they'd outshine his generation.

The ledger was in the trunk of the SUV. Fletcher had picked through it, but had realized after just a few minutes that it wasn't a quick job that could be done in the front of an automobile. To analyze and cross-reference the accounts with enough of an eye for detail to find something amiss, he'd need to have hours and space to lay the documents out at his disposal.

All the new information he'd obtained got factored into his thinking as he drove west. There weren't a whole hell of a lot of new facts, but what he got he made the best use of. Quadrado's email had covered all the points he'd asked of her, except the one he felt most likely to break the case open. There had been no mention of her consulting a geo-profiler. A point he had rammed home in his reply.

With everything to do with the case now emptied from his brain, Fletcher turned a corner so he was on 10th Avenue South. His senses were on high alert although he saw no immediate threat. Cars were parked on the street outside most houses, though one had its front end crumpled from an impact that had buckled and lifted its hood.

Clay's house was halfway along and had a battered VW camper parked in front of the waist-high chain-link fence surrounding its front yard. Fletcher saw no lights shining from the windows of either Clay's place or those of his immediate neighbors.

A house he passed two doors along had music belching from one of its windows: a foul-mouthed rapper complaining about his girl sleeping with someone else, although the rapper's choice of words was less than politically correct.

Fletcher pulled a face at the music and lengthened his stride to escape the auditory pollution. His own taste in music had always been firmly in the rockabilly camp despite that being the source of much derision from his former fellow Royal Marines.

With a brief reconnoiter done, Fletcher collected the SUV, retraced his way around the block and parked in front of the VW camper. It wasn't what he considered good practice to have the escape vehicle so close to a site where things may get physical, in case someone got the license plate, but as he was planning to break into Clay's house and extract information from him using whatever means necessary, he felt it was more prudent to have the SUV close at hand.

He could have, of course, walked up to the door and knocked. The door might be answered, and it might not. If it was answered, he didn't for one second expect Clay would admit to any involvement in what had been happening on the farms. At best he'd laugh at Fletcher, at worst, Fletcher would be marked out as a threat. Fletcher had no issues using himself as bait, but that was a slow process and people were dying, so he needed to expedite the acquiring of answers. Appearing in someone's house with a gun in your hand very quickly establishes a balance of power. The shock of an unknown gunman materializing in what is thought of as a safe sanctum recalibrates people's thinking. Instead of offense, they think of defense. Their security has already been breached and may be again. This makes them afraid and fear makes people cooperative.

With the SUV parked, Fletcher did a rapid weapons check, pulled on the thin leather gloves he kept in his kitbag and prepared to breach Clay's house.

A look up and down the street saw no pedestrians, moving vehicles or twitching curtains. Unlike a lot of the better areas, Ventura Village clearly didn't have a neighborhood watch. Fletcher knew how these streets worked. Residents would look out for each other, but only to a point. Most would abide by the wisdom of the three wise monkeys and see, hear and speak of no evil.

Fletcher took the four steps to Clay's door in two strides, the lock picks ready in his gloved fingers. Since being forcibly recruited by the mysterious figure who'd sent Quadrado to his Georgia jail with a deal, he'd upped his training regime with the lockpicks as he knew a moment like this was coming his way.

The lock to Clay's door was basic. Fletcher had it picked in less than thirty seconds.

A look up and down the street as he grasped the door handle.

His eyes picked out no witnesses.

Now was the moment of truth. This is when he'd find out if Clay had bolted the door or latched a security chain.

He twisted the handle and pushed. The door opened and he was inside and closing it behind him as the first assault came his way.

CHAPTER FIFTY

Geoffrey Elliott leaned back in his recliner and began reading on his tablet the information Fletcher had sent. Even hamstrung as Fletcher was without official backing and infrequent updates from Special Agent Quadrado, his progress was nothing less than impressive.

The investigative techniques used weren't as finessed as those taught at Quantico, but by the same token, Fletcher lacked the resources given to FBI graduates.

Fletcher's thought processes brought the odd whistle of appreciation as Elliott admired the concise way he'd outlined his thinking to Quadrado. Even the requests Fletcher was making of Quadrado were inspired for someone who had no formal training. Had Elliott been running the case, he'd have brought in a geo-profiler when he'd noticed the locality of everything.

The story of how Fletcher had fought with the agricultural contractor and snapped his arm at the elbow brought a smile to his lips. In a life-or-death situation, Fletcher had not just survived, but had shown enough restraint to disable his opponent and bring him in alive. He liked that Fletcher could exert such self-control, although he'd prefer him to not show such consideration to the Hashtag Killer if in a similar position.

The wrecked SUV was a shame, but he and the other heads of agencies such as the CIA and NSA, who'd banded together to recruit Fletcher as their personal blunt instrument, had each dropped a million bucks of taxpayer's money into a slush fund to cover any expenses they'd incur from the missions they set Fletcher, so the cost of one middle-of-the-range SUV was negligible if Fletcher passed his audition. The kinds of missions they had in mind for him were worth far more to them than a tiny fraction of their budgets.

A bone of contention for Elliott was Fletcher's assumption the sabotage to the farms was part of the homicide case. He felt that it was too far-fetched to believe animal rights activists were killing people. The hashtag carvings on the foreheads of the victims had all the hallmarks of a serial killer trying to make a name for himself.

This killer was good, he recognized that. He'd never shied away from admiring the ingenuity and oftentimes brilliance of the killers his agency was designed to apprehend. Admiration could be given without favor. Respect without shame. Dumb criminals got caught by their own stupidity. Smart ones by a local PD. It was the best of the best who came under the FBI's microscope and as director of the FBI he wouldn't have it any other way. Although the death toll in Wisconsin was rising far too fast for his liking. There needed to be a resolution to this case and fast. It was only a matter of time before the killings garnered a wider attention, and when that happened, he'd have to pull Fletcher out lest his blunt instrument become compromised.

There was also the possibility of further escalation to contend with. Serial killers only received official recognition as such when their tally reached five. The Hashtag Killer was at three, and should he reach five, there would be a clamor for the FBI to step in and stop him before he could kill again. If that happened, it would be another reason for him to pull Fletcher out. Another fail.

Elliott brought up the email program he used for his clandestine projects and sent Quadrado a message.

TELL FLETCHER THAT IF THE CASE ISN'T SOLVED BY
MONDAY, HE'LL BE STANDING TRIAL IN GEORGIA. AS FOR
YOU, YOU'LL BE REASSIGNED TO EVERY CRAPPY OUTPOST
I CAN THINK OF UNTIL YOU QUIT.

SOTER

CHAPTER FIFTY-ONE

Fletcher's nose crinkled at the smell attacking him. It was the sweet smell of dope mixed in with the sourness of wet dog, and rounded off with the toxic pungency of lentil-infused farts.

Clay's house was pretty much as he'd expected it to be. There was a rumpled disarray about the place, although untidy as it was, it wasn't dirty.

The second assault to come Fletcher's way was from a basset hound. All droopy ears and sorrowful eyes, it cantered his way a little. Then thought better of it and sat itself down in a side-saddle slouch, looking at him as if wanting a treat and expecting a kick.

Fletcher cursed his lack of forethought. Clay was an animal lover. Someone who led protests, encouraged others to stand with him and tried to save animals from what he deemed unhappy lives or cruel treatment. It stood to reason he'd have a pet or two at home. It wasn't so much a surprise, as something he ought to have expected.

He'd gotten lucky with the basset. Clay could have rescued a small yappy dog like a shih tzu, or a larger, more feral one like a Doberman or German shepherd.

All the same, he hedged his bets and took a moment to bend down and ruffle the basset's elephantine ears.

With the canine greetings dealt with, Fletcher stalked his way through the house. He had his pistol in his hand and was scanning the rooms over its sights, his finger curled ready to depress the trigger if need be.

The downstairs was devoid of all life beyond the basset and three terrapins in a tank. Clay's kitchen looked to be a hygiene disaster waiting to happen, but that wasn't Fletcher's concern. He'd come here for answers, not fine dining.

He looked at the stairs. Threadbare carpet sheathed them in what had once been a busy pattern. The bannister had once been painted white, although it had discolored with age and had more chips than the nearest 7-Eleven.

Fletcher did his usual thing on unknown stairs and took them two at a time, his feet kept tight to the edges to minimize any creaks they might make.

Very much to his surprise, he got to the top of the flight without a sound louder than the lazy scratching from the basset's rear leg.

He could go left or right. Left had one door and that door was open to reveal a bathroom. Right had two doors and there was a third dead ahead. One of the three would be where Clay was if he was home. Another was probably a storage closet.

Fletcher ran through the building's footprint in his mind. The door ahead of him would most likely be the closet and the two to his right would lead to bedrooms. He took a step into the corridor, again keeping his feet to the side to minimize the risk of squeaky flooring. He could go left or right. In the end it was an easy choice.

The moaning made the decision for him. The moans weren't of pain, they were of pleasure.

As cruel as it might be to interrupt someone in the throes of passion, it's also damned effective. Their senses aren't attuned to anything beyond the fire in their loins. They're distracted from danger and therefore much more vulnerable to surprise. They're also naked, a state which makes the majority of the population feel vulnerable.

Fletcher's hand curled round the door handle and he stepped into the room, his pistol seeking out Clay and whomever was with him.

CHAPTER FIFTY-TWO

Clay froze when he saw the pistol pointed his way. The naked woman on top of him didn't freeze. She was too busy scrambling off the bed trying to protect her modesty as she slid out of Fletcher's view.

Fletcher didn't know what might be hidden from his view. It could be that the scraggly-haired woman was only concerned about him getting an eyeful, or on the other hand, she could be reaching for a weapon.

The soldier in him made him assume the worst. He adjusted his aim from Clay to her.

"Hey, lady, hands where I can see them." She stopped moving, her hands at the edge of the mattress. "Good. Keep them where I can see them at all times. If you give me a problem, you'll suffer and it will be your own fault."

"It's okay, sweetie. I promise, it'll be okay." Clay's voice was that of a seasoned orator. Strong, confident and strangely commanding for a man held at gunpoint. There should have been a tremor of fear, a catch of some kind in his throat or, at the very least, questions to Fletcher's identity and purpose. That there were none of these things was odd, but Fletcher didn't give them brain space at the moment.

Fletcher kept the pistol aimed between Clay and the woman ready to react if either of them moved. Sweetie might be Clay's wife or she might be a casual fling he only met hours earlier. It didn't matter.

While keeping an eye on them, Fletcher flicked glances round the room. It was a continuation of the rest of the house. Eclectic furniture of varying ages and conditions. Clean but not tidy.

A pair of jeans and a tie-dye dress lay on the floor at his feet. He bent to grab the dress with his free hand and tossed it across the bed. "Put this on." Fletcher kept his gun on Clay. His eyes focused on the man rather than the naked woman. "Need I explain what'll happen to lover boy here if you try anything stupid?"

"No."

From the corner of his eye he could see her moving as he took his first proper look at Clay. The man would never again see forty. He had the hair of an eighties rock star although his receding fringe added a seedy edge to his appearance. His eyes were dull, something Fletcher connected to the smell of dope in the house. Clay's body was trim with a clutch of graying hairs on his chest. Whether he worked out, ate well, or didn't eat too often wasn't something Fletcher cared about.

"Nnngh."

The grunt from Sweetie was all the warning Fletcher got of the lamp that was arcing its way towards his head. As he ducked he saw the collection of shells decorating the lamp's base and the growing frame of Sweetie following her missile.

The warning prevented the lamp from connecting with Fletcher's face, but it hadn't come soon enough for him to get fully out of its flight path. As he ducked, his gun arm reflexively rose to protect his head.

He wasn't quick enough and the heavy lamp passed over his arm and caught the top of his head with enough force to daze him. Sweetie's hands clawed at his gun arm, trying to break his grip on the pistol.

Fletcher had been trained by the British Navy as a Royal Marine, one of the elite regiments. All the drills he'd been taught, the firearms training and the hours of executing unarmed combat moves over and over until they were instinctive had honed not just his skill base, but his muscle memory.

Sweetie had flopped on the bed gasping for breath before Fletcher even had time to work out how to deal with her without causing more injury than was necessary.

It had been a palm strike to the solar plexus that had stolen Sweetie's breath. Delivered by instinct and a desire to survive. Fletcher realized his response had been proportional. There was no telling what Sweetie might have done had she gotten the gun from him. His one strike had nullified her as a threat while also making sure she survived the experience. Had he driven knuckles into her throat he could have crushed her windpipe. That hadn't happened and although he was pleased with his response, any pride he felt was more than erased by the fact his chivalry had allowed Sweetie an opportunity to strike back, and, more pertinent to his upbringing, he'd struck a woman. Yes she was a combatant, but only in the same way a toddler is when they slap their parent's leg.

He'd lost control of the situation and he knew he needed to retake it and fast otherwise he'd have nothing but problems.

Clay had sat up and was cradling Sweetie, telling her to stay calm and take steady breaths. His words were heeded and Sweetie got enough control of her breathing to allow her to shoot a look of hatred Fletcher's way as she clung to her lover.

Fletcher watched with interest. Clay and Sweetie had unwittingly shown their relationship to him. Their actions displaying the depth of their feelings for each other.

"I told you what would happen if you tried anything. Consider that a start to your schooling in how things are going to be for your immediate future." Fletcher's tone was cold. He needed them to fear him. "You, Clay. I know you're an activist. I know you stir people up to protest. You champion boycotts and I'm of the very strong opinion that you won't be averse to a little sabotage here and there—"

The verbal response from Sweetie was predictable in its ferocity. Fletcher paid it no heed. He'd been sworn at by sergeants and sergeant majors. There was nothing Sweetie could say that would be more insulting than a drill instructor intent on transforming young boys into hardened fighting men had shouted at him.

"Enough already. You might want to calm down and listen for a minute. Only one person in this room is holding a gun and it's not either of you. I don't want to harm you if I don't have to, but I'm here to ask you some questions and I won't be leaving until I have answers. You two just have to figure out whether you're going to choose the hard or the easy way."

"Ask your questions and then get outta our home."

"As I was saying," Fletcher tossed a disinterested look at Sweetie, "you're an activist and something of an agitator. There've been a lot of minor attacks on farms east of here. Sheds going on fire. Milk being spoiled and other such things. I think you're either behind it, or know who is." Fletcher bobbed the tip of his pistol at Clay. "So far three people have been killed. All three murders took place on dairy farms. The way I see it, you're either looking at a homicide charge, or an accessory to homicide at the very least if you know who's behind these attacks and murders."

"You're not a cop." Sweetie's chin jutted as she spat the words at Fletcher. "You ain't shown us a badge."

"I've shown you my gun. Maybe you ought to remember that."

"Pah."

Clay's hand found her arm. "Sweetie. I think we need to stay cool, okay?" Fletcher wasn't sure if Clay was buying thinking time or calming Sweetie before she did something stupid again. He licked his lips and then levelled his gaze Fletcher's way. "Your thinking is so lazy, dude. Something happens at a place where there's animals so you come round here and hassle us. You haven't shown a badge. Not even when she mentioned it. I don't think you got a badge. I think you're one of the farmers or maybe a private eye brought in by them. You've come in here and made threats you haven't followed up on. You're bluffing and it's time you folded because we don't know what you're talking about and even if we could help you, we wouldn't."

"Yes. You tell him, honey." Sweetie managed to show affection to Clay and hatred to Fletcher without changing her expression. "Those dairy farms you're talking about, they're nothing more than milk factories. The cows never see the sun. They don't get to walk in meadows and graze fresh grass. Everything about their lives is geared to making sure they produce as much milk as humanly possible." A pause as she realized the ridiculousness of her last sentence. "Well, animally possible."

In other circumstances Fletcher would have found amusement in her linguistic aberrations. The problem was, they were both right. Clay's call on him bluffing was right. He wasn't going to do either of them serious harm, and while he'd seen no evidence of cattle being mistreated at any of the farms he'd visited, he got Sweetie's point about the cattle being nothing more than natural resources to be mined until they ran dry.

"Look, dude, we all know that you're not going to pull your trigger, so you might as well haul your ass out of here."

Fletcher pulled his trigger. The suppressor muting its noise to a sharp cough.

His aim had shifted from the couple to the tangle of legs beneath the thin sheet. There had been a space the size of a paperback book where the sheet had sagged flat onto the mattress. His bullet hit the space dead center and buried itself in the mattress.

"You're wrong." Fletcher leaned over, placed the end of the suppressor against Clay's knee and looked him in the eye. "You know how this goes. You refuse to talk. I start a countdown. You either talk or have your kneecap smashed so bad you'll walk with a cane for the rest of your life. You've got another knee and two elbows I can shoot without having to worry about you dying."

Beads of sweat ran down Clay's face. When he spoke the authority had gone from his voice and been replaced by fear. "Wait. I can maybe help you. Please, though. You gotta believe me. It's not me that's doing it."

CHAPTER FIFTY-THREE

Fletcher removed his pistol from Clay's knee, took a step back and perched his butt against the top edge of a dresser. "Talk."

All hint of bravado had escaped Clay and he looked to Sweetie for reassurance. She gave him a tight nod and shot a glare Fletcher's way.

"First of all, I need you to understand that while I abhor the factory farms and how they treat their animals, I'm not some crazy fool who goes around setting fires and sabotaging things." Another look Sweetie's way. "Yes, I protest against them and try to get people to boycott dairy products. Yes, I'm a vegan. But you have to believe me, I'm not a killer. I believe in the sanctity of life for all of God's creatures. Jeez, I'm pro-life. I'm against the fur trade. I've protested against hunting, fishing and all forms of cruelty to animals. I've not eaten food with a face for thirty years and I'll never eat it again. All the food I eat is organically grown. Jeez, dude, the animals on this planet deserve the same freedoms we have, don't you think?"

"To a point. The fit will always prey on the weak." Fletcher bobbed the pistol to keep Clay talking. There was no point in getting into a debate on the merits of veganism, or the moral principles of rearing animals for the sole reason of using them as a foodstuff. It wasn't a topic he was well-informed on and, as a devout carnivore himself, any point he made would be wasted on Clay. "You said you could help. Nothing you've told me so far isn't anything I couldn't have guessed for myself. Start helping."

Clay licked his lips. Wiped a trail of spittle from his chin with the back of a shaking hand. "Please, tell me you believe I'm not the killer you're talking about."

"We'll work on that assumption." Fletcher turned the screw a little; Clay needed pressure to keep him talking. "For now."

"It wasn't me. I've been out of town. Haven't I, Sweetie?"

"He has."

"That doesn't prove anything. In fact, it takes away any chance you had at using Sweetie for an alibi."

"Wait." Sweetie rose to her knees causing Fletcher to gesture that she sit down again. "Bill was speaking at events. I filmed them live for our Facebook page so his message could be spread far and wide. When were those people killed?"

Fletcher gave her the dates.

"We were in Fargo for one of those." She pointed at the phone on the bedside table. "I can prove it if you let me get my phone."

"Get it, but I warn you, his kneecaps will be shot out if you try calling for help or anything like that."

Sweetie crawled across the bed to retrieve her cell. With it held in a way that allowed Fletcher to see the screen at all times, she brought up the video, showed him the timeline and a portion of the feed that showed Clay speaking in front of a banner proclaiming, "Fargo Against Animal Cruelty."

"Okay, you've proven you're not the killer. But you knew that, anyway, so how can you help me?"

"This won't come back on me, will it?"

"That depends. I'm getting bored with hearing nothing useful from you. So bored I'm starting to think you might need some nine-millimeter encouragement. You give me what I need and you're cool. You keep jerking me around and I'll have to encourage you. If you sell me a line with the intention of saving your skin and then running off, well, I'll find you. I found you tonight. Until I walked in here, you didn't know I was in your house. The next time I come for you, the first you'll know about it will be the white-hot pain of your kneecap disintegrating."

"Jeez, dude. Why you gotta be so down on me? You're one cynical dude, dude. Your chakra must be all over the place." Fletcher made as if he was going to step forward. His pistol pointing at Clay's knees. "Okay, okay. There's this dude. He came to the meetings a few times. He was right on message. Had been in some groups out west but he'd come home to Minneapolis. He was something of a legend. Fifty arrests to his name without more than a night or two in jail. He'd infiltrated labs and released animals that were used as test subjects, and he'd often torch the labs once he'd got the animals out. He knew what he was at, but he was hardcore. Like total hardcore. If anyone on the animal rights front is your killer, I'd say it'll be him."

"What's his name and where does he live?"

Clay looked at Sweetie and got another nod from her. "He's known as Weasel." A shrug. "They say it's because he can weasel himself into anywhere he wants to be. It might sound odd to you, but trust me, he's very slick, very charismatic. A lot of the times he's gotten into labs to cause trouble, he's done so by talking his way past guards and even the evil scientists testing their products on animals."

"And where does he live?"

A shake of the head. "I don't know the address. I was only there once, but it's in Bloomington."

"Would you recognize the place again?"

"Yeah, I think so."

"Then get dressed, we're going on a road trip."

CHAPTER FIFTY-FOUR

Clay tried to protest at Sweetie coming along. He argued there was no need for her to leave the house. In a lot of ways he was right and Fletcher would much prefer to have one hostage to worry about instead of two, but he couldn't risk Sweetie calling to warn Weasel he was coming or alerting the cops to his behavior since bursting into their bedroom.

Fletcher paused everyone in the hallway. "This is how we do it. Clay, you're driving with Sweetie up front. I'll be in back and I'll have my pistol aimed at your spine the whole time. Take my word for it that I'll cripple you for life if you try anything clever."

Clay led them along the path to the SUV. As soon as he opened the door he stopped. "Dude, I'm not driving this car. Not getting into it. Pull your trigger if you have to, but there's no way I'm sitting on leather. We can take my camper instead, but I'm not sitting on those seats."

Fletcher could feel his grip on the pistol tightening. This could be an elaborate bluff, or it could be a genuine stance. One way or another, his bluff had been called and he had to make a decision.

"We're taking my car." He ground the pistol into Sweetie's ear. "What if you get blankets from the house and sit on them? Will that ease your conscience or do I have to hurt you?"

"Bill, honey. Blankets won't be so bad, will they?"

"They'll do." Clay's tone had changed again; fear giving way to a righteous anger.

They all filed back to the house and Sweetie collected two blankets from the closet on the first floor.

Five minutes later Clay pulled away from the curb and set a course for Bloomington. His driving was a tad erratic, but not so bad Fletcher was concerned he was trying to pull a move of some description. More that he was used to the meager power of his camper van and was struggling to adapt to the more modern and faster SUV.

As it was after midnight there was little traffic on the roads and they made good time. Clay's driving became more assured as he got to grips with the unfamiliar vehicle.

Nobody spoke until they pulled off the I-35W into Bloomington itself and even then it was Clay murmuring to himself as he tried to recall where to go.

Fletcher had worried Clay was using this as a ruse, but he'd paid close attention to Sweetie when Clay had been telling him about Weasel. Her face had shown neither surprise nor bafflement at Clay's words, which suggested he'd been telling the truth.

All his initial doubts returned as he shot glances out of the window. Where Ventura Village was down at heel, Bloomington was a district of prosperity. The houses were all set back from the roads with sizable lawns in front of them. The cars on the drives were new models, imports and top of their ranges. Each house was spacious and boasted two-car garages.

There was no hint of vandalism to be seen and while you never knew what went on behind a closed door, it was a fair bet the greatest extent of drug problems around here would involve waiting in line at the pharmacy.

Fletcher had to speak out. Had to stop Clay wasting his time with a wild goose chase. "This doesn't look like the kind of area where someone known as Weasel would live. You're not trying to get one over on me, are you?" To emphasize his words he lifted his pistol from where it was aimed at the back of Clay's seat and pressed it against the knuckle of spine that was showing above his shirt.

"Easy, dude, easy." Clay's voice held enough panic for Fletcher to feel he was in control.

Sweetie twisted in her seat. Her bare shoulder close to a patch of unblanketed leather. "He's not trying to get one over on you. Weasel lives out here somewhere. His family has money and he keeps himself dressed regular to help him get into places. Bill and me, we're free spirits fighting for the animals. Weasel? He's the kind of guy who looks at home in a swanky-assed restaurant. It's how he works. How he gets into places people don't want him to. Your ideas of animal rights groups are all clichés. Bill gets support from doctors, accountants and lawyers. You don't have to be a beatnik—or even a vegan—to care about animals."

Chastened, Fletcher eased back in his seat and returned his pistol to its former position. Sweetie had a point. He ate meat all the time. Big juicy steaks and pastrami, baloney or ham sandwiches were his go-to meals. Chicken, lamb and pork all graced his table on a regular basis. Yet he still cared about animals. He hated to see them suffer, and he loved Wendy's shih tzu, Wilson, almost as much as she did.

When she'd campaigned for a dog, he'd done the usual macho man thing of arguing there was no way he'd be walking any dog whose back didn't reach knee height, but she'd known her own mind and had chosen the shih tzu pup with its piranha-esque bottom teeth over the cute Labradors and friendly faced beagles he'd suggested.

They'd been binging on the show *House* when they got the pup, and as Wilson was House's best friend, he jokingly proposed it as a name for the shih tzu. Wendy had agreed in a flash and Wilson was now a major part of their family unit.

"Hey, dude."

"Yeah?"

"Keep yourself cool, right. I know Weasel's place is in this area, I just can't remember where exactly. I'm going to have to drive around a little until I see it. Don't worry, I'll know it when I see it, there was this big ass tree in the front with a treehouse."

Fletcher had already noticed how Clay had slowed and was taking long hard looks at the properties he was passing. He liked that Clay had felt it necessary to explain his actions. It showed that, although scared, the man was thinking with a clear head.

What he didn't like was the prospect of not finding the house they were looking for.

"How long is it since you were here with him?"

"About two years, maybe three tops."

This wasn't good news. Three years was a lot of time for memory to fade. There was also the possibility time had escaped Clay. Fletcher knew from his own experience that what he often thought of as a year or two turned out to be four or more. If that was the case with Clay, it could be five or more years since he was here. Weasel could have moved on, repainted his house or Clay's memory could just fail him.

It all sounded like he was being set up for failure. As he was considering what to do, Clay eased the SUV to a halt at the side of the road and lowered the passenger window. Fletcher took a cautious look. There was nothing remarkable about the house, except it had a huge stump in the center of its lawn.

"This is the place." He turned to look Fletcher's way. "Go on then, do your thing."

"What, and leave you here in my car, with the keys? I don't think so." Fletcher put his empty hand between the seats. "Keys, please. As before, you lead and I'll follow. If Weasel answers the door, you two disappear and forget all about me. If he doesn't and you try running, you'll get a bullet in your backs."

"Jeez, dude. What is it with you and threats? I mean, you interrupt us when we're getting funky, threaten us. Malign our ideals, drag us here at gunpoint so you can do God knows what to a man whose ideals we share, and you're still laying heavy crap on us when we've done everything you've asked."

"Just do as I say and there'll be no more threats. But you can consider them implied."

Clay opened his door wide and clambered out. A light rain began to speckle them as they crossed the sidewalk and made their way to the front door.

The knock Clay gave wouldn't have woken even the lightest sleeper, so Fletcher brushed past him and gave the door a proper thumping.

Nothing happened for a minute so Fletcher gestured for Clay to knock again.

He did so with his former gentle consideration of the door's paintwork.

"Knock like you're trying to wake someone."

Clay increased the power he put into his raps on the door and a light came on.

Before the door was even open they heard grumbling. It was a man in his sixties who opened the door. Bald head, a white tee that was losing its fight to contain his paunch and a pair of blue-and-white striped shorts.

"The hell you want banging on my door at this time of night?" He squinted at them, rubbed his eyes and took a better look. "Are you cops? Is it that son of mine in trouble again?"

"No, sir. We're not cops." Fletcher was at the back of the three, his pistol hidden by Sweetie's back. "But we are looking for your son."

Weasel's father peered at Clay. "I know you. You're another one of them damned animal lovers, aren't you? Well, you can take a hike, buddy. You and your kind have gotten him into more trouble than enough. He's been gone on one of his escapades for months now. Not sure if he'll ever come back. His momma's cried all her tears for him. You find him, you tell him to let his momma know he's alive and then to keep away so he can't break her heart no more."

"We will, sir." Fletcher turned away from the house. Wherever the mysterious Weasel was, his folks didn't know. He had an address for the family now. Quadrado could run her searches, find out his real name and see if he had a record.

He passed the keys to the SUV to Clay.

"Where we going now?"

"You're going home. Where I'm going after that is none of your business." As Clay drove, Fletcher typed out yet another email to Quadrado.

CHAPTER FIFTY-FIVE

Quadrado was fighting sleep by the time she pulled into the motel. Her yawns were getting wider by the minute and she'd guzzled three energy drinks to prevent her falling asleep at the wheel.

The first thing she did was scan the parking lot for Fletcher's SUV. It was missing which meant he was out doing his thing. This was both good and bad. Good because everything he did progressed the case, even if what he achieved was nothing more than the elimination of a dead end. Bad because she wanted to speak to him face-to-face. She owed him apologies. One for the message she'd been instructed to send him. One for the tardiness of her responses to his requests for information and a big one for involving him in this case.

More than anything, she needed to speak with him so they could brainstorm ideas. She had yet to tell him they had been given a deadline, and she was intrigued to know why he wanted this man known as Weasel run through the system. He'd given her broad strokes in his email, but she knew Fletcher well enough to be aware there was always an underlying train of thought with him that he didn't always communicate until he'd gone over every angle in his own mind.

The deadline was harsh and unnecessary in her mind. Fletcher was working his butt off and she'd be doing the same. With the Hashtag Killer's victim count rising all the time, there should be a full-scale investigation, yet Soter hadn't called in any other resources. This wasn't how things should be. A vicious killer being trailed by a mercenary and a sole FBI agent. Whoever Soter was, he was testing them both. She was grateful Fletcher had been able to avoid prison after what happened in Georgia, but she couldn't help but think Fletcher had escaped the frying pan only to end up in the fire.

With one thing and another to contend with, she'd not bothered to book herself a room at the motel. It had been her intention to stay with her folks, but with the time well after 2.00 a.m., she didn't want to go round waking them up, so she walked across to the motel's reception.

It wasn't a welcoming place. Eight by twelve with a large counter in the middle, it had a bored woman filing her nails while listening to soul music.

"Hi. Have you any rooms? I don't need anything fancy. A single will do."

"Sorry, sugar, we're fresh out. Don't quite know why, but we ain't been this busy in a long time."

Quadrado thanked the woman and returned to her hire car. She'd have to wake someone at Meadowfields after all. Hardly the homecoming she'd planned.

She put in a call to Fletcher before she started the car. If he was close by, they could catch up before either of them got any sleep.

He answered after the second ring, but she could tell from his one word greeting he was as tired as she was.

"Where are you?"

"A half hour out from Minneapolis."

"Damn. I was hoping to see you, but there's no way I'll stay awake until you get back."

"Likewise, but I'm beat now, and I reckon that by the time I get back, I'll be dead on my feet."

Quadrado pulled a face. What he was saying made sense. She knew from the timings of his emails he'd been on the go since early that morning and he was sure to have only had a few hours' sleep after last night's run-in with Steve Heaton.

"Sure. I'm going to go back to Meadowfields. Get some sleep. We can meet up in the morning."

She could imagine his face as he drove. Calm, yet ever watchful. Nothing of any importance got past him.

"You're going to wake your folks at this time of night? Why don't you take a room at the motel? The government can afford it."

"I was going to, but they're full."

"Take mine if you like. I'll just stop at another motel somewhere on the road and bunk down for a couple of hours."

"Are you sure? I don't want to steal your bed."

"It's fine. I'm fighting sleep already so it's probably wise for me to stop and rest anyway."

"Thanks. Either way, I'll meet you at the diner in the morning. What time can you get there for?"

"I'll be there for seven."

Quadrado wasn't planning to use his room until a yawn threatened to dislocate her jaw. If she went home, whoever she woke was sure to want to talk to her. As much as she was desperate to see her family, she knew they'd worry if they saw her quite so broken and exhausted, so she climbed out of the rental car again and went back to the reception.

Two minutes later she was walking towards Fletcher's room with a spare key in her hand and the receptionist thinking she was an airhead for not knowing her husband had already booked them a room.

She unlocked the door, strode into the bedroom and let out a scream when she saw the woman sitting on Fletcher's bed. She thought the receptionist had given her a key to the wrong room, until she noticed the maps taped to the walls and the various notes in Fletcher's neat handwriting.

CHAPTER FIFTY-SIX

Fletcher arrived at the diner in a state of exhaustion that bought him a concerned look from the server.

"The usual?"

"Please." Fletcher lifted the coffee she'd poured and walked to the seat he'd claimed as his own.

As was his way, he'd chosen a seat that allowed him to have a clear view of the room, its entrances and exits and kept his back against a wall.

Quadrado turned up at the same time as his breakfast. He'd wanted to speak with her last night, but he was glad he hadn't. By the time he'd found a motel to get his head down for an hour or two, he'd been on autopilot, his brain too fuzzy with lack of sleep to be able to do anything other than control basic functions.

"You've not wasted any time making friends, have you?"

"What do you mean?" Fletcher paused a forkful of eggs below his mouth.

"Well, let me put it this way, as well as the two fights you told me about, and the fight with Heaton, you seem to have found time to start dating someone."

"That wasn't dating, that was me talking to someone who could give me information." Fletcher pointed his fork at her. "Something *you* were supposed to be doing."

"Tell me, how does getting information from someone turn into a half-naked woman being in your room?"

"Felicity was in my room?"

Quadrado answered his question with a shake of her head. "You trying to tell me you thought it was Felicity? Don't tell me you're seeing more than one person. As if you don't know, it was a girl called Idaho Drake and, judging by the fact she was in her underwear, I'd say it was obvious what was on her mind."

"I'm damned if I know how she got there, or why she was half-naked. I made it clear to her that I wasn't interested in sleeping with her in exchange for information. As for Felicity, you were the one who suggested I speak to her."

Fletcher couldn't help feeling both irritated and flattered at learning Idaho had made the attempt to seduce him. He meant what he'd said to Quadrado, he had no interest in her, or anyone else, and if he'd returned to the motel to find her in his bed, he'd have booted her out.

"I can't believe this. You've only been here a few days and you're creating mayhem wherever you go. What the hell are you playing at, Fletcher?"

"I'm trying to find out who killed your friend." Fletcher's voice was low, but his rising anger had turned it into a hiss. "I can't help it if some young reporter is stupid enough to think I'd tell her all about the investigation, if she offers herself as a bribe. For God's sake, Quadrado, it's time you switched your brain into gear before you open your mouth. You asked for me to be here. It's your friend's homicide I'm here to investigate. And you know what my wife meant to me, know that I'll never be over her death and my part in it. As for thinking I'd let the promise of sleeping with a young girl like her do anything to jeopardize my work on the case, that's the biggest kick in the nuts you could deliver."

Quadrado's eyes flashed his anger right back at him. "Yeah, and what about the bar fights? I warned you the folks round here were parochial, that you'd have to keep your nose clean to get anywhere."

"They pushed at me. I pushed back. That's all there is to it. They were too dumb to learn a lesson. If they'd been good students they would have learned the first time." Fletcher speared the last piece of ham on his plate. "So, are you finished telling me off yet? Because I have some homicides to look into, and I thought that as an FBI agent, they would be higher on your list of priorities than treating me like a naughty boy."

"Damn you, Fletcher. You know solving Jane's homicide is all I care about."

"Then stop riding me for things beyond my control." Fletcher shoved the ham into his mouth to give them both a moment to cool down. "Did you get the information I requested on this Weasel character?"

Quadrado pulled a face. "Yeah, his real name is Nathan Arbutt. He's twenty-eight and has a job with an accountancy firm. He has a list of misdemeanors against his name. I've got searches running on him now. When they're done they'll be emailed to me." She leaned back so the server could place an egg white omelet in front of her. "Did you get a look at the accounts yet?"

"Not yet. I was too busy running around Minneapolis." Fletcher didn't elaborate as he wasn't proud of the way he'd terrorized Clay and Sweetie into giving him information.

"It sounds like Arbutt could be our man."

"I'd like to think so, but I'm not so sure."

"What do you mean?"

Fletcher buttered his last slice of toast. "He's an animal rights activist, right? So he does things to protect animals. To save them from testing labs. You said he's got a list of misdemeanors against his name. I'd have been a lot happier if you'd said that he'd been suspected of homicides or that he'd been arrested for assault. Better yet, if you'd said he'd done time for a crime where violence had been a factor, then I'd feel a lot better about him as our main suspect. Tell me, is assault listed among his collection of misdemeanors?"

"No, it's not." Quadrado's brow furrowed as she absorbed what he was and wasn't saying. "So you now think you were wrong to suspect Arbutt is the killer?"

"I never said he was. He's an okay suspect for the nonviolent attacks, but I definitely don't think we should put all of our eggs in his basket. He's not shown any level of murderous violence before, and the picture I got of him from Clay and his girlfriend is that he's someone who bypasses security with a con trick rather than a baseball bat. Why he'd turn to killing now doesn't make sense. There's also the victims: a farmer's daughter-in-law, a farmer and a farmer's daughter. Surely if you're killing to protect animals, you'd aim for the top of the tree and target farmers all the time instead of their family members." Fletcher took a drink of his coffee. "There's also the locale to consider. The farms round here have suffered a number of attacks that were passed off as bad luck. Why here? Why would a guy from Minneapolis choose Taylor County as his place to kill people and cause havoc for farmers when there's a hundred miles worth of farms between here and Minneapolis?"

"So what you're saying is that you're doubting his motivations, that you don't understand why he's targeting Taylor County and not somewhere closer to home, aren't you?"

"I guess so." Fletcher was hesitant to admit too much about his confusion as he still wasn't sure how involved Quadrado was with the test. "Basically, I haven't yet worked out what motive *anyone* could have for the killings. Let alone an animal rights activist who has no history of violence."

Quadrado bit down on the last of her omelet, her face a picture of deep thought although Fletcher detected a hint of something else there. He paid close attention to her until he realized she was afraid. He waited until she'd finished eating and had sipped her coffee before meeting her fear head on.

"Whatever it is you're holding back, whatever it is that you're afraid to say, it needs to be said and said soon so we can focus on the matter in hand."

"You're not going to like it." Fletcher didn't speak, he just waited for her to spit it out. "Soter emailed me last night. We've got until midnight tomorrow to solve this case. If it's not solved by then, I have to arrest you and you'll be transported to Georgia, where the evidence against you that's been suppressed will magically appear."

Fletcher speared Quadrado with a hard stare. "I'm guessing this Soter character you speak of is the person who got you to offer me the deal in Georgia."

"He is. I had to involve him, Fletcher. He wanted a test case and I want Jane's killer caught. He told me not to tell you, but I couldn't keep it a secret any longer. Not now he's given us a deadline."

"I figured you'd gone to him. You might have thought to tell me sooner. We're supposed to be working together, aren't we?"

"It's not like that, damnit. I didn't have a choice. Would you have done things any different if I'd told you from the start?"

"You always have choices, Special Agent Quadrado. Would you have told me if he hadn't given the deadline?" As much as he was angry with Quadrado, he accepted that she'd been in an impossible situation. Her face wore grief like a coat of makeup and the redness around her brown eyes spoke of many tears being shed.

"Of course I would. I just didn't dare tell you any other way than face-to-face in case our communications are being monitored. Whatever purpose Soter has for you in the future, I figure it'll be far bigger than investigating a homicide in a place like Medford. You were my best chance of getting justice for Jane. I'm sorry if you feel used, but I don't regret a single thing I've done. Tell me, what would you have done in my position?"

Quadrado had him there. In her place he'd have done much the same as she had. "Who is this Soter anyway? It's not a name that means anything to me."

"I googled it. Soter is the name of a Greek daemon of protection."

"That figures." Fletcher rose to his feet. "Come on then, we've got work to do." He dropped a few bucks on the table to cover their breakfasts and set off back towards the motel, his feet taking long strides.

Fletcher had been afraid this would happen if Quadrado had involved the mysterious figure who he now knew went by the name of Soter. When he was investigating one homicide, he'd had time on his side, but with the killer having struck twice more, it was inevitable Soter would get antsy about his lack of success. What he suspected had originated as a test had grown into something bigger and with the body count climbing, there was no way he could be left on the playing field if he wasn't getting results. Sooner or later the local cops would increase their numbers to the point where he'd be surplus to requirements. He knew the role Soter wanted of him was that of a troubleshooter who could be dropped into problems and expected to solve them with either brains or brawn. He'd proven his brawn in Georgia, so this case must be about showing his brains.

Quadrado caught up with him, her boots clacking on the sidewalk as she trotted to keep up.

"There's more bad news, I'm afraid. I got the email about Nathan Arbutt. He's been in the South Idaho Correctional Institution for the last two months."

"So he's definitely not our man. Brilliant, our only half-decent suspect wasn't that great and he's just been struck off the list." Fletcher glared at Quadrado. "Anything else?"

CHAPTER FIFTY-SEVEN

Fletcher retrieved the files on the accounts from the trunk of his SUV and put them on the motel room bed. Quadrado was standing in front of the maps he'd taped to the wall, her face screwed in concentration.

"Do you see how there's a definite epicenter on the crossroads?" Fletcher used a pen as a pointer. "All the farms I've circled have suffered either an outright attack or a piece of bad luck that may have been a disguised attack."

"I see it. I saw it last night and again this morning, but I didn't know what the circles meant."

"Now that you do, what do you make of it?"

"It seemed like too much of a coincidence to also have homicides in the exact same place as so many random attacks."

Fletcher nodded his agreement. It was this thinking that had led him to suspect that everything was the work of the animal rights activists. With the closest known activists now ruled out, the field was wide open for activists from elsewhere in the country to be the perpetrators, if it even was animal rights activists behind things. He needed to find another thread to pick at because he couldn't visit every known animal rights group in the country to question them.

"Don't get snippy with me again, but if Idaho has been in here, she'll have seen all this as well. My dime to your buck says she took photos and notes of everything she thought might be important. At some point she's going to use that information to make a splash."

"Well duh. That was my first thought."

Fletcher let the implied insult slide. With the deadline hanging over his head, there were better uses of his time than sniping at Quadrado. As always since arriving in Medford, he needed more information. "Can you call your brother? I want to know if any of the farmers had more trouble last night. And if any of those standing guard caught or saw anyone? When you've done that, can you take a quick look at other animal rights groups who may be involved, just so we can rule them out of our thinking? I'm not against the theory, I just feel we made a mistake by focusing our attention on the nearest group. Ideally, the ones you're looking for will have a history of violence from some of their activists."

The unknowns about the case were endless and it took all of Fletcher's willpower to put aside the threat hanging over him and spend his time worrying about Soter's deadline. His first point of call was the files on the farms' accounts. He got out his notepad, jotted down the four farms' names in a series of columns and started compiling his own old-fashioned spreadsheet from the sheets he'd bribed the receptionist to print for him.

Fletcher knew Quadrado could have compiled it quicker on her laptop, but that would give him the raw data without any understanding of it. By taking on the task himself, he was absorbing the facts as he built the spreadsheet. He got context and could differentiate feed merchants from contractors and vets.

Quadrado was speaking to her brother. He could hear her, yet to him her voice was nothing more than a background noise to be ignored. She'd tell him what he needed to know when the call was finished, so there was no point listening to her side of the conversation when he could be getting on with something else.

With more bodies piling up he'd always been aware of the time pressures on him, but now he'd been given so little time to solve the case, every second was precious.

Column after column was filled on his spreadsheet. Pages were torn off his notebook and laid on the bed to create an overview yet nothing was speaking to him.

The numbers he was dealing with boggled his mind. Farms might seem like quiet slow-moving businesses, but the money they turned over astonished him. From the payments they received from dairy companies to bills from contractors and suppliers, the numbers were often in the five-figure region and rarely below four.

Tractors and other machinery were more expensive than he'd thought possible until he factored in the complexity of the equipment and the limited number of sales the manufacturers could make.

The size of the numbers he was looking at gave him an understanding of why there were so many farms declaring bankruptcy. A poor yield or an expensive piece of equipment breaking down could be enough to make the payments coming in smaller than the ones going out. It was little wonder the farmers affected by the attacks were so livid. It wasn't just their property that was under attack, it was their livelihoods and the whole fabric of their lives. Running a farm wasn't just a job you chose to do, it was something you were born into, something you accepted from an early age. There were long hours, constant worries and hard work on a daily basis.

Page after page was laid on the bed until Fletcher's hand was sore from all the writing.

Quadrado touched his arm to get his attention. "Fletcher?"

"What?"

"I've said your name three times now. You were miles away."

"In case you've forgotten, I have less than forty hours to solve this case before I'm thrown into jail on a homicide charge. My best leads have been a bust and, unless the killer walks up to me and confesses, it's not looking likely that I'm going to identify him, much less lead you to wherever he is before you slap a pair of cuffs on me. But please, accept my apologies for being distracted when you're wanting my attention. If only I was as perfect as you are when it comes to responding to requests for information or help."

As soon as the words came out Fletcher regretted them. Quadrado wasn't the one putting the squeeze on him, Soter was. She didn't deserve his ire, Soter did.

"Can it, Fletcher." Quadrado was in his face in a way that would have made him punch a man. "My friend was killed and I trusted you to find her killer. I've had to juggle my case back in New York, your emails and Soter's requests for updates. I've worked my ass off to get here to help you. This whole thing has turned to crap, but I still trust you'll figure it all out, so don't give me any of your attitude because I'm just as pissed at this as you are."

"Oh, you are, are you?" Fletcher was trying to rein in his temper, but he knew it was a forlorn attempt. "You're not the one being threatened with jail. In fact, from what I recall, you're the one who's making the threats. You might have been the messenger today, but that doesn't excuse that email you sent the other day."

"What email?"

"The one with the picture of a court and a link to Georgia's stance on the death penalty. That was real cute of you, *Special Agent Quadrado*, real cute."

Fletcher watched as Quadrado backed away and sat on the room's only chair. Her face was ashen, and her hands were raised as if she'd witnessed a shocking sight.

"You think I sent that of my own volition? That I choose to be so nasty to you?" Her face changed from the professional FBI mask she'd been trying and failing to display all morning. Now there was real fire in her eyes as her frustrations and grief-fueled anger poured out. "You saved my life, you're here investigating the murder of my best friend. How can you think I'd be such a bitch to you? I was ordered to send it by Soter. I've already told you I figured they were monitoring our communications. Do you think I feel good about sending it? That I enjoyed putting the pressure on you? Damnit, Fletcher, I thought you knew me better than that."

Fletcher's anger left him. All he had left was a sense of shame. Quadrado was a good person, she was kind, generous and while she was tough, she was also genetically programmed to see the best in people.

He wasn't. He was cynical. He'd seen too much, experienced too many betrayals, and heard too many lies to be anything else. She had had a lot of the same thought processes as he had regarding Soter and that was to her credit.

"The email came from you. I guessed you might have dialed him in, but I had to know. Have to be sure that you have my back. I know that now. Friends again?" He stepped towards her and offered his fist to be bumped. "The guy who's pulling our strings, this Soter, what say we get our heads together and work as a team, see if we can solve this? I don't want to go to jail. Don't want you to have to arrest me."

Fletcher's knuckles didn't so much get bumped as punched. He took the gesture for what it was. She'd forgiven him, but for the time being she was still sore at him. He could live with that; he was sore at himself for getting so angry with her. She was the only help he had available to keep him out of jail, and getting on her bad side could only be a foolish thing to do.

"I spoke with Peter. A milk tank was holed over by Rib Lake. The hole was near the bottom and all the milk drained out. The farmer there has had to delay milking his cows until he can fashion a patch on the tank."

"Was the farmer one of the ones who was guarding his farm?"

"No."

One small word with only two letters could say an awful lot.

Fletcher could see Quadrado had more to say so he gestured for her to continue.

"Peter had other news. Elsie Renard at White Birch is talking about selling up."

"So quickly? Her husband isn't even buried yet. Surely this isn't the time to be making decisions."

"I agree, but you don't know the Renards. Their son, Tom, worked White Birch with his father. Walt wanted him to take over when he retired, but while he's a good worker, Tom hasn't got a head for business. There's a good chance you'll have seen his wife there when you visited. She's a real mother hen."

"Is Tom their only child?"

"No, there are two brothers and a sister who've moved away, none of them want a farming life. We've all known that when Walt's day was up, White Birch would be sold. It's just a surprise it's happening so quickly."

Fletcher got what Quadrado wasn't saying. Tom wasn't clever enough to run the business and his family knew it. "What about realtors and so on? Surely there's been no time to put the farm on the market?"

"Elsie didn't want it being sold to an out-of-towner, so she got pretty much straight on the phone to her neighbor, Robert Kearney, from Calvertsholm. And from what Peter was saying, he's made her a fair offer. It'd be good if she accepted it. Robert is a decent guy and has had a terrible run of luck recently. And he's been looking for more land for years now. Folks round here would prefer that to someone new coming in."

Calvertsholm was one of the farms next door to White Birch; one of the four on the crossroad whose accounts Fletcher had been going over that morning. It was also where the fire in the barn had been two days ago.

So far as he could make out, the timing of the sale wasn't great for anyone, as from what he'd seen of Kearney's accounts, he was making money, but unless he had a nest egg stashed elsewhere,

he would be stretching himself to buy White Birch. He pushed
the thought from his mind and turned back to the accounts of
the farms; maybe he'd find something somewhere in them that
would give him a decent lead to follow.

CHAPTER FIFTY-EIGHT

"I still say you're wasting your time looking over the accounts. No offense, but unless you're a forensic accountant and haven't told me, I don't see what you expect to find."

Fletcher ignored Quadrado's grousing. She had tapped into the police databases and taken a look at the autopsy notes for Marcia Jamieson. As with Jane, there was no sexual element about her homicide, so he was trying to follow the money. The oil he'd found had been tested and had been proven to be a generic brand. Once the killer was found, a comparison against oil from his vehicle would help secure a conviction, but without a suspect to focus on, the oil was useless as a clue.

The only people he could think of who'd benefit financially from any of the homicides were the Renard family. The farm being sold with such haste made him think they were cashing in at once. Fair enough, the one son, Tom, wasn't fit to run the farm himself, but under his mother's guidance he could surely have coped for a month or two until Walt had been buried and the ground had settled on his grave.

That hadn't happened though. Whether Tom or any of his siblings would inherit at this stage was anybody's guess. There was also the question of whether Elsie Renard had seized an opportunity to repay her husband for his philandering. That was still a thought Fletcher couldn't shake.

The two female victims had no wealth for anyone to claim. One was a farm owner's daughter-in-law, albeit one who stood to inherit her family farm one day in the future, the other a daughter. Neither had a claim on the farm. If Carl was a partner of Greenacres Farm, she would have gotten half his share in a divorce, but there was no financial gain to be had in her death.

He turned back to his spreadsheets and cursed the world in general. The farms all used the same suppliers, be they feed merchants or contractors. They sold their milk to the same chain of dairies and bought and sold their cattle from the same market. They even used the same company for the artificial insemination of their cows.

The odd item would vary from farm to farm, but they were either small value or big-ticket items. A google search on his phone had told Fletcher the expensive items had been bought from companies selling agricultural machinery. For the most part the tractors he'd seen on the various farms were John Deeres, but there were exceptions and he figured that like auto dealerships, tractor brands would all have their own franchises.

One by one he scoured the various spreadsheets he'd created.

"Hey." Fletcher waited until Quadrado looked his way. "What do you know about the Kearney guy paying someone to drill core samples?"

A tight smile caressed Quadrado's mouth for the briefest of seconds. "That's just Robert being Robert. He's always looking for ways to strike it rich with one daft scheme after another. I bet he'll be dreaming of a super-farm now he's made an offer for White Birch." Quadrado's smile widened although there was fondness in her voice. "Over the years he's looked into eco pods for vacationers, turning the farm into an adventure center and giving up the dairy to grow exotic herbs and spices for the restaurant market."

"So he had the drilling done and struck out, did he?" Fletcher didn't expect an answer and Quadrado didn't give one. Kearney had spent over fifty grand with the drilling company and nearly as much again having the core samples analyzed. "Does he have a lot of money behind him? I would have thought a better way to get rich is to not squander what you've already got."

"He's got money but he almost only ever spends it on things he hopes will generate more. His pickup is ancient, but he won't replace it as he says it does all he needs it to."

"What's he like as a person?"

"He's okay. He's just your average guy. He's tighter than most, but he mucks in and helps out others like the rest of the folks round here."

Quadrado's phone emitted a shrill ring that startled Fletcher. He'd figured she'd have had a gentler ringtone, or have it set to a piece of music she liked.

A hand was flapped in his direction as Quadrado listened to the caller. He tuned into her side of the conversation.

"What, both of them? Oh, their poor family." Sorrow creased Quadrado's face as she listened some more. "We'll be there as quick as we can." She ended the call and looked at Fletcher. "There've been two more homicides. A farmer and his wife were found on their front porch. Both had been killed with a single stab wound to the heart, and before you ask, yes, they both had the hashtag on their foreheads."

CHAPTER FIFTY-NINE

While Quadrado drove, Fletcher bent his mind to what he knew about the latest homicides. Bettsina and Ken Pickworth were in their sixties and were known to be of good health. Like most other farmers in the area they were well liked and respected by the rest of the community.

Quadrado had filled him in on their family. They had none. After a series of miscarriages, they'd given up trying. Ken had a sister he hadn't spoken to for thirty years, but other than her, they had no living relatives. According to Quadrado, they'd been talking of selling up for quite some time.

This line of thought made him consider the money aspect again. To erase the nagging doubts about Kearney in his mind, he put a call in to the drilling company and pretended to be Kearney.

When he asked about minerals or ore found, he was referred on to the laboratory where the core samples were sent. The person he spoke to gave him a number to call.

All he got from the call to the laboratory was a recorded message telling him the lab would be closed until 8.00 a.m. Monday. Monday was too late for him. Monday was after Soter's deadline. On Monday he'd either be in a Georgia jail or on his way to one.

With yet another avenue of investigation turning into either a dead end or proving to be out of reach, he bent his mind back to the latest homicides.

Ken Pickworth had been branded with #4 and his wife, Bettsina, with #5. This meant the killer was keeping to his habit of scoring his kills. It also indicated there had been no other kills that had gone undetected, as the sequence of numbers was intact.

In all there was no great information to be learned from what they had so far, but he was hoping there would be someone at the farm who'd seen or heard something. The latest accounts he'd been studying were for the Pickworths' farm, Broken Spur.

Quadrado had taken a road out of Medford he was unfamiliar with, but as she'd grown up around here, he trusted she knew where she was going.

As they pulled off the road and followed a track to the farm, Quadrado's phone emitted its shrill ring. Like the good FBI agent she was, she'd hooked her phone up to the car's hands free and took the call, alerting the caller they were on speaker and who was listening.

"Zeke. It's me." Peter's voice was recognizable to Fletcher. "You know how bad luck comes in threes? Well I've just heard that Robert Kearney was attacked last night too. He said someone tried to stab him, but he managed to fight back. He says the guy ran off before he could get the better of him."

Quadrado beat Fletcher to the obvious question. "Did he describe the guy he was fighting with?"

"He said the guy was wearing a ski mask. Said he was carrying a knife. I tell you, Zeke, he was damn lucky not to get himself killed."

Fletcher kept an ear on the conversation as he thought about this latest revelation.

Robert Kearney had a farm bordering the crossroads. He'd been targeted and then the killer had moved on to Broken Spur, where he'd killed the Pickworths.

Once again the crossroads was at the center of everything. Kearney's reasons for having core samples taken from his farm seemed less important to Fletcher in light of this recent news.

CHAPTER SIXTY

Broken Spur was the same as any other farm in the area. Or at least it would be if you discounted the throng of police vehicles, concerned neighbors and smattering of press.

Fletcher hung on Quadrado's heel as she used her badge to get past the deputy who was trying to preserve the scene from those trying to get close enough to have a good look. A feisty woman with a New York accent and a notepad in her hand was giving him the hardest time. As he passed her he was enveloped in a wave of perfume that was toxic enough to be sold by the gallon.

Idaho Drake was off to one side doing a piece to camera. It was in his mind to go across and ask her live on camera what she thought she was playing at by tricking her way into his room, going through his notes and stripping to her underwear. It was a bad idea and one that was sure to backfire against him. All the same, he wanted to let her know what he thought of her. He contented himself with sending her a fiery look she didn't notice and stalked after Quadrado.

A pair of detectives were in conversation with each other at the edge of a screen that had been erected. Old Cop was off to one side and when he saw Quadrado he marched over. His body language screaming dominance. Fletcher wasn't sure if his problem was that Quadrado was a woman, was younger, or that as an FBI Special Agent, she outranked him. For the moment he held back.

"Dammit, Zeke. Don't you go pulling any jurisdictional bull on me. This is a case for Medford PD."

"Have you solved it, officer? Do you have any suspects?" Fletcher stood his ground as Old Cop strode over to confront him for the barbed questions he was throwing around. "Are you going to lock up some more people on account of them not being locals?" The chuckle from one of the detectives was faint, but it was clear he wasn't the only one to think Old Cop was an ass. "If it helps, your answers should be: yes, yes and of course not."

"Damn you, Fletcher. This is a crime scene. You're a civilian, you shouldn't be anywhere near here."

"He's with me." Quadrado stepped between Fletcher and Old Cop. "There've been five kills now. That officially counts as a serial killer. Make no mistake, I'll be calling this in to the FBI as soon as I've ascertained a few facts to put in an initial report." She cast a look towards the detectives. "You guys got a problem with that?"

"No, ma'am. We've got nothing and would be glad of the FBI's help." The one who answered was handsome in a rugged way.

Quadrado laid a gentle hand on Old Cop's arm. "Look, I know Ken was a good buddy of yours. But you have to admit, this is running away from the Medford PD. Nobody wants any more deaths."

Upon hearing Old Cop was close to one of the victims, Fletcher felt a pang of guilt for prodding him. All the same, he wasn't prepared to offer an apology as he was sure it would be thrown back in his face.

He gave Old Cop what he hoped was a respectful nod and sidestepped to a place where he could see behind the screen. What he saw wasn't pretty. Ken and Bettsina Pickworth lay side by side on the porch, their hands touching in a final moment of tenderness as their blood pooled and mingled beneath them.

Fletcher had seen many dead bodies. Had made a few. Yet rarely had he seen such poignancy in death.

It was people like the Pickworths and the other three victims who deserved his best efforts. As much as the case was a trial of his own abilities, it was also about catching an indiscriminate killer so the dead could go to their graves knowing justice had been served.

As best he could without going any closer and potentially contaminating any evidence, Fletcher tried to work out how the kills had went down. There was a splash of blood on the handrail at the front of the porch. Ken was nearest the railing and Bettsina central.

In his mind he mapped it all out as he'd done with Jane Friedrickson. Ken's feet were in line with the door. If the killer had stood beside the door waiting for Ken and his wife to emerge, he'd have been able to replicate the backhand stab that he'd used on Jane. Ken would have staggered forward, his hands going to the rail for support. His legs would buckle and he'd go down never to rise again.

Bettsina following behind him would have seen nothing except her husband's collapse until he slumped onto his back. She'd have gone to him at once leaving her exposed back to the killer. An arm round her throat would have drawn her hands upwards and then it'd be simple enough to pierce her chest and leave her to die beside Ken. It was only the blood staining the front of her blouse that told Fletcher she'd been killed this way. If it had been him, he'd have slid his knife in from behind. She'd never have known he was there until she was dying. In the brief seconds the arm had been around her throat, she'd have felt fear like she'd never experienced before. Maybe the killer had whispered something to her. Maybe he'd taunted her.

With luck, a scraping of Bettsina's fingernails would unearth something to identify the killer.

Fletcher knew wishing for forensic evidence to solve the case would give the wrong outcome for him. It wouldn't matter by then. It was the middle of Saturday morning, by the time the evidence had been collected, analyzed and a suspect had been identified and captured, it'd be too late for him.

If he was to solve this case, he had just over thirty-seven hours to do it and no leads to go on. To make matters worse for him, Quadrado was on the point of calling in the FBI, which would mean he'd be shunted even further towards the sidelines. All the same, he *had* to solve the case. Not just to ensure his liberty, but to maintain his self-respect. Failure was not an option.

CHAPTER SIXTY-ONE

With two more homicides to add to the list, Fletcher's brain was bulging with all the information he had crammed into it. The beginnings of a headache were already showing and although he'd normally pop a couple of Advil to help manage it, there was no way he was going to take anything that might dull his wits.

Quadrado was inside her sedan putting in a call to the FBI field office in Eau Claire. She'd be summoning support. It was the right thing to do with a serial killer on the loose. He knew that. Believed it. Dreaded it.

He walked around the sedan to give his body some of the exercise his brain was getting; with each new circuit he widened his route.

The fact all four farms adjacent to the crossroads had seen homicides or, in the case of Kearney, attempted homicide, the greater his conviction was that something about the crossroads or the land surrounding them were important to the killer. Whether it was someone like the contractor Mick Barkel, who felt they'd been screwed over, or someone as yet unknown was beyond him, but with the imminent arrival of the FBI, there was no time for defeatist thoughts.

As he passed her window, Fletcher shot a look at Quadrado. Her face was grim as her fingers drummed on the steering wheel.

All Fletcher wanted was to get back to the motel where his notes were. Where he could reconnect with his spreadsheets and work the evidence he had while he still had some time on his side.

Another three circuits round the car saw Quadrado in the same position.

Fletcher began to think about the killer as a person. He had no experience as a profiler, but without getting an expert involved, he had to do the best he could. Quadrado had informed him about the profile she'd requested from her friend, Heidi, but until that profile came through, all he had was guesswork.

The autopsies of Walt Renard and Jane had suggested a right-handed assailant, which was of little help at this time. The forehead carvings were all done with enough expertise to be clearly legible, therefore the killer was adept with a knife. Chefs, farmers, butchers and a dozen other professions could be included in this assessment. It could be the killer had a lifetime of hunting experience to aid his cause, but actually worked as something benign like an accountant or lawyer.

If the killer was ex-military it would explain a lot with regards to the cleanness of the kills. Only Walt Renard had received more than a single stab to the heart to kill him. That spoke of a level of professionalism, which in turn told of training. Fletcher knew his own training had instilled certain moves into him with such a depth of muscle memory that he was able to react physically long before conscious thought had a chance to dictate his actions. This ability had saved his life on many occasions.

The downside was that if some jerk fronted him up in a bar, he had to fight to control himself, as if the man stepped too close, or made any kind of threatening gesture, Fletcher would land him on his ass in a flash. That in itself wouldn't be so bad, but Fletcher's training had instilled in him the philosophy that if you had to hit someone, you made sure they stayed down and didn't get up to have another go. In a public place, they called that level of violence assault no matter how much the jerk had asked for it.

The killer having a background in law enforcement would also make a lot of sense. He'd know how to limit trace evidence. How to make sure the kill site was as bereft of clues as possible.

So far the only definite links to the victims were the proximity of their homes and businesses, with the exception of Marcia Jamieson who bucked this trend. Where she fitted in was a mystery to Fletcher, although he did have the beginnings of an unpalatable idea regarding her involvement.

For all someone with a law enforcement or military background would be best suited to the homicides, there was more than enough information in the public domain for a civilian to execute the kills. There were hundreds if not thousands of tutorials online when it came to self-defense moves and tactics. There were also a myriad of TV crime dramas and true crime documentaries that showed the extent of how forensic evidence was used to catch killers. All of this meant anyone intent on taking the life of another could research their killing methods and learn how to avoid detection with relative ease.

Another five circuits and his glance at Quadrado showed her wringing the steering wheel as if it was a motorcycle throttle and she was in a life-or-death race. Her lips were moving and from the way she was spitting words out, it was clear she was arguing a point.

The early afternoon sun held enough warmth to bring sweat to Fletcher's brow as he marched around Quadrado's sedan. His back was to the car when he heard its door slam.

"Fletcher."

He'd already turned and begun to return to the car. Quadrado's expression didn't suggest good news.

"What's up?"

"Eau Claire aren't sending anyone until Monday." She held up her cell for him to see and then passed it his way. "Read that."

Fletcher took the cell and read the email she had open. It was from Soter and informed Quadrado that there would be no FBI involvement until the midnight on Sunday deadline had expired.

The email was telling and it brought out different emotions in him. While he was pleased to get a clear run, he also felt the victims deserved to not have their deaths turned into a test of his abilities. Who knew how long it would take to catch the killer? How many more people would be murdered before he was caught?

"This is crap, Fletcher. Complete and utter crap. Soter's playing games with lives. I didn't sign up for this. He should be sending agents out here right now."

For all he'd seen Quadrado pissed before, this was a whole new level. "I agree." He did, although he would have used a far stronger adjective than crap and added a serious amount of adverbs before it.

She flapped a hand at him. "Oh well, that's okay. You agree with me. Everything will be fine, then." A shake of her head. "And there was me thinking we were up a creek without a paddle. Thinking you'd end up in jail."

"That's enough." Fletcher held her by the shoulders and looked down into her brown eyes. His fingers gripping enough to hold her still, but not so hard that he'd cause her pain. "I'm glad you don't want me to go to jail. I sure as hell don't want to go there. But if we're going to make that happen, then we need to focus. Soter is testing us. Seeing what we're made of. I've guessed all along that this case was a trial for me, but until today, I hadn't realized you were being tested as well."

"Didn't you? Why not?"

"It makes sense that he'll want to see what I'm made of, but I hadn't figured you'd be tested as well."

"It's nice to feel trusted to do our jobs, huh?" A guilty look crossed her face.

"What have you done?"

Quadrado looked as if she was about to be sick. "When your request for a profiler was turned down, I called in a favor from a friend. I went behind his back and broke his rules. That's sure to flunk us if he finds out."

"I'm not so sure." Fletcher leaned against the sedan and raised his face to the sun for a moment's thought. "We're an off-the-books team, aren't we? My guess is that he'll want us to use unconventional methods, to overcome obstacles and circumvent protocol. The more I think about it, you calling in a favor behind his back is exactly what he'll want you to do."

She exhaled a long hissing breath, the earlier fury still on her face. "Damn you, Fletcher. I guess we better hope your logic is the same as Soter's?"

Fletcher gestured at the sedan. "Let's go back to the motel and my notes. We need to go over everything again while factoring in these new homicides." He reached his hand towards her. "But first, give me your handcuffs."

"What are you up to?" Quadrado's face wore skepticism like it was the latest fashion as she handed over the handcuffs.

"You'll see."

Fletcher walked behind the reporter's SUV and saw she was chatting with her cameraman. He caught her eye and waited for her to join him by the door that was left open. Where he stood they were out of sight of everyone except the cameraman.

"Mr. Fletcher. Reconsidered your options, have you?" Her smile was knowing.

"I thought you were bluffing about your offer. Then I heard about you being in my room, and well… you could say I've changed my mind."

"Interesting. What do you say we meet up at your motel? I can be there by three."

Fletcher leaned in as if he was going to kiss her. She bent her head as the fingers of his left hand grasped her right wrist. He lifted her arm until it was beside the SUV's open door. He whipped the handcuffs from his rear pocket and snapped one ring around her wrist, and the other around the open hoop of the door's window frame.

"Let's get a couple of things straight, shall we? One, you don't try and bribe me again. I have integrity and can't be bought. Two, your attempts to use seduction as your bribe are degrading for you, and quite frankly, disgusting to me. Three, you don't break into my room and go through my stuff. Four, your viewers can see through you, they don't particularly like you. Sooner or later your station bosses are going to realize this and replace you. I'd suggest that you change your ways or expect to lose what you've already got."

"Damn you, Fletcher. I'll ruin you for this."

"You can't ruin me, there's nothing I value that you can take away from me." Fletcher took four steps away from the SUV, stopped and fired one last parting shot. "Good luck finding a key for those cuffs."

It was an asshole's trick to leave her like that, but Fletcher's pride was too strong for him to let her intrusion into his space pass without some form of retaliation.

CHAPTER SIXTY-TWO

The sandwiches they'd picked up from a deli were long gone as Fletcher and Quadrado bent over the notes strewn all over the bed. His back ached from being stooped over, but it was the least of his worries.

"Tell me again about the Pickworths. You said they were thinking of selling up the farm. Have you any idea what the sister will do with the farm she'll likely inherit?"

Fletcher paced back and forth as Quadrado spoke. There wasn't much room to move in the motel room, but physical exercise got his blood pumping and he wanted to make sure his brain was as oxygenated as it could be.

"From what my pop has told me about it in the past, theirs was a falling out that would never be resolved. She'd hated the farming life and everything about it."

"Really? And there was no chance of a reconciliation?"

As someone who'd been fostered then adopted, Fletcher always struggled to understand how some families couldn't resolve their differences. When you've had nobody, the desire to have a loving family dynamic life is either all-consuming, or it's absent altogether. He'd gotten lucky and been adopted at the age of nine. For his foster parents to do that had meant everything to him. Upon leaving home he'd joined the Army, transferred to the Royal Marines after basic training, and found himself with an additional family. When you're in life-and-death situations with people, the bonds that are created are unbreakable. Family meant everything to him, and when he'd had differences of opinion with them, he made sure that all arguments were kept low-key, regardless of how strong his emotions or conviction in his position might be.

"None. I guess that if the sister does inherit the farm, it'll be sold. If they'd planned to leave their money to charity or someone else, it'll still end up on the market unless it's left to someone with a farming background."

Fletcher fell silent to think about the whole connection. The crossroads were the center of things and he was beginning to wonder if it was the farms or the farming families who were the real target. What he couldn't yet work out was who could gain from this and how they would achieve that gain. He voiced his thoughts to Quadrado.

"I can see why you think that, but you're not aware of the challenges facing dairy farmers. It's tough to make a living unless you have a certain acreage and head of cattle. Even then it's hard work to turn a profit. There's more money to be made in contracting than there is in farming these days." She cast a glance in the general direction of Meadowfields. "Pop is often complaining about how much harder it is to make money farming than it used to be. More and more dairy farms are going out of business. Pop hasn't said as much to me, but Peter's told me Meadowfields has been close on a couple of occasions. How would anyone stand to gain from the farms going bust?"

"That's what I hoped you might know." Fletcher pulled a face. "If he hadn't also been attacked last night, I'd have said Robert Kearney making an offer for White Birch was suspicious. We need to look at the hard facts. All four farms bordering that crossroads have seen at least one homicide or an attempted homicide. If it's not the farmers who are the target, it has to be the farms."

"It can't be. There's dozens of farms round here that are just the same as the ones by the crossroads. Hundreds even. You're wrong, Fletcher. We need to consider other angles."

"Maybe we do." Fletcher plucked his keys from the dresser. "I have an idea, but I need to check a couple of things alone before I say anything about it, in case it's a wild goose chase. I'll be in touch."

Fletcher climbed into his SUV and started the engine. His ideas were all about the farms and he needed a break from Quadrado's company while he dug into them.

CHAPTER SIXTY-THREE

Quadrado picked up the Medford PD's reports on the latest two homicides. As with the others, nothing of note had been found at the kill site. The coroner's initial inspection of the victims had suggested he expected to find they'd been killed by the same knife that had ended three other lives.

No matter what she tried, Quadrado couldn't make any sense of the homicides. Fletcher's insistence the crossroads was at the center of things didn't work because of Marcia Jamieson. She'd been killed more than forty miles away. Had she not borne the same hashtag signature as the local victims, Quadrado might have thought she'd been killed by someone different to the others.

What Fletcher was looking into was a mystery to her. He had a knack for unusual thinking, and could often bring ideas from the left-field as well as follow clues in a more traditional fashion. Rather than waste time trying to second guess what his latest idea was, she was content to let him do his own thing for the time being.

Quadrado's feelings towards Fletcher were the source of much introspection for her. He was a smart guy with a sharp wit, yet he could be infuriating without even knowing it. Cynical and hard-nosed, he was a killer who had no qualms about inflicting pain or ending lives. He was haunted by the murder of his wife, yet he was kind to others and, for all his cynicism, he wasn't misogynistic, racist or had any of the other traits she found deplorable. He'd saved her life, yet he drove her crazy. And there was the fact that if he did identify the killer, his own life was at risk. For all he was more than capable in his own right, they were tracking a deadly killer and she'd never forgive herself if anything happened to him because she'd requested his help.

If a friend had explained those feeling to her, Quadrado would have suspected the friend had a thing for the guy in question. That wasn't the case for her, though. Although Fletcher was good enough looking, she'd never once felt any glimmer of a physical attraction to him. Her feelings towards Fletcher were of gratitude, exasperation and fear. Not fear of him, but fear for him. Putting aside the twin threats from the killer and the possibility he'd face the homicide charges hanging over him, Fletcher possessed a side to him that was self-destructive in its stubbornness to see things through to a conclusion he found satisfying. He didn't know how to quit, how to accept defeat. Should it come to it, she knew she didn't want to arrest him. There was also the question of whether he'd allow her to do that. His morals and principles would prevent him from harming her, but he could put her into an impossible situation by resisting the arrest or going on the run. Though she knew those same ideals might also see him acquiesce and accept his fate with dignity.

A beep from her phone had her scrabbling to check the email that had come in. It was from Heidi, the geo-profiler. Quadrado opened the email while mentally crossing her fingers it would give her the solid lead she was so desperate for.

Heidi had done her usual high standard of work. She'd assessed all the data Quadrado had sent her, including the update from this morning, cross-referenced the known factors and made informed suggestions based on the regionality of the killings.

In short, Heidi's report stated that the area surrounding the farms by the crossroads was of great importance to the killer. Marcia Jamieson's homicide was an aberration Heidi suspected was rooted in a personal dislike of her or her family, rather than the main reason driving him to kill farmers in his chosen area. She also suggested it was a seemingly random killing to throw off the investigation and divert police attention from the crossroads. The carvings on the victims' foreheads was the killer's way of instilling terror as it was a suggestion more people would die, while also doubling as a display of the killer's prowess by laying claim to each of his victims.

An addendum to the report suggested anyone who lived within three or four miles of the crossroads could be at serious risk, as Heidi was convinced the killer would strike again and again until he'd achieved whatever twisted aim he had.

The idea that she was also being tested by Soter was one that galled Quadrado. She'd been through more tests than she could remember to earn her place in the FBI. There had been refresher courses and many lectures on procedural doctrines and professional ethics, yet here she was, being tested again with the passing grade potentially being subject to her achieving results by methods that contradicted everything she'd been taught.

As much as it was alien to Quadrado to think this way, she knew she was being driven by a desire to bring justice to the door of Jane's killer, while also repaying Fletcher for saving her life. Her own pride wanted her to be the one to solve the case, but if she was first to the solution, she'd make damned sure Fletcher got the credit instead of her.

She checked her texts and found a message from him suggesting they meet at the diner in a half hour.

CHAPTER SIXTY-FOUR

Fletcher clocked the atmosphere as soon as he stepped into the diner. There was a hush in the room that was wrong for the number of people sitting at the Formica-topped tables. In any eatery, there's a clatter of cutlery and crockery, chatter from the patrons and discussions with servers. All of that was happening, except it was muted.

The cause was obvious as soon as his eyes picked out Quadrado. She was alone in his usual booth and there were two guys in front of her.

It was a story as old as time. A girl alone in a public place like a diner or bar might garner a certain amount of attention. A pretty girl will often get more than attention. The two guys would be hitting on her, testing their pickup lines to see if they could get a bite.

Fletcher eased a shoulder against a wall and let the situation play out in front of him; with the research he'd done having paid dividends, he could spare a minute to let Quadrado handle the situation. He made sure she could see he was there if needed. It was instinctive to want to tell the guys to take a hike, but he respected Quadrado too much to act like an overbearing Neanderthal and waltz in to her rescue unbidden.

The guys were average working men around the same age as she was. They wore construction clothes that were coated with dust and other stains. Fletcher guessed they'd be working in the area and desired some female company. Whether they had a wife or girlfriend at home was a moot point to them if the way they were hitting on Quadrado was anything to go on.

One still wore his tool belt, while the other sported a style of flat top that had gone out of fashion years ago.

Tool Belt placed his palms on the table and leaned towards Quadrado. Whatever he said to her wasn't well received, as she shook her head and shrank back a fraction. Flat Top slid into the seat opposite her and tried his luck.

Someone as pretty as Quadrado would be used to unwanted attention. She would have built up her defense mechanisms, learned ways to say no that would be heeded by the majority of men. She opened her mouth, raised an arm and pointed to the door.

They said something to her that brought a distasteful look to her face and made for the exit.

As they walked towards him Fletcher eased his shoulder off the wall and began crossing the room to join Quadrado.

Flat Top bumped Tool Belt's arm to get his attention. When he spoke his voice was loud enough for the whole diner to hear. "That damned beaner is a total lesbo, dude."

It was a typical act of face-saving bravado from the guy. All the same, Fletcher couldn't let such a slur pass.

His right arm came up in a halt gesture. "Stop right there, guys. I'm a friend of the woman you've just been speaking to and I'm sure she doesn't care for the way you've just insulted her. I think it would be polite of you to turn around, go over to her table and apologize."

"Screw you." Tool Belt drew himself to his full height. "Who are you, the Good Manners Police?"

"I told you, I'm her friend. If you want to know who I represent, that'd be the Royal Marine Corps."

Flat Top eased himself into a wider stance and set his hands ready for combat. Tool Belt did the same and mirrored his buddy's martial arts position.

CHAPTER SIXTY-FIVE

"Guys, I'm telling you now, and I'm telling you once and once only, I don't have time for this. Go make your apology and leave, because if you don't—" Fletcher let the threat hang. His hands were loose at his sides and he'd eased himself on the balls of his feet ready to move with pace when required.

"As I already said, screw you."

"Your choice." Fletcher raised his voice so the whole diner would be able to hear his words. "This pair of jerks just insulted a local girl, a local girl who I might add is an FBI Special Agent, and are refusing to apologize. Now it looks as if they're going to get physical with me. I want you all to know the facts before I kick their asses."

Flat Top looked at his buddy. Whether he was looking for instruction or backing, Fletcher didn't know. Didn't care. They'd crossed a line and he was about to kick their asses back to the right side of it.

Neither of them backed away or made any move to stand down. The news about them trying to hit on an FBI agent wasn't enough to make them think twice about getting into a fight.

"Enough." Quadrado stepped in front of Fletcher and flashed her badge at the guys. "My name is Special Agent Zoey Quadrado and I will arrest the crap out of anyone who starts a fight in here." She jerked a thumb at the door. "Now beat it before I change my mind and let him kick your asses."

Flat Top and Tool Belt did as they were told, so Fletcher led Quadrado back to the booth.

"What was all the macho bull about? I'd already told them to take a hike and I don't need you to make assholes apologize to me. If I want an apology I'll get it myself."

Fletcher knew she was right. Now Flat Top and his buddy had left, he realized he'd wanted the fight more than the apology he was asking for. It was the looming deadline that was behind it. For all he was trying to stay calm about it, he was worried, and that worry was manifesting itself as misplaced anger and nervous energy.

He should have followed his own lead and left Quadrado to deal with it. All he'd achieved was a waste of time and yet another reason for Quadrado to be mad at him.

She filled him in on the results from the geo-profiler. He was pleased to hear there was someone who backed up his theory about the crossroads, although he wasn't sure how having support was any help at this stage.

"What do you figure?" It wasn't quite an accusation or an "I told you so," but it made his point.

"That to a degree you were right about the locality of the kills." She pursed her mouth. "Although I'm not sure we needed a geo-profiler to work out that there was locality."

"Maybe not, but it does give an interesting theory regarding Marcia Jamieson, while also hinting at a different motive for the crossroads killings. Have you checked the investigation into her killing? Are the cops looking at Marcia and the rest of the Jamieson family to see if they have any enemies?"

"It'd be nice if it was that easy, wouldn't it?" Quadrado gave a tired smile. "So what have you got, Fletcher? What's this idea you've been following up?"

"Your talk about Broken Spur probably being sold got me thinking. I know I'm an outsider to this world, but from what I understand, farms are generally handed down from generation to generation and are only sold when there's no family member left, or the ones who are can't keep them going. Sure, some will sell due to bankruptcy or for other reasons, but for the most part, they stay in a family for generations." He looked at her and saw the nod of agreement. "I know I could have asked you the question, but I wanted an accurate answer rather than an anecdotal one. So I went to the library and used their computer to look up the records for Taylor County. Specifically I looked at the farms which were sold. According to Google, Taylor County is just over two and a half thousand square kilometers or a shade under a thousand square miles. Wikipedia states there were a thousand and ninety farms in 1995. I took a look at the sales of farms between then and now. There weren't many of them. In fact, I'd go so far as to say that considering I was looking at a twenty-five-year period, there weren't many at all. This caused me to dig even deeper and I looked at the sales of farms in the areas surrounding the crossroads. None of the farms in this area have changed hands at all in that time."

"I could have told you that."

"I know you could. And I mean you no insult when I ask if you could have told me with certainty the things I researched as hard facts. For instance could you have told me that while the majority of farms that were sold were bought by neighboring farmers, or at least ones whose farms were close by? Could you have told me that while farms were growing in size, two neighboring farms were only purchased once in the space of five years in the whole county? Could you have told me that not once in the time frame had neighboring farms been sold within a year of each other?"

"You're right, I couldn't, but what are you getting at?"

Fletcher licked his lips before speaking. "I think someone wants the farmers to sell up. I think someone wants to buy the farms for themselves and they're killing people to make the sales happen."

CHAPTER SIXTY-SIX

Fletcher ordered a flat iron steak with extra fries from the server and accepted the refill of coffee she offered him. He needed the energy the food would give him. As he so often did, he'd made sure his meal was packed with protein and carbs. Quadrado went for a Caesar salad.

While they waited on their meals coming, Quadrado picked at his theory. That was fine by Fletcher, he'd picked at it plenty himself.

"So, working our way through the victims, let's look at each one individually so I can follow your logic."

To Fletcher she had a skeptical quality about her tone. He wasn't offended by it. In her position he'd be the same and he welcomed her picking at his theory as she was smart enough to spot any faults in his logic.

"Fair enough." Fletcher gestured at her. "Do you want to start?"

"Jane doesn't fit with your theory. Her in-laws own the farm and her husband is set to take it over when his father eases off."

"You're right. I had trouble with that too. But here's the clincher—she was only going to milk to do Carl a favor as he'd been up all night. Carl was the one who was supposed to be walking round the corner not her."

Quadrado's hand flew to her mouth and she blinked back tears. "You mean she was killed for nothing. That her death was a mistake?"

"If my thinking is right, that's what happened." He gave her a moment to compose herself and then picked up the tale. "Walt Renard's homicide has already precipitated the sale of his farm. I think Elsie Renard offering it to Kearney first will have thwarted the killer's plans for the time being. It may explain the attempt to kill Kearney, although I think he'd have been targeted at some point anyway."

"What about Marcia Jamieson, where does she fit in? She was a farmer's daughter and there are a clutch of brothers in line to take the farm on anyway, either singly or as a partnership."

Marcia's place on the list of victims was the most suspect and the reasoning Fletcher had for her inclusion was the most outlandish part of his theory. "Can I come back to Marcia?"

"Whatever, it's your theory."

The sudden tiredness in Quadrado's voice touched something in Fletcher. For the first time he considered her position during the last week. Her best friend had been killed and she wasn't able to look into the homicide herself. As a backup option, she'd contrived to have him involved and Soter had agreed to the request although he'd set conditions of his own to test them both. She'd had to deal with his pressing for answers, the case she was working as an FBI agent and whatever bull Soter was sending her way while trying to grieve for her friend. Sleep would have been a rarity for her, as when she got through her workload, she'd have had time to think of the friend she'd lost.

"Okay, jumping forward to Bettsina and Ken Pickworth. You yourself said earlier that their farm will surely go up for sale." He paused to slurp his coffee. "Now, if as I suggested, Carl was the real target instead of Jane, what do you think would happen to Greenacres Farm?"

"It would eventually get sold. Carl's folks have more or less retired in terms of the help they give him. All his father does is criticize and belittle him. I've never understood how Carl hasn't turned round and told him where to get off."

"That's pretty much what I thought regarding the future of Greenacres Farm. So, three homicide sites would have resulted in three sales. Now we have to look back at the third homicide before we try to predict the sixth."

Quadrado pulled a face then straightened her features as the server approached with their meals.

"I still can't see how she'd fit the pattern."

"Neither can I, and that's why I think she was chosen as a victim."

They both fell silent as the server put their food in front of them. Once she'd left Fletcher picked up some fries with his fingers and pressed them into his mouth.

"You mean she was killed for the sole purpose of messing with the investigation?"

"Exactly. There's no logical connection between her and any of the other victims. Her folks will be devastated by her homicide, but it's not likely that they'll sell because of it. She might not even have been specifically selected as the victim. It could have been any member of her family who happened to be available. To my way of thinking it was a random killing at a specific location. The name of the victim didn't matter to the killer, all that mattered to him was that he recorded a kill somewhere else than near that crossroads. He was screwing with the investigation. Making us and the cops wonder where he'd execute his next kill. I think he might well do the same for number six."

"That poor girl. And if you're right, murdered just to try to cover the tracks of a killer." Her eyes turned his way with a beseeching look. He guessed she wanted him to explain how someone could do such a thing. He couldn't. He was as bereft of understanding as she was. Finally she spoke again. "You said about predicting the next victim. Who do you think it'll be, assuming it's not someone else random to throw us of the scent?"

"Robert Kearney. The killer has had one go at him already. I reckon he'll be back to finish the job. If my theory about Jane being the wrong victim is correct, he might also go after Carl Friedrickson again."

"You're right." Quadrado made as if to stand. "We should go warn them."

"We should. But first we eat. We're both close to running on empty and the killer strikes in the early hours of the morning. We've got hours and I need to pick your brain before we go our separate ways again."

"What do you want to know?"

"I want you to tell me about Robert Kearney and the people whose farms border the four at the crossroads. We need to identify anyone who might be a potential target. Start with Kearney; I want to know who owns his farm, what family he has and so on, and then do the same for all the other farms abutting the four."

Fletcher took out a notepad and jotted details as he listened to Quadrado. Kearney was the sole owner of Calvertsholm and had no family who were likely to take over the farm. This meant that if anything happened to him, his farm would be sold. It explained the attack the previous night and, if Fletcher's theory was correct, put him squarely in the killer's sights.

Long term, it'd be straightforward to see who bought the farms and then look for evidence linking them to the homicides, but the number of people who would die before that happened was unknown and waiting to see couldn't be sanctioned in any way. And that was without factoring in the deadline that loomed over him.

Before long, Fletcher had several pages of notes and a list of people who looked to be prime targets.

When they'd covered all the possibilities from the farms ringing the four at the center of things, Fletcher eased out of his seat and stretched his muscles. "Right, we've now got something to go at. You're the local so I think it's best if you go round and warn the farmers who we've identified as high risk."

"What are you going to do?" Quadrado flicked a strand of hair from her face as she looked at him.

"I'm going to find out more about the core samples that came from Kearney's place. Maybe it's not the farms themselves that are important, but what's under them. I think that someone knows something about what's under that land that wasn't in the report."

"How are you going to do that? The lab is closed until Monday."

"If you get me the names and addresses of a couple of their lead analysts, I'll do the rest." He gave her a steady look. "The less you know, the happier you'll be."

CHAPTER SIXTY-SEVEN

The last traces of daylight were dipping below the horizon when Quadrado exited her sedan and went towards the homestead at Calvertsholm. The sounds and smells of a farm were familiar to her and triggered a real sense of nostalgia.

She'd grown up running around Meadowfields and other farms with Peter, Jane and a clutch of other kids of a similar age. Parental care at the time had been little more than an instruction not to get into trouble and to be home in time for dinner, or in the winter months, before it had gotten dark. They had been good days, when innocence had made the future seem the most magical place on earth. What she wouldn't give for a game of hide-and-seek in the corn rows with Jane again. Or a trip to the river where they'd swim and splash each other as they shrieked their delight.

Robert Kearney walked out of a barn before she could get to the house. He had a shotgun in the crook of his arm and his face was a mess of cuts and bruises. One eye was swollen until there was nothing more than a slit to look out of. His cheeks bore grazes and bruising, a nasty split above his good eye looked raw and painful and there was a general swelling to his face that spoke of a brutal exchange of punches.

"Hey, Zeke. Good to see you. How's life as a feebie?"

"Good, thanks." She gave a little wave at his face. "I'd ask how you are, but I can see for myself."

"Nothing wrong with me that won't heal. I got lucky, he didn't bust any of my teeth."

Quadrado wasn't sure if he was joking or being serious. For someone as tight with money as Kearney was, an expensive trip to the dentist would add a grievous insult to the injury already received.

"I'm not here officially, but I suppose you've heard that I'm looking into the homicides with a friend of mine."

"Yeah, I've heard. It's a good job you are, as the local cops, well…"

He didn't have to finish his sentence. Everyone in the area knew the Medford PD weren't capable of anything more than keeping order and doling out traffic tickets. It was the primary reason she'd drafted in Fletcher.

"I'm not going to beat about the bush, Robert, you were attacked last night, and while you did very well to defend yourself, you were a target then and we think the killer will come back to finish the job he started."

Kearney patted the shotgun. "Let him try. I'll not get caught by surprise a second time."

"Can you talk me through what happened?" Quadrado found herself doing one of the shrugs she found so irritating when Fletcher did them. "I've read the reports from the cops who spoke to you, but as you said before, well…"

Quadrado leaned against a wall and listened as he talked. Robert Kearney was someone she'd known and liked since childhood. He was fifteen or so years older than she was. Always helpful and kind. He'd given lifts to her and her friends as they were walking back from one of their childhood adventures. And there was that time in the Tavern where he'd stepped in when a drunken stranger had squared up to Peter. Since his parents had passed, he'd been a regular Thanksgiving guest at the Quadrado house and made for good company with his repertoire of impressions and jokes.

"It was the middle of the night. I was tired from keeping watch after what happened with my barn, so I busied myself fixing a problem I've been having with the feeder mechanism when I heard a noise behind me. Like a shoe scuffing a stone against concrete. I spun round and there he was. This masked man with a knife in his hand. He came at me with the knife raised, like he was going to stab me *Psycho*-style. I managed to block his arm and then we fought. Damn he was tough. Punched like a mother... er, flipper."

"What about the knife, did he try and stab you again?"

"He did, but I'd grabbed a wrench to use as a weapon. I must've caught his knuckle as when the wrench deflected the knife he yelped and dropped it. We traded some punches and I clocked him one with the wrench. He went down to one knee; I thought I was winning but he hit me in a place no man likes to be hit."

"What did he do then?"

"He grabbed his knife and was coming for me so I rolled towards where I'd left my shotgun." He patted its stock. "He saw what I was going for and ran off before I could shoot him."

"Sounds like you were lucky."

"I guess so." A determined look filled Kearney's eyes. "So was he. So help me, if I get another chance at him, he won't be running off again."

Quadrado ignored the admission of intent to kill, or at the least cause grievous injury. She didn't blame Kearney for wanting to defend himself and his property. "What can you tell me about the guy who attacked you? I know you've said he was wearing a mask. Was he tall or short, fat or thin? Did he speak at all? Did he have anything distinguishable about him at all?"

Quadrado went through each point one by one with Kearney, trying to build a profile for the killer. By the time they'd finished, she'd learned the killer was of average height and build, had blue eyes, white skin and a hell of a hard punch. Kearney hadn't noticed anything unusual about him. His hands were gloved and had appeared normal in size. There had been no tattoos showing on the exposed parts of his arms where the gloves ended just short of the jacket.

"Do you know if any of your punches managed to bust your attacker's nose or lips?"

Quadrado was hoping for a blood sample. That would give them a solid lead, a person to apprehend and that above anything else was what they needed.

"I don't know. I didn't see any blood, but that doesn't mean I didn't make him bleed. That ski mask of his would have hidden it anyway. I wish I could be more help. I really do."

For another half hour, Quadrado pushed and probed as she sought to dig out any slight detail that would help them. The fight had taken place at the edge of the milking parlor, and by the time the cops had arrived, a hundred cows had trodden past destroying evidence with their feet and lack of toilet training.

Kearney's descriptions of the attacker's knife were vague. It was long and thin, silver in color and gripped in the attacker's left hand. The coroner's reports had stated a long thin knife had been used for the homicides. This backed up their theories that the killer was also Kearney's attacker. It also interested Quadrado the knife had been held in the attacker's left hand. Only about ten percent of the population was left-handed. This cut down the list of potential suspects in a massive way. Or at least it would if they had a list of suspects. The counterpoint to this was the coroner's reports on Jane and Walt had suggested the attacker was right-handed. Could they be ambidextrous? Or had Robert or the coroner made a mistake?

"What are your plans for tonight, Robert?"

"You asking me on a date, Zeke?" Kearney's mocking smile diffused any seriousness he might have imbued in his question.

"Hardly." Quadrado knew he was just being his usual jokey self. "I'm asking you where you're planning to sleep. I don't think it's a good idea for you to stay here alone. I'd be a lot happier if you'd stay at the motel or go over to your girlfriend's place."

A lazy shake of the head. "Not going to happen. Number one, the only person I'll ever allow to drive me off Calvertsholm will be an undertaker. Number two, I'm not paying for a bed in a motel when I've got a perfectly good one here. Number three, I'm not dating anyone so that's not an option. Don't you worry about me, I'll be fine."

She talked to him for another ten minutes, trying to persuade him to leave the farm, but eventually walked away, warning him not to take the law into his own hands.

By the time she fired up the sedan, Quadrado was torn between asking the Medford PD to send someone to guard Kearney and pitying him for having to face this alone.

CHAPTER SIXTY-EIGHT

Rochester, Minnesota wasn't a place Fletcher had even heard of until a few hours ago. It was where the core samples taken from Calvertsholm had been sent for analysis. From what he'd seen of it so far, it appeared to be a typical Midwest city with its good and bad areas.

He had two names and addresses from Quadrado's look into Kasson Analysis. The lead analyst, Vince Whitman, and his assistant, Quint Gilligan.

As the lead analyst, Whitman was the more probable of the two to be a key holder, so it was his house Fletcher was sitting outside. Not the best neighborhood in town, but by no means the worst. The house was large enough to be at least a three bedroom. The car on the drive might be a minivan, but it was a new model and polished well enough to reflect shards of light from the streetlamps. Before coming to this part of town, Fletcher had visited an ATM and maxed out every card he had with him.

A light was on in an upstairs room and there was the flicking of lights from a downstairs room that spoke of someone watching TV in a darkened room.

It told him the house was occupied. With the time approaching midnight on a Saturday, he'd been unsure as to whether he'd find either man at home. But someone was in Whitman's house. The question was: did Fletcher knock on the door or let himself in and surprise Whitman so he was sure to have the upper hand?

For once he decided to do things with the least upheaval for those whose help he needed.

His knuckles rapped on the green panel door.

A woman answered the door. She was late forties to early fifties and had the look of someone who'd ambushed more than one bottle of wine.

When she spoke her voice was earthy with enough slurs to suggest she'd spent the evening with a glass in her hand. "Who are you? We didn't order a pizza."

"I've dropped by to see Vince. Is he home?"

"He's sleeping." A giggle as a finger went to her lips, poking her nose in the process. "Shhhhh."

"Could you wake him for me? I'm afraid it's important. It's to do with his work."

She closed one eye to better see him. "He tests soil and rocks in a laboratory. What's so important you have to come knock-knock-knocking on our door at this time of night?"

Fletcher ignored the way she'd mangled her words and raced to find a plausible answer. He could hardly claim he needed something tested in an emergency. There was also the growing fear in him that Whitman would be as drunk as his wife and would be more passed out than asleep.

"Why don't you go wake him and then you'll find out." Fletcher aimed for a friendly tone, although he'd got the toe of one boot in the door so the woman couldn't slam it in his face. "Trust me, it's to your advantage to hear me out."

"Whatever you say, sugar. Let's go wake him." With that she turned and lurched her way into the house.

Fletcher followed her into a spacious lounge that had a sixty-inch TV and more ceramic thimbles than he knew existed. They were on racks fixed to the walls, lined up in display cabinets and there were a dozen sitting on top of a magazine-strewn table.

A man lay in a rumpled heap on a recliner that had leather upholstery and a near horizontal position. Beside the recliner, a table held a glass of amber liquid and an ashtray filled with cigar butts. The smell of stale alcohol and cigar smoke was offset by the dime store perfume Mrs. Whitman appeared to have bathed in.

The sole of her bare foot was placed on the front of the recliner and, with what appeared to be a practiced move, she pressed down and brought Vince Whitman to a more upright position.

He grumbled in his sleep and snuggled against the stained leather, so she gave his forearm enough of a slap to create an audible crack.

Whitman grunted, cleared his throat and opened an eye as curses fell from his mouth.

"Vince. There's somebody here to see you. Says it's to do with the lab."

Whitman levered himself to a more upright position, fished a pair of glasses from his shirt pocket and peered at Fletcher. "Who the hell are you?"

"My name isn't important. What I want is information about some samples that were tested at Kasson Analysis. I have a thousand bucks in one pocket, and a gun in the other. It's up to you which pocket I put my hand into."

"He'll take the thousand bucks." Whitman's wife flumped down in a chair next to his. "Cash up front, if you don't mind."

Fletcher dropped a glare onto her. "I'm calling the shots here. You have to trust that I'm a man of my word. If I get what I need, you'll get your money and you'll never see me again."

"Hold up a moment, buster." Whitman had straightened himself and was looking at Fletcher with eyes that were bloodshot but focused. "What exactly do you want from me?"

"I want to know about the results of some samples you tested, who at the lab would have access to those results and what you told the customer who paid for the analysis."

Whitman eased himself forward and reached for the shoes that were beside his chair. "We'll need to go to the lab."

Fletcher had figured as much. Kasson Analysis would handle countless samples. To expect a worker to remember one in particular was asking too much.

CHAPTER SIXTY-NINE

Other than Whitman giving directions, the journey to the lab was silent. Kasson Analysis was nothing like Fletcher had expected. In his mind the labs would be a huge sprawling complex with hundreds of employees, machinery so complex it'd need to be built by engineering geniuses and analysists with IQs above one fifty.

If it hadn't been for the sign above the door naming the company, Fletcher would have suspected Whitman had brought him to a random warehouse.

Whitman entered first, keyed a code into an alarm panel and switched on the lights. What Fletcher saw was a neat office workspace. Three doors led out of the room. One at the back he guessed would lead to the parts of the warehouse where the samples were tested and two at the side he figured from the width of the building led to welfare facilities.

"So, want to tell me which samples you want the results of?"

"The ones taken from Calvertsholm Farm in Taylor County, Wisconsin."

Whitman started laughing. At first it was a nervous chuckle that grew into belly laughs that shook his whole body.

It took him a couple of minutes to regain his composure. Time Fletcher spent getting more and more impatient.

"That's priceless. I should have known it'd be that one. Of all the samples, all the earth and rock we've analyzed over the years. You have to ask about *that* batch of samples."

"What are you talking about?" Fletcher was growing uneasy. The fact Whitman remembered the samples meant there was something memorable about them.

Whitman didn't answer. He walked to a file cabinet, rifled a number of pages then plucked out a file. "Here you go. Everything you want to know is in here."

With the file laid on a desk, Fletcher scanned his eyes over every one of the pages. Nothing he saw jumped out at him as the reports were all in geological terms.

"What am I looking for?"

"Here." Whitman's finger jabbed at a particular line among a list of minerals found in the samples tested.

Fletcher looked at the words on the page. He could look all day, but without googling the terms or getting Whitman to explain them, he'd never understand what they meant.

"What are lateritic nickel ore deposits?"

"The mother, grandmother and every female relative you can think of lodes." Like all scientists, Whitman was evangelical when speaking on his chosen subject. "Lateritic nickel ore is generally near the surface so it can be open-cast mined. That's much cheaper than the deep extraction mining which they do for sulfide nickel ore deposits. The people who are sitting on the land over this ore will be richer than Croesus when they sell."

"How big is the deposit likely to be?"

Whitman held his hands wide. "There's no way of knowing without taking more samples from the surrounding area, but there are patterns and lateritic nickel ore deposits are usually big, and by big I mean they stretch for miles around." Whitman seized a sheet of paper from the file and thrust it under Fletcher's nose. "It's like coal mines used to be. You don't just get one bit. If you're lucky you find a decent seam. This is the richest seam I've heard of. Mines will run anywhere from between a half percent to two percent for a really good one. These samples are at an unheard of 2.5 per cent. I tell you, buster. Short of finding solid gold or diamonds, there's not much that could have topped these samples. The way the shape of the seam is looking from the areas tested, it's a sure thing to say this guy is sitting on only a tiny fraction of it."

Everything became clear for Fletcher. Calvertsholm was sitting above the ore and there was a strong chance that a rich seam would also extend under the other farms. Nickel was in ever greater need due to the rise of its use in batteries, and with the auto industry moving towards electric cars, there would be a hugely increased need for it.

Fletcher grabbed at the file and looked through them until he found a map of the farm. "Was the ore found all over the farm or in a specific location?"

"The samples which contained lateritic nickel ore deposits were found in this area." Whitman's finger showed an arc right where the crossroads was. "The farmer who commissioned these samples will be worth hundreds of millions for what he has under his land. As for the folk who own the land beyond that, I'd guess they'd get billions of dollars provided they strike the right deal. It's my estimation, based on thirty years of experience, that the deposits only just touch this guy's farm, that they extend away from this point for several miles.

It was all Fletcher could do not to let out a low whistle as he contemplated the numbers at play. They were more than enough to incite someone to use homicide as a way to get their hands on the farms.

CHAPTER SEVENTY

Now that he knew where the money angle was coming from, Fletcher had to work out who knew about the farms sitting on top of rich nickel deposits. These would be his list of suspects. It might be late and he might be exhausted, but for the first time since learning of his deadline, he had the feeling he might just meet it.

As much as he wanted to call Quadrado, he knew his priority was to extract all the information he could get from Whitman before he did. He could speak to Quadrado on the drive back to Medford unless his investigation took him elsewhere.

"These deposits, who would know they existed? I'm guessing that as well as your client, your lab workers, your boss, whoever owns the company and a secretary or two?"

Fletcher didn't want to think about how many people each of the people in the know might have told.

"It's actually fewer people than you might think. I ran these samples myself. There's only two of us who work in the lab and Quint was on vacation. For all that this is huge news, we do have a level of security about what we do. I told Quint when he came back from his vacation but I didn't tell him where the samples came from. With the sums of money involved in a find like this, we operate on a need-to-know basis. Apart from myself, the only person from Kasson to know about these deposits existing is our owner and he is my direct boss."

"Is it possible he'd tell anyone about them, you know, sell the information on?"

Whitman gave a vehement snort. "You're joking, he's so tight-lipped he wouldn't tell you the time if you asked."

"What about a secretary who'd send the reports out? They'd be sure to know, wouldn't they?"

"You've no idea of the scale of what we do. We have a number of guys who put different slices of the core samples into a variety of instruments for testing. Those machines feed their data to our computers. We also have other slices undergoing chemical analysis for different minerals and elements. Those results also go into the computer. The guys who undertake the work on the slices aren't geologists like me. They're regular guys who we've trained to do repetitive processes. Believe me when I say there's not one of them who understands what they're doing. As for a secretary sending out reports, we tend to handle larger public contracts as well as a few private ones. For the most part I translate the week's findings on a Friday afternoon and email it to whichever customer we're working for that week. In the case of private samples like the ones we're discussing, that was four days' worth of work and the report would be emailed off the day we had all the information collated."

"Okay. So it's just you and your boss who'd know about the deposits." Fletcher held up a silencing hand. "You said you'd told your colleague Quint about the nickel deposits, without saying where they'd come from. Say he wanted to find out which samples you were talking about. Could he do that from your office records?"

"I guess he could, but he's no interest in money. His parents are rich. He's only got a job here until his trust fund matures and then he'll be moving into the family business."

"Which is?" Fletcher knew existing wealth didn't stop most people wanting more money; in fact it was often the case the more money people had, the more they wanted; and the information held in an unlocked drawer of the Kasson lab was worth many millions to the right person.

"Medical research. Quint's family were involved in the Mayo Clinic from the early days. They're all scientists and Quint's way of rebelling was to not follow them into that kind of lab. His life revolves around tinkering with cars and motorbikes. Guess he likes getting his hands dirty."

Quint Gilligan was Fletcher's top suspect for the sharing of the information. By getting his hands more metaphorically dirty with a trading of information, he'd be able to escape the family shackles, perhaps even eclipse his family's wealth. He'd be truly independent and could work on his vehicles as much as he wanted to.

"Okay. What about your cybersecurity, does your server have firewalls, anti-virus protection and are they password protected?"

"All of the above. Mr. Morton takes such things very seriously." Whitman took his glasses off to clean them. "Maybe you should be looking at the other end of the transaction for the leak. Maybe it's the client's secretary or accountant who's spoken out about this? What does it all matter anyway?"

"People are being murdered on the farms where the deposits are. Your client is lucky to be alive—he came face-to-face with the killer last night. Someone is using homicide to drive people into selling the farms." Fletcher pulled a face. "I don't mean to sound mistrusting, but are you able to prove to me that you informed your client about what's under his land?"

Whitman shot a look of pure venom Fletcher's way. "As it happens, I can." He crossed to a computer, entered a long password and opened an email program. There was a lengthy list of files which he scrolled through until he brought up his correspondence with Robert Kearney.

Whitman had used layman's terms in the report and had spelled out the size of the windfall coming Kearney's way.

Kearney had responded with a polite thank-you followed by a threat to sue Kasson Analysis for a breach of confidentiality should this information ever be shared.

"There's one last thing I have to ask. How do I know that you've not sold this information on? After all, you've taken my thousand bucks without knowing who I am. That tells me two things: number one, you can be bought."

"And what would number two be?" There was amusement in Whitman's voice rather than offense at Fletcher's accusation.

"That you're not worried about getting the company sued. This suggests to me that you've already sold the info on once so a second time doesn't matter. You've worked out I'm not representing a large company as they don't send their men out late on a Saturday night with a thousand bucks to make the finds. They'd entrap you somehow and then blackmail you into feeding them everything they wanted."

"There is, of course, a number three you haven't mentioned. You show up at our home and lay down a very polite threat that either I take your thousand bucks to do what you want, or you use a gun to make me do it. Tell me, in my position, what would you have done?"

Fletcher wheeled away from Whitman, exited the lab in a series of long strides, and climbed into the SUV sickened at what he'd become. He was now a tame thug, sent to get whatever was needed from innocents using whatever methods he deemed necessary. It had been the same with Clay and Sweetie. They hadn't deserved to be startled then threatened either. The coercion of bad guys would never give him the slightest pause for thought, but the fact he'd threatened innocents to further his own ends wasn't something he could ever be proud of.

As always with the case, there were far more questions than answers and the biggest question of all was who else knew about the nickel deposits.

CHAPTER SEVENTY-ONE

Fletcher put in a call to Quadrado as soon as the wheels of his SUV began turning. She needed to know what he did and he wanted to find out what she had to say about her own investigation.

She answered on the third ring, and although she sounded tired, it only took a few words from her to assure him her brain was still running at top speed.

"So, Fletcher, these nickel deposits you're talking about, they're worth a fortune, right? Yet Robert never mentioned them. In fact when I asked him about the drilling he had done, he told me it was a waste of time and money."

Fletcher ran through the reasons for Kearney to lie. The obvious one was he wanted to keep his windfall secret. Yet there wasn't a lot to gain by keeping it secret as his land was only above a small part of the nickel seam. Except soon he wouldn't be in the same situation. White Birch was slap-bang above the ore and he was about to become its new owner.

Everything clicked for Fletcher. He'd looked past where his focus should have been aimed. Everyone investigating the homicides had.

Before he voiced his suspicions to anyone, he needed more confirmation. "Kearney was beaten up last night, wasn't he? How did his injuries look?"

"He had some superficial cuts and bruises; they looked painful, but nothing life-threatening."

"Did he tell you about the attack? If he did, can you walk me through it?"

Fletcher listened to Quadrado with great care as he drove with an increasing abandon. His thoughts weren't pleasant ones and he wanted to get back to Medford as soon as he could.

There was a hundred and seventy miles between Rochester and Medford. Three hours driving at the speed limit. He pushed his right foot down until he was at a speed that would see him arrive in two. At this time of night traffic was light so—as long as a cop didn't stop him—he would be able to drive without interference from other road users.

He continued his conversation with Quadrado. "Okay. What do you make of his story?"

"What do you mean?"

"I think he's lying. And I think he's lying because he's the killer. Think about his story. The killer made a noise that alerted Kearney and allowed him to defend himself. That's out of character. The killer hasn't made a mistake before now. Not when creeping through people's houses. Not when waiting for them to come into range."

"That's preposterous. I've known him all my life."

"Think about it, Quadrado." Fletcher paused while he overtook a station wagon that was traveling at less than half his speed. "He's the only one who's survived an attack by this killer. A killer who picked up his knife and ran off when it became clear he couldn't finish the job he'd come to do. He's also the only one to know about the nickel ore. He's also the one who swooped in and offered to buy White Birch within a day or two of Walt Renard being murdered. How much more evidence do you need?"

"Don't get cute. I'm still trying to get my head round this."

"Then you better get your head round things a bit quicker. Meadowfields is also located where the ore is expected to be, so you need to keep your family safe for tonight. Either hole them up in the house and don't leave until I get there or get them away to somewhere safe."

"We're all in the house together. It's probably best we stay where we are." The line went so quiet Fletcher began to think she'd hung up on him. When she spoke again her voice was faint as if she was thinking aloud to herself. "Your reconstructions of the kills. Did you work on the theory the killer held the knife in his right hand?"

"Yeah. Statistically speaking more people are right-handed than left. Why do you ask?" As he waited for her answer, it came to him before she could speak. "Kearney told you the killer held the knife in his left hand, didn't he?"

"Yes."

The one word from Quadrado was enough to confirm Fletcher's worst thoughts. Robert Kearney was trying to drive his neighbors into selling up so he could buy their farms. Once he had a certain acreage under his control, he'd be able to sell to a mining company and sit on a beach somewhere counting his money.

The attacks on the farms would be his doing too. They'd start off by being a way to cause unease among farmers. Perhaps drive some to bankruptcy. The attacks on Calvertsholm would have been him camouflaging his actions by including his own property in his litany of destruction. The same for the attack he claimed to have survived. A few bangs about his own face with a padded fist to cause some swelling and a cut or two and he'd be hailed as a hero, instead of a villain for the people he'd murdered.

"You need to call this in; get a SWAT team to take him down."

"I know. I'm on it."

As Quadrado cut the call, Fletcher urged the SUV to add another 10 mph to its speed. He wasn't sure why, but something was telling him that his part in events was a long way from over.

CHAPTER SEVENTY-TWO

The beep from his phone was enough to wake Geoffrey Elliott from his sleep. A holdover from his days as a regular FBI agent, he'd trained his subconscious to alert him to certain sounds whether he was awake or not.

The beep he'd assigned to the email account he used to contact Quadrado was such a sound.

At this time of night, a message from her could mean several things. His first concern was that Fletcher had absconded from the case rather than face the consequences of failure. The psych profile he'd had drawn up on the man refuted this idea, but there was no telling how someone would react in a situation until they were embroiled in it. Next up was the idea Fletcher had succeeded in pinpointing the killer. A darker thought crossed Elliott's mind and he gave his fingers a mental crossing that there were no more victims. It already looked bad the FBI had been kept out of the investigation and if someone else was to die, there could be repercussions right back to his office.

The worst thought he had was the killer and Fletcher had met and it was the killer who walked away. He'd invested a lot in Fletcher, in getting the backing of his counterparts at the other agencies, to have him fail on a test mission was unthinkable, and he'd be sure to lose face with his peers if that was what had happened.

He fumbled his glasses on and read the message under the covers so as not to wake his wife.

Elliott smiled in the darkness. This was the best possible outcome. There might not be enough real evidence such as forensics and eyewitnesses to guarantee a conviction, but he agreed with Fletcher and Quadrado's choice of suspect. Although a lot of the theorizing was based on circumstantial evidence, everything made sense. Kearney stood to gain hundreds of millions, or possibly billions of dollars, if he could buy up a few of the farms. He had to be the killer.

To Elliott, Kearney was vermin and he only had one solution for vermin. Plus, what he thought was the best way of dealing with a killer like Kearney would double as a final test for Fletcher.

He rose and left the bedroom. No matter how deep a sleeper his wife might be, the conversation he was about to have was one he didn't want her hearing any part of.

CHAPTER SEVENTY-THREE

Quadrado picked up her phone expecting the call to be from Fletcher. It wasn't, no number was displayed on the screen. Her hands trembled as she stabbed the answer button.

A disembodied mechanical voice asked if it was speaking to Special Agent Quadrado.

"You are. Who is calling?"

The voice didn't answer. Instead it went into a series of instructions. Orders really. As each new sentence was completed, Quadrado felt her stomach churn and her skin prickle with unease at the instructions she was receiving.

There was no doubt in her mind that she was speaking to Soter. Once the orders were complete she was told to repeat them back to Soter. She did as she was bidden and as soon as she'd finished, the call was cut.

Quadrado grasped the arm of her chair hard enough to make her fingers ache. Damn Soter. Damn Robert Kearney. And damn Grant Fletcher for being such a macho asshole and getting her involved in this crazy series of events. She calmed a little and realized none of this was Fletcher's fault.

She knew what she had to do. Knew what she *must* do. She didn't want to do it, though; not in any way could she envision a scenario where Soter's instructions made for the best resolution.

Her orders went against everything she believed in. She hadn't joined the FBI to do things like this. She'd joined to hunt criminals so they could be brought before the courts.

All the same, orders were orders, and as much as she hated herself for obeying them, Robert Kearney had to be stopped, and Fletcher had to be kept out of the judicial system.

Quadrado cursed her decision to inform Soter. She'd thought it best he be the one to summon a SWAT team, that he be made aware she and Fletcher had solved the case and identified the killer. It hadn't been in her thoughts Soter may have other ideas on the case's outcome. As soon as she'd heard Soter's instructions, she recognized both she and Fletcher were being handed a final test. She'd known that in her role as an FBI agent, there may come times when she may face death to protect life; what she'd never envisioned was that she might have to order someone to take a life. Order was the wrong word. Fletcher wouldn't take orders from her and she'd never give them. All the same, she'd have to pass on Soter's directive.

She rose from the seat and picked up the keys to her sedan. There were two things she had to do and they could be done at the same time. First off she had to learn where Kearney was, and second she had to bring Fletcher up to speed. As she went to leave the house, she turned back and went to her father's gun cabinet. The key was where it always was, on a hook hidden in one of the drawers below. There was a rifle, a shotgun and a pistol. She took the shotgun and pistol plus spare ammunition for both. The shotgun was an old-fashioned side-by-side one and only held two cartridges, whereas the pistol was a revolver. Both would stop a man. Kill him. Yet neither left too great an error for margin as once their ammo ran out, they were slow to reload, and she wasn't familiar with either weapon. This meant that if she had to pull the trigger, she couldn't afford to miss.

Both weapons were loaded onto the passenger seat of her sedan and she set off towards Calvertsholm. As she dialed Fletcher's number to give him the latest news, she realized Soter's words had been spoken so there'd be no digital evidence of his orders and that his instructions had been a final test, not just for Fletcher, but for her as well.

CHAPTER SEVENTY-FOUR

The traffic around Eau Claire was light enough for Fletcher to keep his foot close to the floor, although he'd eased back to a more respectable speed. Towns meant cops. Cops meant the risk of being pulled over and a lengthy delay. Delays were bad. He needed to be in Medford, yet he was better to be a few minutes later than he'd prefer, than being held up for hours by a small town cop with a big city attitude.

He was just getting onto Highway 29 and gunning the SUV's wimpy engine back towards three-figure territory when Quadrado's call came in. Whatever she was calling about wouldn't be good, he was certain of that. As his hand reached for the phone, his foot pressed down on the gas pedal.

"What's up?"

"I had a call from Soter."

Fletcher's heart sank. Soter wouldn't be the guy's real name, but there was no doubting that he was a tough man who had his own agenda for them.

"What did he want?"

"I emailed him to summon a SWAT team to take down Kearney." There was a guilty pause. "I thought it was for the best. I'm sorry, Fletcher. There's no SWAT team coming. We've been instructed to take Kearney down ourselves. To quote him, and believe me, I don't like repeating these words, we're 'not to bring Kearney in, we have to find him and make it look as if he's the sixth and final victim of the Hashtag Killer'."

"I see." Fletcher did see. Quadrado would have been keen to show Soter they'd achieved their mission. The fact they were being tested would make her want to prove herself to Soter. To show they were both up to the task at hand. Regardless of the content of her email, she'd have also had his best interests at heart too. For all they fought, the bonds that had been forged between them in Georgia were strong.

It had been naïve of her to contact Soter before a SWAT team was summoned. Now she had their orders, any other course of action would be seen as disobedience and would condemn their mission to failure.

Rather than criticize her, he parked his anger and thought about what they needed to do. First off, they had to locate Kearney. The idea he might be out killing again was Fletcher's biggest worry. If that was the case then they'd have to try and intercept him before he struck again. He was too far away to run any kind of surveillance operation himself. That would all have to be down to Quadrado.

"Where are you?"

"In my car on the way to Calvertsholm."

"Good. I'm not familiar with the place and I've looked at so many farms this week, they're all blurring in my mind. Remind me, what's it like in terms of access? Are there roads in and out or could he drive across the fields?"

"There's a track that's the only real way to get in and out as there are ditches or woods that make up his boundaries."

"Good." Fletcher thought for a moment. He knew what he'd do, but it was different asking Quadrado to do it. She might be an FBI agent who'd undergone rigorous training in weapons, but he was an ex-Royal Marine. His training had been in camouflage, surveillance, concealment and he knew more ways to kill a man than he cared to remember. To set her up where he would establish himself would be a folly. There was only one thing for it, he'd have to trust to luck that Kearney would either rest tonight, or would only take the basest precautions on his own property. "What I need you to do is to find a spot that lets you see his lights if he leaves the farm, yet is far enough away so that you're not visible until he's out on the road. Can you think of somewhere?"

"Yeah, I know a place."

"Go there at once. As soon as you're there, park your car but leave the engine running and turn your headlights off. Also, keep your foot off the brake pedal as you don't want to give away your position with the brake lights. Make sure your doors are locked, and if you see any sign of him coming for you, haul ass like you've never hauled ass before."

"Do you think he'll come for me?" Quadrado had tried to hide it, but there was no mistaking the quiver of fear in her voice.

Fletcher didn't want to scare her for no reason, yet she had to be made aware of the facts. If he was in Kearney's position and he found someone watching, he'd see Quadrado as a threat. A threat requiring elimination.

"I don't know. I'd just feel better if you did everything possible to not let him know you're watching him." He had a thought. "Are you armed?"

"I've a pistol and a shotgun with me."

"Good. When you park, keep the pistol in your hand and the shotgun close. The pistol is a better weapon in a confined space."

"I'm pulling up now. It's something of a make-out spot in a clearing of a small wood. There's no one else here so I should be okay, right?"

Fletcher didn't answer. His heart was thinking of her sitting alone and isolated watching and waiting for a killer. It would be an unnerving experience for anyone. Before long, she'd hear imaginary threats. Misdiagnose sounds as the killer stalking his way towards her.

His brain was telling him that if Quadrado was scared, she'd be more alert to any real threat Kearney might present to her. It was cruel not to give her any level of comfort to allay her fears, but being alert was her key to staying alive if Kearney spotted her, so he was content to let her question go unanswered.

She was in position, and he was just less than an hour away. The SUV was slow to respond to the extra pressure on the gas pedal, but he saw the needle begin to creep higher.

CHAPTER SEVENTY-FIVE

Quadrado kept her eyes on the track leading from Calvertsholm to the main road. She was alert to everything as she watched. The hoot of an owl. The rustle of the trees around her as a breeze blew their thinner branches back and forth. The fingers gripping the pistol were stiff and sore from the pressure she was exerting, yet try as she might, she couldn't summon the nerve to swap it to her weak hand in order to flex them and give her circulation a chance to recover.

Whether Kearney would go on one of his missions or not wasn't something she could know. A major part of her hoped he'd stay put so she and Fletcher could go to his place in the morning and bring him down. That would be the easy solution. Walk up as if making a routine visit, whip out their guns and effect a textbook arrest. Nobody would have to die. Nobody would be in any kind of danger anymore and the farmers of Taylor County could go about their business again without fearing for their lives. For all Fletcher was a killer, he wasn't a cold-blooded one. So if they got Kearney to surrender to them, she knew between her and Fletcher they could concoct a story. One where murdering Kearney and making him the sixth victim of the Hashtag Killer didn't have to happen.

A different, more primal part of her psyche was hoping Kearney would emerge again. That she and Fletcher would be able to hunt Kearney down. If he resisted arrest and Fletcher had to get rough with him, that would be fine by her. He'd killed Jane. The best friend she'd ever had. That anyone could ever have. But vengeance wasn't part of Quadrado's genetic makeup. An eye for an eye didn't sit well with her belief system. A second wrong didn't right the first.

If it was to be a brutal takedown, she wasn't sure if she could pull the trigger when it mattered. Only once had she had to pull her trigger during the line of her duty, and although she'd missed her target and kept her composure at the time, when she'd gotten home that night she'd voided her stomach at the thought she might have taken a life.

Fletcher didn't have that problem. He was baked in a different mold to her, to most of the people she'd met. He could take a life or inflict grievous injuries and rationalize them away without a second's thought. In a lot of ways he was like the killers she hunted. Yet by the same token, he was a good man.

She wished he was here with her now. Not just because he'd make her feel safe, nor because he'd know what they should do next, more because he'd be calm, focused and set on his course. Her heart was thumping, her ears were beginning to imagine sounds she was convinced were the omens of an attack from Kearney and the longer she sat alone in the crappy rental sedan, the more she was realizing just how exposed she was.

It would be nice to crack a window to make the noises she heard clearer. To alleviate some of the condensation that was building up in the car. No way was she going to do that. To open a window, even the tiniest crack, was to afford Kearney a way to access the car's interior.

In an effort to calm herself, she cast a glance over both shoulders and saw nothing. There was enough moonlight to show the shape of trees and bushes, but not enough to make them anything more than shadowy outlines.

Quadrado brought her eyes back to the track from Calvertsholm and saw there were lights moving along it. Her pulse quickened as she put the sedan into drive and prepared to follow Kearney.

Kearney could go one of two ways when he joined the road. Left, away from where she'd secreted herself, or right, towards her.

She offered up a prayer Kearney would turn left. For all she was hidden away, if he was heading out to kill, his levels of vigilance would be every bit as high as hers.

He turned right. It was a road she knew well. It went west towards Perkinstown. Arrow straight, it offered little chance for subterfuge, yet it also had few junctions before Perkinstown, therefore he'd be easy to follow at a safe distance.

She eased the sedan out from the make-out site as soon as his taillights were out of view.

With her lights kept low, she picked up the pace until she had built enough speed to rein Kearney in.

As soon as the red glare from his taillights was visible, she eased off the gas, slipped her cell onto her lap and put in a call to Fletcher.

Before he could answer she saw the crimson sparkle of Kearney's brake lights. Quadrado's earlier prayers were blasphemous compared to the ones she was now making. She knew where Kearney had pulled over. Knew the area well. There was a wood there, perhaps five acres in total, with a small lake in the center and trees she'd climbed as a child.

Meadowfields—her childhood home—lay a mile away and there were no other farms in the vicinity. There was another, Westlands, off at a tangent, but Meadowfields was closer. Inside her parents, Peter and his wife and their newborn baby all lay sleeping.

Her foot pressed down on the gas. As she passed where Kearney had pulled off the road, she spied his vehicle and a shaft of moonlight picked out a solitary figure leaving the cover of the wood and setting off towards Meadowfields.

With the threat to her family now confirmed, all thoughts of clemency towards Kearney had disappeared from Quadrado's mind.

She dialed Fletcher again and put the cell to her ear.

"He's moved. He's going across the fields towards Meadowfields. Towards my family. He's around a mile away."

The response from Fletcher was exactly what she wanted. Calm, assured and best of all, he was close by. She listened as he gave her a series of instructions. They would be obeyed. For all she was an FBI Special Agent, stalking a killer at night was a job for a soldier. A job for Fletcher.

CHAPTER SEVENTY-SIX

Fletcher punished the SUV's engine until he got within a mile of Meadowfields. After that he slowed so it was barely turning over. As he'd instructed Quadrado to do, he drove the last mile to the farm without lights. She had maybe a five-minute head start on him, so he ditched the SUV at the end of the track leading to the farm and silently jogged the two hundred yards to Meadowfields.

There wasn't a light on in the house. This was a good sign so far as he was concerned. It meant that Quadrado had followed his instructions and done nothing to alert Kearney there was anyone awake.

He'd told her to gather her family in one room. To stay low, so no shadows gave away their movements to anyone watching the house. He'd told her to cover the door with the shotgun and the windows with the pistol. She'd tried to argue that she ought to be outside with him, but he'd told her she had to protect her family and the best way for them to do that was to split up. Taking enemies down in the dark was his thing. He was the one who was a trained killer. As good as she might be, she'd only learned FBI levels of self-defense. He'd been trained by the Royal Marines. He'd provide the first line of defense, she the last.

By his thinking, Kearney was arriving in plenty of time. Milking wouldn't start for another two hours, so Kearney had a while to set up his latest ambush.

In a sideways appreciation of his opponent, he had to give him credit. The man was making the same moves he himself would:

parking away from the kill site, using the cover of darkness to shroud his movements and making sure that he had a sizable time cushion to prepare his kills. For all he wasn't on home territory, there was a good chance that, as a neighbor, he'd know his way around Meadowfields anyway.

Fletcher was now moving at a fast jog. Quick enough to cover the ground in a hurry, but not so fast as to leave him breathless. Luck was on his side as the homestead of Meadowfields was a lot closer to the roads than most of the farms in the area. This meant he should arrive there before Kearney did.

To Fletcher's right was a small ditch. He kept an eye on it as he continued towards the farm. Halfway there he spotted what he was looking for. An area where there was exposed soil. He bent over there, splashed some water onto the soil, rubbed his hands into the dampened earth then smeared his filthy hands across his face. A second splash got him another pair of fistfuls and he scrubbed the gloop around his neck. As camouflage went, it was rudimentary at best, but rudimentary was still better than nothing. His clothes were either black or dark anyway so they didn't need covering and he was careful not to get his feet wet lest his boots squelch and give voice to his movements.

The closer he got to Meadowfields, the more his vigilance grew. His eyes were now becoming accustomed to the dark, although he hadn't yet developed what he thought of as the optimum level of night sight.

Meadowfields wasn't a place he was too familiar with, although he had a rough mental picture of it.

He was pleased to find his memory was more or less accurate, although if he'd been asked, he'd have said the milking parlor was much closer to the house than it actually was.

Now that he was at the farm he had two main things to achieve. Number one was finding out where Kearney was, and number two was setting a trap for him to walk into.

The setting of a trap for Kearney was something Fletcher was confident about. He knew Kearney's methods, had re-enacted them in his mind often enough. Kearney would look to install himself at a point where someone rounded a corner or exited a doorway.

There was a straight walk from the house's main door to the milking parlor meaning the only corner to be rounded was at the edge of the parlor building.

As that would be the route taken by anyone leaving the house to begin milking that meant there were two ideal points Kearney could choose from as the location to ambush his next victim. There was a barn across the way which would make a good place for Fletcher to hide out and watch both locations.

The problem with holing up in the barn was that it'd be difficult to stalk closer to Kearney once he was in position. All the same, it would give Fletcher the best chance of observing.

He ducked round the parlor building and stalked his way to the barn. A side door allowed him access and he left it ajar enough to surveil both the parlor and the house.

Rather than work on nothing more than assumptions, Fletcher made his way around the barn and looked through a hole in the sheathing timbers where a knot had fallen out.

He had a good view of the route Kearney would be approaching from, so it ought to be a case of watching him approach, waiting until he'd assumed a position at either the house or parlor, and then stalking forward until he was able to disarm Kearney.

As plans went it was simple and straightforward. Simple was good. Fletcher had more than enough experience to know the more complicated a plan, the more there was that could go wrong.

CHAPTER SEVENTY-SEVEN

Fletcher held his stance peering out of the knot hole and watched as Kearney approached Meadowfields. He kept his breathing steady and tried to control his heartbeat. Moments like these were worse for him than the ones when he was in a battle situation. It was a time to hold your nerve, to believe in the plan and to summon courage ready for the fight that was coming.

Sometimes battles would be thrust upon you in an unexpected fashion such as the attacks in the bar, or the fight with Steve Heaton. These were easier to deal with in many ways; there was no time to consider the consequences of failure or for nerves to take hold.

Fletcher much preferred the moments when training and survival instincts took over. To wait in anticipation of battle was to allow the mind room to conjure up negative energy and destructive thoughts. To combat these natural traits, Fletcher turned his mind to his daughter. Wendy had lost one parent, and he was damned if she was going to lose another. Missions like this might involve him risking his life at times, but there was no way he was going to allow a greedy wack job like Robert Kearney deprive Wendy of his presence in her life. For all Soter wanted him to kill Kearney and brand him with the hashtag, that wasn't what Fletcher wanted to do. He had no issue taking a life when necessary, but to take one in cold blood wasn't something he could ever be comfortable with. Screw Soter, he was going to bring Kearney in alive and damn the consequences.

Kearney's approach was subtle. He was stalking towards Mead-owfields. As he neared the farm, he was taking more and more of a slow approach. Fletcher could see Kearney's head swivel as he scanned the areas in front of him.

The route he took saw him circle the barn, so Fletcher returned to the doorway. There were no openings Kearney could use to enter the barn other than this door and the main one which was large enough to admit a huge tractor and was set on rails to slide open or closed.

Fletcher reached a hand behind his back and retrieved his pistol from the waistband of his jeans. He'd have much preferred to have a shotgun or an assault rifle instead of the pistol, but he hadn't wanted to deprive the Quadrado family of their best defensive weapons.

It was too dark for Fletcher to see if Kearney was carrying anything more deadly than his usual knife as his target stalked past the doorway. The fact all of Kearney's kills had been done with a knife boded well for Fletcher in that he wasn't known to use a firearm. That, of course, didn't mean he wouldn't have one on him to use in an emergency, and Fletcher was too experienced not to assume Kearney wouldn't have other weapons on him.

With Kearney just six feet away from him and moving slowly, Fletcher knew he'd never get a better opportunity to take his target down. He could shout an instruction, and use his gun to intimidate Kearney. Most people would obey, but Kearney would be sure to weigh the odds. To calculate whether a desperate attempt to escape was worth the risk of potentially being shot instead of facing a life in jail.

Fletcher didn't want to kill Kearney. Not when that was what Soter wanted. Wanted him to become. It wasn't his place to execute someone and, while he was comfortable with taking a life as worthless as Kearney's, he was also conscious that another homicide on his record would give Soter even more leverage over him.

As all of this went through his mind, he eased the door a little wider and took his first step towards Kearney.

CHAPTER SEVENTY-EIGHT

Step by careful step, Fletcher pursued Kearney as the killer made his way to the corner of the milking parlor. His old training was second nature when it came to placing his feet. Heel, outside, then the ball of each foot caressed the dusty concrete of the farmyard.

Ahead of him, Kearney was moving with a similar caution, although his forward momentum was greater than Fletcher's as he headed to his point of ambush.

For Fletcher, silence was everything. He wanted to have his gun against Kearney before the man even knew he was being stalked. A careless noise would alert his prey, allowing him time to mount a defense. That wasn't what Fletcher desired as he wanted the takedown to involve the least possible chance of resistance from Kearney.

He was eight feet behind Kearney and losing ground so he picked up his pace. As he moved his eyes were flicking back and forth between the ground looking for obstacles and his target, trying to recognize any signal in Kearney's body language that his approach had been detected.

The air was full of farmyard smells so there was little chance of Kearny smelling him. Fletcher didn't smoke and while it was many hours since he'd last stood in a shower, other than the fast jog from the road to Meadowfields, he'd not done much to build up a sweat and the aromas associated with rigorous exercise.

Seven feet. Kearney was perhaps ten from the parlor wall. When he got to his post, he'd be sure to look around and see Fletcher coming his way. Worse, when Kearney got within maybe five or six feet of the parlor, it was probable he'd quicken his pace on the last few steps so he could assume his position against the wall.

Five feet away from Kearney who was maybe seven from the parlor wall. The pistol was held firm in Fletcher's hand, yet not so firm he couldn't maintain the grip for hours. His right forefinger was straight, ready to curl inside the trigger guard when he put the gun to Kearney's head.

Fletcher's breaths were shallow, his muscles coiled and tensed with enough power to snap into action when required. He could see Kearney's empty hands at his sides, but that didn't mean they couldn't pluck out a concealed weapon if the need arose.

When the numbers got to four and six, Fletcher made his move. As the toes of his right boot made contact with the concrete of the yard, he used his body's momentum to propel himself forward.

The quick steps he took forward were complemented by his left arm snaking around Kearney's neck, while his right went to jam the barrel of his pistol into Kearney's ear.

At least that's how it should have happened. The step was good. So was the arm he wound around Kearney's throat. The gun was due to arrive a millisecond later so his choke arm didn't get in the way of his gun arm.

It was this tiny window of opportunity that Kearney utilized. His body twisted forward into a hip toss that had Fletcher airborne before he had time to counter the move.

CHAPTER SEVENTY-NINE

Rough farmyard concrete didn't make for a soft landing. Fletcher's shoulder jarred with enough force to rattle his teeth. All things considered, it could be worse; had Fletcher's head been the first part of his body to slam down, he could be dealing with a concussion, or at the very least, a dizziness that might prove fatal. There was no time to marvel at the speed of Kearney's reactions or wonder if he'd made a mistake and alerted the homicidal farmer of the imminent attack. This was now a fight for survival with a known killer.

The gun was still in Fletcher's hand, but Kearney had a grip on that arm and was trying to bang his hand against the concrete in order that he'd release the weapon. That couldn't happen.

With Kearney on top of him, Fletcher was at a disadvantage as they struggled for control of the gun.

The knife Fletcher carried was in a sheath at his back meaning he couldn't get to it, so he used his free hand to throw punches as best he could.

A prone position isn't one that favors punches. There's no room for a backswing and the weight of an opponent on top of you prohibits any meaningful forward motion.

Fletcher had been trained for a fight like this, so he gave up on the instinctive attempts to punch upwards at Kearney's face, positioned his arm at right angles to his body and swung a ground scraping blow that veered upwards, his arm curling at the elbow before his fist crashed into the side of Kearney's torso.

The punch bounced off with little effect. Rather than repeat the action hoping for a different outcome, Fletcher changed his tactics. The knuckles of his right hand were bruised and sore from Kearney's attempts to smash his grip on the pistol. All the same he bent his wrist in an attempt to bring the pistol to an angle where he could shoot Kearney. At the same time he used his left hand to claw at Kearney's face to distract him from what was happening with the gun.

Kearney's hand on the pistol barrel pressed with too much weight for Fletcher to compete, and before he could hook a finger into one of Kearney's eye sockets, the farmer had squirmed off him in a way that exposed Fletcher to the same broken elbow move he'd used on Heaton.

As well as being trained in how to apply such holds, Fletcher had learned how to counter them. He hauled backwards on his gun arm, dragging it until his elbow was behind Kearney's grasp and safe from being bent the wrong way.

He continued to claw at Kearney's face as they grappled for the pistol. Strong fingers attempted to prize his free of the weapon and bend them backwards. Fletcher knew that he needed to again change his tactics, so he stopped clawing and used his thumb and fingers to squeeze on Kearney's throat. The pressure on his gun hand paused long enough for Kearney to grab the little finger of his left hand and bend it back until the bones snapped with an audible crack.

Kearney used Fletcher's howl of pain as an opportunity to resume his assault on the gun hand. With Fletcher's efforts to aim the gun at Kearney and their writhing struggles, Fletcher's right arm was now pointing along their bodies.

A knee from Kearney found Fletcher's groin. It wasn't a full contact, but it was still hard enough to send waves of pain radiating from Fletcher's crotch.

Fletcher realized he was being picked off by Kearney, so he did the only thing he could do with the gun. He pulled the trigger.

Not once, or twice, but again and again until the magazine was empty. There was a burning sensation down his leg from the discharge of so many bullets in close proximity to his flesh. Kearney and he yelped in the same moment and then resumed their battle. It wasn't the first powder burn Fletcher had received, and he was happy to work on the principle that compared to a gunshot, a powder burn was nothing to worry about, regardless of how much it might sting.

As a lethal weapon, the gun was now useless. On the other hand, it wasn't something to be fought over anymore.

"Hah. Fat lot of use it is now you murderous—"

Kearney released his arm and threw two hard punches into Fletcher's face, breaking his nose and loosening a tooth while also making a pulpy mess of his lips. Fletcher absorbed the blows secure in the knowledge that his ploy had worked. Kearney had given up on the gun as a weapon and was now trying to subdue him until he could pull his knife. The gun was still in Fletcher's right hand and while no longer able to spit bullets at Kearney, it was still a solid lump of metal that could inflict damage in a different way.

Fletcher put everything he had into crashing the pistol into the side of Kearney's head.

There was a quasi-metallic thud and for the first time since they'd begun fighting Kearney had taken a blow that had rocked him. His eyes went glassy and there was a muted ferocity to the next punch he threw at Fletcher's face.

As Fletcher was winding up his next blow with the gun, Kearney was the one to change his tactics.

He rolled off Fletcher and produced a long boning knife from a sheath on his hip as he stood. Its blade one and a half times the size of the fist Kearney had wound around its handle.

Not that he needed it, but the knife was a final item of proof Kearney was the Hashtag Killer. The coroner's reports on the victims had all stated the knife used as a murder weapon was long and thin, just like the one in Kearney's hand.

Fletcher rose to his feet, dropping the now useless pistol and produced his own knife. If Kearney wanted to make this a mano a mano affair, that was fine by him.

CHAPTER EIGHTY

Fletcher and Kearney circled each other. Both focused on the other's movements. Fletcher was watching Kearney's eyes as much as the boning knife he held. The eyes were always the key, they gave away intent.

Kearney's eyes flashed and the knife in his hand swung in a contained arc that left a ribbon of blood pouring from a cut on Fletcher's arm.

The way Kearney was holding his knife told Fletcher a lot about how good his opponent was. Instead of the traditional method of holding a knife as if about to chop vegetables, he held it in a backhand position with the back of the blade against his forearm. It was the way Fletcher held his knife. The way he'd been trained to hold a knife. How much training Kearney had gone through was unknown, but from the way he was behaving, Fletcher was certain the farmer had a far greater than average knowledge of how to use a knife in a fight situation.

Fletcher knew he had two choices, continue using his own knife and trade moves with Kearney until one of them got a telling strike, or drop his knife, go on the defensive and wait for Kearney to make a mistake that would allow him to grab Kearney's knife arm with both hands and break a bone that would finish his opponent.

Kearney advanced. As the one who had most to lose, he was always going to be the one who needed the fight over the soonest. Fletcher had no need to get away. No need to get back to a farm and pretend that everything was normal. Except Kearney couldn't do that so long as Fletcher lived to tell people about him being here. To have any hope of getting away from this, Kearney would have to silence Fletcher in the most permanent way.

Another step from Kearney saw Fletcher retreat then feint a lunge forward. Kearney was too quick to get caught out and swung his knife in a defensive sweep that would have drawn more blood from Fletcher had he actually been trying to connect.

Twice more Kearney advanced and twice Fletcher used the same move.

"That all you got, punk?" Kearney ignored Fletcher's taunt as, again, Fletcher feinted an attack.

Kearney anticipated the move and gave his now standard counterstrike. Fletcher was ready for him and, although Kearney's wild slash was close enough to his body to have him feel the sting of another cut, he pressed forward as soon as the farmer's arm was returning to its original position.

Fletcher's knife flashed sideways towards Kearney's chest only for a raised forearm to block the blow. Nonetheless, Kearney now carried the most serious knife wound. Fletcher watched as the farmer tried to clench and unclench his fingers without success. Somewhere in the gaping wound on his arm a tendon or ligament must have been severed.

Still Kearney pressed forward. Insults spilled from his lips as he tried to goad Fletcher into making a mistake.

Fletcher threw back an insult of his own. "Pah. You're nothing but a greedy fool. Killing people just so you can get rich from the nickel ore under all these farms. That's what you are, a greedy asshole who's twisted himself into a serial killer."

Kearney's eyes widened. "You know about the ore? Don't say that, I'm not a serial killer."

"What about the folks from White Birch, Greenacres and Broken Spur? You saying that wasn't you? Or the girl from over Greenwood way? That not you either?" The serial killer jibe was needling Kearney so Fletcher used it again. "If you killed them all, you're a serial killer and that's how everyone will think of you."

"I had to kill them. I know them, they were fools. Don't you see? They wouldn't have sold up to a mining company and there's no way a mining company would open up a mine for the ore under my land. They'd want more."

Kearney lunged forward with a wild swing causing Fletcher to jump back so as not to have his stomach opened.

"I'm gonna gut you, then kill all the Quadrados. Know what, I'm thinking that maybe leaving you here will make for a good diversion. That you'll be the perfect scapegoat. You'll be known as the serial killer. Not me."

Fletcher didn't answer. The time for talking was past. It was time for action.

Another feint, another defensive slash from Kearney and another telling wound from Fletcher. This time he'd aimed at Kearney's upper arm and scored a direct hit. Kearney's arm now hung at his side and—in the breaking dawn light—he could see the crimson sleeve Kearney's blood was creating.

With the advantage now all his, Fletcher circled Kearney to keep the wounded farmer's injured side at his mercy. There was no doubt in his mind that Kearney was still a dangerous opponent, as this was the first time since being tossed over his hip Fletcher had possessed the upper hand.

"Give it up, Kearney. You're finished."

"Screw you." Even as he spoke Kearney lunged forward his knife sliding on a diagonal arc up towards Fletcher's right shoulder.

Fletcher use his own knife to deflect the slash and found his arm raised as high as Kearney's. Unlike Kearney he still had a free hand that worked and while his right arm wasn't in an optimal position to strike, his left was free and there was an inviting amount of Kearney's torso exposed. He threw a thunderous left into Kearney's side.

It was a move that may have saved Fletcher's life as Kearney's downswing arced the boning knife into his shoulder rather than the side of his neck.

The boning knife hit bone as Fletcher's knife stabbed at Kearney's upper arm and drew a primal howl from the man. It would have been as easy to direct the strike at Kearney's neck, yet Fletcher still wasn't looking to kill him if he didn't have to.

Kearney pushed Fletcher back, dropped one shoulder and then hit him like a linebacker sacking an unprotected quarterback.

Fletcher was driven backwards until his body slammed into the wall of the milking parlor. Due to Kearney's low position, Fletcher's arms were outside the farmer's body and he had no idea what Kearney's knife was up to.

The first thing Fletcher did was thrust Kearney away from him. All it did was create room for his opponent to attack. The farmer reversed his grip on the knife and arced it upwards, its path arrowing a course that would see it slide under Fletcher's bottom rib and into his heart.

Fletcher managed to get his left arm in the knife's way, but he received a further vicious cut for his trouble.

Kearney went to repeat the blow, so Fletcher dropped his own knife and wrapped two hands around Kearney's wrist as the next swing came upwards. Instead of blocking the blow as he had with the first attempt, Fletcher was aiming to alter its trajectory away from him.

The boning knife slid under a rib, through the pericardium and into a heart. Blood gushed downwards over both men as Kearney's eyes lost their luster and his legs their strength.

CHAPTER EIGHTY-ONE

Fletcher stumbled and lurched his way to the house, yelling for Quadrado.

An upstairs window opened and she appeared, concern all over her face.

"It's over. He's dead."

There wasn't a part of him that didn't ache. Not an area of his body larger than the back of his hand that wasn't slick with blood.

Fletcher got to the porch and wrapped an arm round a post to give him support as Quadrado barreled out of the door. Her feet slid on the porch's deck as she tried not to crash into him.

She looked shocked at his condition and he could see she was caught between wanting to hug him and not daring to touch in case she hurt him further.

At her heel was Peter, his wife and Quadrado's parents. All of them looked at him as if he was the prize exhibit at a freak show. He could have cared less. He'd completed his mission, stopped a killer and he'd soon be going home. Back to Utah, to Wendy and Wilson the dog, and all the joys of being a parent. He couldn't wait. In fact, if it wasn't so far, weakened as he was, he'd set off walking.

"Mom, Libby, get some towels, clean water and the first aid kit. Peter, take the shotgun and go check Kearney really is dead." A part of Fletcher knew Kearney was beyond help. If he wasn't already dead, he would be long before the EMTs got here. "Pop, can you bring a chair over?"

With her instructions given, Quadrado pulled her phone and, from what Fletcher heard of her side of the conversation, called 911.

Quadrado's father got a cane chair from the porch and brought it over. It had a sloping back that was semi-reclined so Fletcher stayed on his feet. He had two reasons for doing so: the worst of his injuries were to the upper part of his body; by staying upright, he'd minimize the flow of blood to his worst cuts. His second reason was more altruistic. The cane chair looked new and its cream cushions would be ruined by the blood coating his body.

Quadrado passed off the phone to Libby and took a step towards him with a pile of towels and a basin of water.

"Hell, Fletcher. Look at the state of you. Are you okay?"

"I'll be fine. Couple of shots of Novocain and a few bandages and I'll be as good as new."

"Did you... you know, mark him with the hashtag?"

"No. If it had been at his place I would have. To do it here would have been wrong and raised more questions than enough."

Fletcher let go of the post so the Quadrado women could start treating his wounds and promptly fell into an untidy heap.

CHAPTER EIGHTY-TWO

Quadrado parked in the lot and climbed out of the rental sedan. It was a full twelve hours since Fletcher had collapsed on the porch and she'd not had a minute to herself since.

Along with giving statements, liaising with Soter to have the heat removed from Fletcher for killing Robert Kearney, she'd had to wrap up her and Fletcher's end of the investigation, retrieve his SUV, clean out his motel room and what seemed like a million other tasks.

She'd kept in touch with the nurses at Medford's Medical Center. Fletcher had received three pints of blood, had his wounds sewn up and the last she'd heard, he was resting.

It was him she was here to visit. She knew that he'd want to know about the loose ends of the case and she was sure his priority would be getting home to his daughter and making sure his name was clear with regards to Kearney's homicide.

The hospital had its usual sterile aroma and the seemingly chaotic energy it always had. Due to the abundance of available building land, it was a large low building rather than the multi-storied hospitals that Quadrado had grown used to since moving to New York.

Quadrado's shoes squeaked on the hard floor covering as she stalked her way towards Fletcher's room. Her mind awash with conflicting emotions. She was delighted Jane's killer had faced a form of justice, although she'd have given her last cent to reverse time and have her friend alive and well. The counter to the pleasure at having solved a tricky case was the methods that she and Fletcher had had to use to do so. That Fletcher had killed again, this time to protect her family, was something she felt both sorrow and gratitude for.

As exhausted as Fletcher was after the fight, there had still been enough of his logical brain working for him not to carry out Soter's instruction and put a hashtag onto Kearney's forehead.

She entered Fletcher's room and found him sitting on the edge of his bed trying to push his legs into a pair of blood-soaked jeans. He showed no signs of embarrassment at the fact he was only wearing his underpants.

"Here." She lifted the carryall she'd packed in his motel room and put it onto the bed. "I figured you'd need fresh clothes."

"Thanks."

Fletcher leaned over the carryall and rummaged until he found a shirt and a clean pair of jeans.

"You going home?"

"Yeah. It's time I was back." He gave her a curious look. "So what's it going to be? Are you here to arrest me or not?"

"Not." Quadrado let the first smile of the day touch her lips. "I'm here to offer you a ride to the airport, to say a proper thank-you for protecting my family and to let you know how things have ended."

Fletcher huffed out a long breath as he eased his legs into the new jeans. "A ride would be appreciated. So, tell me, what's the verdict? Will Robert Kearney's homicide be added to the list of things Soter has to blackmail me with, will the Medford PD arrest me as soon as I get outside?"

"There's to be no arrest and, so far as I can tell, Soter seems pleased we've got a result. You have to remember, he doesn't want you to fail."

"I think you'll find it's us rather than me." He did one of those infuriating shrugs of his and for once it didn't bug Quadrado.

"So what's on the agenda for you when you get home? Surprise your daughter with a military-style homecoming and then take a few days off to recuperate?"

Fletcher held her gaze for so long she thought he was trying to have a staring contest.

"I'll be back at work tomorrow morning at seven o'clock sharp. I have a mortgage to pay and mouths to feed. As for the homecoming surprise, that's not my thing and I'll have Wendy meet me at the airport knowing exactly what time my flight lands."

As Fletcher dropped his hospital robe onto the bed, Quadrado took in the number of bandages swaddling his body.

"I thought you forces guys went in for that."

Fletcher winced as he pulled on his shirt. "Some do. I don't. That's not my kind of thing." He paused as he bent to look at the buttons he was struggling to do up. "You know how my wife Rachel was in the US Army?" Quadrado nodded. "One time I was home when Rachel was deployed. I was on pins the whole time waiting to hear how she was. I'll never forget how I felt worrying about her then. Nor—before Rachel—the way my mother looked at me when I flew back home after my first tour in Iraq."

Quadrado didn't speak. Didn't want to break the spell. Gone was the action hero who'd delivered a report before allowing his injuries to floor him. This was another side of Fletcher she was seeing, the sensitive side, one that allowed her to meet the real him, the father and husband instead of the killer.

"We got back. Ninety-seven of us walked off that plane after a hundred of us flew out. Two were in hospital with life-changing injuries and Smudger, Smudger was in the cargo hold. We waited until the hearse came for him. Lined up and saluted him before we went to see our loved ones. And you know what the most amazing thing was? We talked on the flight back. And any one of us would have taken those odds on the way out." He pulled at his collar until it was comfortable. "Anyway, we get our bags and walk into this big room at the airport. All the wives and girlfriends, husbands and boyfriends too. They all ran over to us. Kids were scooped up and cuddled. After saying goodbye to Smudger like that, it didn't feel right to be feeling so happy. My mum hugged me harder than she ever had before. Then she stood back and held my shoulders at arm's length while she inspected me. She looked me up and down to make sure I was okay and then she looked into my eyes, into my soul. I never could hide anything from her. She saw the change from awkward kid to a killer in me and I saw her fear for me in her eyes." Fletcher lifted the carryall, went to swing it over a shoulder, winced and let it hang by his knee instead. "All that outpouring of emotion you see on those videos, that's months of fear manifesting itself as relief. It's the sleepless nights spent worrying. It's the dread every time there's news of a casualty in the press or a TV news show. It's missing a loved one on special occasions and for everyday interaction. It's the constant fear the empty chair at the table might always be empty. It's jumping when there's a knock at the door. Don't get me wrong, I love watching those videos, but I know them for what they are. Those wobbly-kneed sprints, the tear-streaked faces and the sheer joy of those who've been surprised, that's about them being released from fear. My family have been put through hell whenever I've been at war, just the same as every other military family the world over. To not release them from that fear at the earliest possible moment seems cruel to me. It's not just soldiers who make sacrifices and that's something not enough people appreciate."

Quadrado still didn't speak. It wasn't that she was being respectful to Fletcher's opinions, more that she didn't trust her voice to behave itself. He'd spoken with such raw honesty, such self-awareness that it was hard to equate him with the man who'd collapsed on her parents' porch twelve hours ago after killing a man in a fight to the death.

She wiped the tears away and held the door open for him. He gave a nod and then led the way out of the hospital like he was the visitor and she the patient.

It was only when they were in her car that she trusted herself to speak again.

"So home for you. Back to New York for me after the funerals and all the loose ends are tied up."

"Yup." Either he was now in a melancholy mood or he was embarrassed by his outpouring and keeping his answers short.

"Just FYI, Kearney's house was searched. He'd plotted out the possible size of the ore deposits and had details of the farms where the Hashtag Killer had struck all taped to a wall."

"Yeah?" Fletcher turned his face her way. "I'm guessing that your folks' place was one of the farms above the ore. Do you know what the plans are now that everyone knows they're sitting on a goldmine?"

"You'd guess right. So far the ore side of things has been kept contained. It'll break out, of course it will. I told my pop this morning and he says he doesn't want to see Meadowfields turned into a hole in the ground. I dare say there'll be others who think the same way and others who'll only see the dollar signs. Time will tell."

"It always does."

Quadrado wanted to move the conversation away from a subject she had so many mixed feelings about. "I saw a news report from Idaho Drake. As you were the guy to crack the case and thwart the killer, she had to give you a positive spin. You could tell it was false though. She must hate your guts for that stunt with the handcuffs." Quadrado let a giggle escape. "The local cops told her their keys wouldn't work as they were FBI handcuffs and they made her wait there until after the evening broadcast. From what I've heard, she'd tried to do something with her back to the vehicle but her cameraman couldn't get an angle where the handcuffed arm didn't look odd."

"Good enough for her. I hope for her sake that she rethinks her strategies; otherwise she'll end up being fired."

After all the trouble the journalist had caused him, Quadrado found it heartening to hear Fletcher speak with such grace. It was as if his move to immobilize her had leveled any score he might be keeping against the reporter. "Anyway, who do you think Soter is?"

"Some top ranking FBI guy. The director, deputy director or someone at the same kind of level in another agency that we've been passed onto. Whoever it is, he's got serious clout and more than enough material on me to keep me dancing to his tune. The name or position doesn't matter." A huffed breath. "I know a guy who could probably trace the emails and get me a name without being detected, but getting a name won't help me. Soter could announce himself to me and I'd still be powerless against him."

With that Fletcher leaned back against the headrest and closed his eyes. Quadrado let him be, he'd more than earned a rest.

An hour later she was shaking his hand and thanking him one last time before he went to board his plane. The sedan seemed empty when she climbed behind the wheel and checked her phone before setting off.

There was an email.

I'LL BE IN TOUCH. SOON.

SOTER

A LETTER FROM JOHN

I want to say a huge thank you for choosing to read *Final Second*. If you did enjoy it, and want to keep up-to-date with all my latest releases, just sign up at the following link. Your email address will never be shared and you can unsubscribe at any time.

www.bookouture.com/john-ryder

I had great fun writing *Final Second* and I hope you enjoyed the read. After Fletcher's escapades in *First Shot*, I was keen to show a somewhat different side to him in his second outing and therefore I made this case one where he had to use his brains more than his fists. Of course, it wouldn't be a Fletcher story if there weren't at least a couple of dustups, but I felt it important to show that he's got a good brain on him, although his intelligence will always be limited by my own.

I'm from a farming family myself and I chose the setting of dairy farms for no other reason than it is something I am familiar with. You may have thought while reading the farms seemed rather small for an American-set story, but I did a fair amount of research into the size of farms in Taylor County and the farms are more or less accurate in terms of acreage. Following on with this thread, there are a lot of arguments both for and against intensive farming of the type described in the story. I pass no comment either way as I can see both sides of the debate and I hope this was reflected in Fletcher's position as both a carnivore and someone who cares about animals.

The central premise of the story, where the pot of gold is buried under the farms, is one I hope you didn't work out too soon, but if you did, I'd like to think you didn't suspect it would be for a mineral ore that's becoming more and more important to our society now there are so many battery-powered devices that are part of our everyday life. As part of my research for the novel I watched some online videos about the mining process, and while the engineering and mechanical machines are very impressive, in their scale, what is not so impressive are the scars the mines leave behind them.

I hope you loved *Final Second* and if you did I would be very grateful if you could write a review. I'd love to hear what you think, and it makes such a difference helping new readers to discover one of my books for the first time.

I also hope you'll subscribe to my newsletter for updates on me and my writing as well as following me on social media.

John

JohnRyderAuthor

@JohnRyder101

johnryderauthor.com

ACKNOWLEDGMENTS

As always I'd like to thank my family for the support they've given me and my writing. Special thanks go to the team at Bookouture, starting with my wonderful editor Isobel Akenhead, whose liberal use of the red pen can oftentimes be frustrating, but she is invariably right (she's insisting I say these last five words. In fact, I quite literally have a gun to my head as I'm typing this) and she certainly improves my writing. Kim, Noelle & Sarah in the publicity do a fantastic job of getting the word out there and guys in the back who manage all the marketing and digital analysis also do a great job.

The world of crime fiction is a tremendously supportive one; from authors of all levels of success and fame, to readers to bloggers, editors and agents, I'm immensely lucky to have such a great network and I cherish their friendship far more than I ever tell anyone. My Crime and Publishment writing gang are all among my closest friends in the genre and they've shared my journey. I raise a glass to each of them and thank them for their friendship.

Finally, dear reader, I come to you. The many hundreds or thousands of hours I spend planning, writing, editing and polishing each novel is done in the hope that I can entertain you for a few hours with a rattling yarn or a mystery whose solution you need to learn the answer to. After all, without readers I'm nothing more than a typist who's not very good at typing.

Made in the USA
Middletown, DE
01 June 2021

40829983R00176